Hotel
Paradise

Hotel Paradise

BRIDGET ANDERSON

ARABESQUE®

HOTEL PARADISE

An Arabesque novel

ISBN 1-58314-726-8

www.kimanipress.com

Printed in U.S.A.

ACKNOWLEDGMENTS

I'd like to thank Shirley Harrison, Adrianne Byrd, Shelly Fouad and the helpful folks at The Penn Center on St. Helena Island.

This book is dedicated to Margaret, James Sr. and James Jr. And of course, to my husband, Terry, with love.

Chapter 1

"Welcome to Hotel Paradise, Mr. Monroe."

Darius Monroe unfolded his six-foot-nine-inch frame from the cramped minivan turned airport taxi and stepped out to inhale the thick salty air. Huge oak trees dripping with Spanish moss flanked the hotel's entrance, welcoming him back to the coast. In its heyday, Hotel Paradise was the only hotel African Americans could stay in on Jekyll Island.

A young man in wire-frame glasses, a starched white shirt, and tan khaki pants held a silver tray balancing a single champagne glass. His southern drawl immediately reminded Darius of his father, his uncles, and home.

"Thank you." Darius took the glass and sipped the chilled mimosa that hit the spot. *Nice welcoming touch.*

"I'm your general manager, Sterling Simpson. On behalf of the staff here at Hotel Paradise I'd like to welcome you, and we hope your stay is a pleasant and enjoyable one." He tucked the tray under his left arm.

"Thank you, I'm sure it will be." Darius glanced back at his luggage being pulled from the taxi, and loaded onto a dolly. A younger man stood there ready to escort him to his room. Darius finished his mimosa and handed the glass back to Sterling.

"If it's possible, I'd like to see my office before I go to my room."

Sterling nodded and instructed the young man to get help before delivering the luggage to Darius's room and told him to meet them back at the office. Darius listened as he noted the huge chunks of salmon-colored paint peeling from the building. He was about to see why AAA gave Hotel Paradise only a two-diamond rating.

Sterling led Darius to his office through the lobby—with its white rattan furniture and salmon cushions that matched the exterior of the building. A large water fountain provided tranquil background sound.

Several employees greeted them with smiles, as Sterling introduced them according to their staff positions. Each one offered his or her condolences for his grandfather's passing and expressed how much he would be missed.

Poppy, as everyone affectionately called Willie Monroe, had been buried three months ago. It took Darius that long to get his coffee shop business squared away and his calendar cleared for this trip.

Two young women behind the front desk greeted him as Sterling knocked on a door to their right. The door opened, and Sterling stepped back to let Darius enter.

"This is the front office where most of the staff work."

The small African American staff were busy moving about the office; some took the time to smile or wave. Darius followed Sterling down a short hallway as Sterling pointed out rooms on either side.

A sign on the door at the end of the hallway read: William Monroe, Owner/Proprietor, Private.

Darius crossed the threshold into the overstuffed, cluttered office. Relatives had come to clear out most of his grandfather's personal belongings, but a musty ointment smell remained in the room. The spiritual presence of his grandfather was needed and appreciated.

"Sterling, how long had you worked for my grandfather?"

"A little over twelve years now," he responded with a polite smile.

Darius didn't think he looked a day over thirty, although he carried himself like a much older man. "So you know this place like the back of your hand?"

"Yes, sir," he replied with a firm nod.

"Great, because I'm going to need your help when I start making renovations." Darius walked behind his grandfather's desk and pulled out the chair.

"Renovations?" Sterling asked with raised brows.

"Yes, I've arranged for a few investors to fly down in a couple of months to look around. Before they show up I think the place could use a little work. Starting with some fresh paint."

Sterling took a step back and crossed his arms. "Excuse me, sir, but I thought you were here to sell the property. Your grandfather talked like that's what the family was gonna d..."

Darius shook his head. "He may have initially thought about selling, but Hotel Paradise belongs to the Monroe family, and I plan to keep it that way. I've got big changes planned for this place." The strained look on Sterling's face wasn't what Darius expected. A sigh of relief that he wasn't about to lose his job would have been expected. Darius sat in his grandfather's chair, which had permanently molded to the size of the old man.

"If you don't mind me asking, what type of changes do you have in mind?" Sterling probed.

"If you're worried about your job, don't be. I'll need somebody with your knowledge to keep running the day-to-day operations of the hotel."

Not ready to divulge his ultimate plan just yet, and taking a cue from Sterling's stressed face, Darius treaded lightly.

"For right now, some minor cosmetic improvements. Although I can't be certain until I've had a better look at the property. How about showing me around?"

Sterling's eyes widened as he uncrossed his arms. "My shift is about over, and I have to hurry to pick up my son this evening, but tomorrow morning after breakfast we can tour the property."

A muscle in Darius's neck twitched as he turned his lips up into a thin smile. "Tomorrow morning, bright and early."

Sterling pivoted toward the door. "I'll have someone show you to your room. Right now, I have to oversee dinner preparations before I leave."

"Before you send someone give me a little while, to get acquainted with the office."

"No problem."

"Oh, one more thing."

Sterling turned in the doorway and glanced back.

"Until I'm more familiar with the staff, I'd like to hold a managers' meeting every morning over breakfast—starting tomorrow. If you'll notify everyone before they leave today I'd appreciate it."

"Yes, sir. I'll let them know. And before I forget, I'd also like to offer my condolences for the unfortunate passing of your grandfather."

"Thank you." Darius leaned back in his seat after Sterling left and clasped his hands behind his head. He'd been forewarned that some of the staff didn't want him here. He hoped Sterling wasn't a part of that crew.

* * *

Two hours later, while Darius skimmed over financial reports he'd asked to have available, a soft tap came at the opened door. He looked up to see the young bellhop standing in the doorway. "Come in."

"Mr. Monroe. I'm here to show you to your room."

Eager now to change out of his travel clothes, Darius closed the file and joined the young man.

"What's your name?"

"Rodell, sir."

This kid's southern drawl was more pronounced than Sterling's, and reminded Darius of childhood friends he'd made during his island visits. "You can drop the 'sir.' Call me Darius."

They left the office, cleared the lobby, and walked out to a panoramic ocean view. None of the beaches on Jekyll Island were private, however, Hotel Paradise sat at the southernmost point of the island, with nothing to its right but marshes. This vantage point gave the appearance of their own private beach, which made the location perfect for Darius's plans.

"Do you get to the islands often?" Rodell asked as they left the main building and strolled alongside the pool.

Darius shook his head. "I haven't been here since I was in high school." He took in the large palms, the tree-covered dunes, and breathtaking view of the Atlantic Ocean before noticing a woman sunbathing topless by the pool. He cut his eyes toward Rodell.

The young man smiled. "It's Paradise, sir. I mean, Darius," he said with a shrug.

"Rodell, let's take the long way. I'd like to get a better look at the property."

Rodell stopped and pivoted. "Okay, then we need to go the other way."

They walked along the front side instead of the oceanview side of the building. The property was larger than Darius remembered. The two buildings holding all fifty-eight guest rooms were adjoined by the lobby. A separate building held the gym and gift shop. His grandfather hadn't neglected the various gardens or the lush landscape, but the buildings were dilapidated. Some of the surrounding undeveloped land also belonged to the hotel, which should interest his investors.

As Darius looked around he could see his vision coming to life. Private chalets with Jacuzzis opening to luscious gardens or ocean views, each with its own personal butler or waitstaff. He only wished his father, Charles, was alive to witness the transformation process.

"So Rodell, how long have you worked here?"

"This is my second summer."

"Did you know my grandfather?"

"Not really, sir. I did meet him once, and I saw him around some, but Mr. Monroe didn't get out much. My dad use to say that before the big hotels showed up, everyone wanted to work at Hotel Paradise. Mr. Monroe taught a lot of black men the hotel trade."

"How do the locals feel about the hotel now?" At one point this hotel meant a lot to the people on the island. However, now Darius wasn't sure how much support he could count on should he need it.

Rodell looked at him and shrugged. "Well, the other hotels pay more, but this is still a good place to work. People were loyal to Mr. Monroe. He was cool with everybody."

"Nevertheless, it takes money to compete with the big boys, and from the looks of this place, my grandfather could have used some help."

"Yes, sir. Holiday Inn's up the road," he said, pointing in the chain resort's direction. "They have fine dining inside of the hotel, VCRs in all the rooms, and something called Victorian tea time. We have a local band that only plays Saturday nights, and a stupid karaoke machine." He looked up at Darius with a twisted smile.

Darius laughed. "Well, that's about to change."

Sterling stormed into his office and slammed the door shut. He kicked out his chair and flopped down onto the seat. This wasn't happening, not now, not to him. He picked up the phone and punched in several numbers before lowering his head.

"Thank you for calling The Shores. May I help you?"

"Yes, I need to speak to Mr. Denton." Sterling waited for the receptionist to connect him to his benefactor.

Several seconds later, a familiar northern accent came on the line. "Sterling, good to hear from you. How's everything in Paradise?"

"Not so good, I'm afraid." Sterling took a deep breath between pauses. "Mr. Monroe's grandson is here. And I don't think he plans to sell the hotel."

"Well…you'll just have to make sure he changes his mind."

Perspiration beaded Sterling's brow as he tapped his pen repeatedly against his desk. "But I don't know if—"

"But nothing… Your children have great futures awaiting them. You're doing what you can to make sure that happens, aren't you?"

Sterling ran a shaky hand across his forehead and finally said, "Yes, sir. It might take a little longer now, but—"

"Just make it happen."

The line disconnected.

Sterling slammed his phone down and cursed himself.

Rodell left Darius at the end suite that had been Willie Monroe's home. The suite was more like a two bedroom ranch home, complete with ceiling fans, a small kitchen, and a dining area. That same musty ointment smell that filled the office lingered here as well. Inside, the opened curtains let sunlight in and revealed a private deck.

The stresses of his everyday life in Chicago were missing. No television, CD, DVD, or MP3 players. A clock radio and a telephone sat on a table in the bedroom, his only link to the outside once he entered the suite.

A loud knock at the front door stopped him from unpacking. When he opened the door, an older man with a salt-and-pepper receding hairline stood there. He wore the tan-and-maroon uniform of the hotel. His complexion was the deep dark brown of an Islander's.

"Hello, can I help you?"

The man stood straighter to meet Darius's height. He searched into his eyes for a moment, and then shook his head before speaking.

"Hello... I'm sorry. It's just that the resemblance between you and your grandfather when he was a young man is amazing."

Darius gave an understanding smile. He'd been told before that he resembled his Poppy. "You knew my grandfather a long time," he stated.

"Oh yes, we was boys together. Grew up right here on the islands." He scratched his head before sticking his hand out, as if he'd suddenly remembered why he'd come by. "I'm Nathan. Mr. Monroe's driver."

"His driver?" Darius laughed as they exchanged handshakes. His grandfather wasn't a rich man, he could barely hold on to the hotel. What in the world was he doing with a driver?

"Yes, sir," he said proudly. "I also shine shoes up in the billiards room on weekends, and I run errands for just about anybody in the office."

Darius took a closer look at Nathan, and realized that with his knowledge of the hotel and the island he was what Darius needed. He was a gentleman who, with just a little cleaning up, could pass for a distinguished butler to the rich.

"It's a pleasure, Nathan." The man's firm handshake and gentle smile also gave Darius hope he had someone else on his side if he needed him.

"I just wanted to let ya' know that my number is by the phone right where Mr. Monroe kept it. It's also in the office by the phone. The old man wasn't much of a driver, so I been driving him around since he was about seventy on account of his bad legs, you know."

"That I do remember. But how did he get back and forth from the office to this suite every night with bad legs?"

"He had a scooter. It's down in the service center. If you ever need it… Naw, I don't see a young man like yourself needing a scooter."

"Let's hope not."

Nathan laughed. "Well, I just wanted to drop by to introduce myself and let you know I'm here if you need me."

"Nathan, it was good to meet you. I'll call if I need a ride somewhere."

"Oh, there's also a hotel car available if you prefer to drive yourself. Just ask Sterling, he keeps the keys."

"Thanks, I'll do that."

Darius closed the door and turned around staring into the cozy little living room with no television. This was his home for the next few months, possibly longer. At one-tenth the size of his condo in Chicago, somehow this suite felt more like a home. He found his suitcase in the bedroom and unpacked. After a quick shower he changed clothes and ordered room service. While waiting, he stepped out onto the deck for a better view.

The heat and humidity hit him in the face, but he'd have to get accustomed to it, like he'd have to adjust to life on the tiny island. How his father lasted until college on such a small island he'd never know. Darius was prepared to get to work and spend the least amount of time here as possible. The hotel's financial outlook was bleak at best. He'd have to turn this place around if he hoped to interest anyone.

Off the deck a small path led to the beach. Darius saw a small boat dock and decided to do a little exploring before dinner arrived. He took the path, which he speculated was created for his grandfather to maneuver with his scooter. Down the beach closer to the hotel he could see families playing in the water and people relaxing on the beach. He took a deep breath and exhaled. His whole body relaxed. The calm before the storm, he thought, and he laughed.

As he turned, a flash of color caught his eye. He spun back around to see a brown-skinned woman in a hot pink two-piece bathing suit with her hair pinned up. She rose from the lounging chair, and his breath caught in his throat. Her curvy body filled her suit to perfection. She leaned over and put something in a bag. His racing heartbeat slowed, but he couldn't get his legs to move as she walked away. With her back to him, he smiled. "Rodell might have been right, maybe this is paradise."

Chapter 2

"So what's your pleasure?" the bartender asked.

"I'll have a white wine, please." Alicia McKay glanced around at the wedding party crowded onto the yacht and wondered if she'd done the right thing. When she called her Aunt Ode—whom she hadn't seen since she was ten—to inform her of her visit, she found out a cousin's wedding would be taking place the same weekend. She didn't know this side of her family and almost cancelled the trip. However, it had taken six months to make up her mind to visit, and if she'd changed the date, she might have never come.

As the bartender set her glass of wine on the counter, a warm, soft hand touched her shoulder.

"Is that all you're having?"

Alicia turned toward the familiar voice. "Hello. Sherri, right?" When Alicia arrived Monday evening her cousin Ruth Ann had introduced her to Sherri and to Sherri's fiancé, Maurice.

"Yes, and you're Alicia. I remember because Nana said you live in Atlanta. We're moving there after the wedding. She also said you came down alone."

"Have suitcase, will travel." Alicia pointed to herself and smiled. She paid for her drink and stepped aside so Sherri could order hers.

"You're brave, girl. I didn't see you when we boarded."

"I was sitting inside. Where's your fiancé?"

"He's on the top deck with the rest of the crowd. Why don't you come join us?"

The crowd, as she remembered them, were a rowdy bunch in town for the wedding. "I think I'll pass, but you guys have fun."

Sherri reached back and touched Alicia's arm before she could walk away. "Girl, you're on vacation. Nana said you're going to be here for a month. Come have some fun. Almost everybody up there's from Atlanta too. We'll show them how to party dirty south style. Besides, there are other single guys here you should meet."

Alicia took one step back. "Okay, now I know I'm staying down here. I didn't come to Jekyll Island, of all places, to get hooked up." She wasn't looking for a man, didn't need a man, and right now she certainly didn't want a man. Nobody, or nothing would interfere with her family research, it meant too much to her. Besides, the wedding party were all in their twenties.

"No, seriously, I'm not trying to hook you up. Some of my coworkers came by themselves, that's all. Girl, I'm getting married in two days I don't have time to play matchmaker."

The bartender set down a tray with four drinks on it. Next to the tray he placed two bottles of beer that wouldn't fit.

Sherri turned around and scanned the room before

stopping at Alicia. She smiled like a big fat Cheshire cat. "Can you do me a favor?"

Alicia responded by raising one brow.

"Can you help me take these up? If you don't want to stay, you don't have to."

Oh, what the hell. "Sure." Alicia set her wine on the tray, grabbed the bottles of beer, and followed Sherri to the top deck.

Steel-band music from the lower deck was piped in via large speakers, and the crowd danced as if the band were on their deck. After being introduced around, Alicia decided to stay.

Sherri and her fiancé Maurice sat in the corner and cuddled and whispered in each other's ears. The uninhibited show of affection brought a smile to Alicia's face. She couldn't take her eyes off the infatuated couple. How they managed to focus on each other instead of the party, Alicia had no idea. Must be love, she thought. Not wanting to be accused of voyeurism, she finally tore her eyes away and sipped her wine.

"Cute aren't they?"

Enthralled by the couple, Alicia hadn't noticed a man sit down beside her. She looked up into his baby-smooth face with delicate—almost feminine—features and trendy cut bleached-blond hair.

"I'm Rorie," he said, offering his hand.

"Hi, I'm Alicia." She returned the handshake.

"Yeah, I know. We're cousins. You probably don't remember me, but the story goes like this. My mom, Sister Sarah, says your mother brought you down to our house when we were kids, and I broke your favorite doll."

Alicia looked at him stunned. "I still have that doll. It's one where you can make her hair long or short. I wondered how come her ponytail wouldn't go back in. She's a keepsake."

He held up his hand. "Guilty, according to my mother anyway."

"Well, Rorie, it's nice to see you again, and I forgive you for destroying my doll."

He held a hand over his chest in a theatrical gesture. "Thank you so much, it's haunted me for years." He crossed his legs at the knees and leaned back in his plastic chair.

"I also heard you're from Atlanta and flew down by yourself."

She shook her head. "News travels fast."

"Small town, baby. I flew down by myself too. But, I don't normally travel alone. Some trips are just better when shared with the ones you love." He winked at her. "If you know what I mean."

She chuckled. "I think I know what you're getting at."

He eyed her with his baby blues—probably contacts—and then reached down for her left hand. "I don't see a wedding ring, so you're not married." He crossed one arm over his stomach and tapped the other index finger against his chin. "Hmm, but you didn't bring the boyfriend either. I know what it is!" He snapped his fingers.

"What?" she asked, enjoying his little game.

He popped his lips reminding her of a drag queen she'd seen on *Taxicab Confessions* late one night.

"You're recently divorced and spending all your new-found fortune."

She frowned and shook her head.

He set his drink down and in a dramatic gesture held his hand up, palm out. "No, wait a minute. Where are you staying?"

"Hotel Paradise, same as you."

He dropped her hand. "Aw hell, you're not wealthy or you wouldn't be staying in that dive." The minute *dive* left his lips he covered his mouth and looked back at the blissful crowd. "Don't tell anyone I said that. But, Maurice and Sherri could have at least sprung for a place with a spa." He retrieved his drink.

"What's wrong with Hotel Paradise?"

He reeled with astonishment. "For starters, it ain't paradise! It's more like Hotel Wannabe."

Alicia laughed more at his animated behavior than at what he'd said. She liked the little hotel with its history, subtle charm, and practically empty beach. It wasn't The Jekyll Island Club Hotel, but she'd chosen to stay there for a reason.

"You know I should stop trippin' and be thankful for the free vacation. Sherri and Maurice are good people."

"They seem like it," she agreed.

The steel band took a break and the electric slide music piped in. The wedding crowd turned up the volume on their party and hit the makeshift dance floor.

Rorie turned to Alicia. "That dance is old as dirt." He stood up. "But, too much fun to pass up. Stop nursing that wine and come on."

He grabbed her arm, barely allowing her time to set the drink down before he pulled her onto the dance floor. She couldn't have said no if she'd wanted to. And she hadn't.

Before the cruise ended, she met a few more relatives, but chatted with Rorie most of the trip. By the time they returned to shore, she knew his life story, including the sad details of his breakup with Al. Rorie was on the rebound and making the most of it.

"You get a good night's sleep. Those are about the saddest eyes I've ever seen." He hugged her like they were old friends.

Unaccustomed to being hugged by people she hardly knew, she initially stiffened. But the warmth and friendliness of his embrace relaxed her.

Her shoulders slouched, as she shifted from one hip to the other. In a soft monotone voice she replied, "I'm not sad…a little tired is all—" she hunched her shoulders "—so, I'll say goodnight and thanks for keeping me company." She waved and walked off.

"Okay, but I'll be looking for you tomorrow," he called after her.

And of that she was sure.

The long and reflective stroll back to her suite bothered her. Rorie had planted something in her mind. She hadn't felt all alone in the world in a long time. Tonight he reminded her of childhood visits to her grandmother's. Her grandmother had always told her, "stop frowning, don't you know children all over the world want what you got. And here you sit looking like you're about to cry all the time." But Alicia would have gladly given the children all her toys in exchange for time spent with her father.

After a warm bubble bath she curled up in bed and pulled out one of her journals. She left her hair tied up in a towel not wanting to deal with it after the humidity had zapped all the life out of it. She opened the journal to a random page and started reading.

The sunset this evening was the most beautiful I've ever seen. We sat under a huge oak tree embracing and cherishing our special love. A love forbidden in most eyes. One day we'll leave this place and go somewhere where we can live freely as husband and wife. But for now, our stolen moments are all I have. The passion-filled kisses from my lover and our soul-stirring love-making sustains me from day to agonizing day. Last night we made love at the edge of Hotel Paradise. This

place has become my home away from home, our ren-
dezvous spot, the only place I feel at peace in my
lover's arms.

A tear slid down Alicia's cheek as she pulled the covers
over her head and drifted off to sleep.

The next morning, Alicia opened the balcony doors and
welcomed the bright coastal sunlight in as the phone rang.
The car she'd reserved was ready.

She spent a minute or two trying to decide what to wear
to her aunt's. The day Alicia arrived on the island she had paid
her first visit. Gospel music continually played throughout the
house and her Aunt Ode Simpson hummed every tune. Not
wanting to offend her aunt now, Alicia folded a short, blue
jean skirt and tucked it back in the drawer. Instead, she
selected a pair of white pants with a red-and-white-striped,
short-sleeved top.

She twisted her hair into something that resembled a
French roll and held it with a butterfly clamp. A pair of silver
hoop earrings, a touch of makeup, and she was good to go.

All that preparation left her only a few minutes for breakfast.
If she hurried she could grab something quick before they closed.

By the time she reached the drab dining room with its
disco-era multicolored matted carpet and aging pink wallpa-
per, the breakfast bar was almost empty. Alicia picked up a
cranberry muffin and asked a nearby waiter for a carryout cup
for some juice.

In the corner of the room she spotted her cousin Sterling
with a group of men who looked like other managers. At one
end of the table, a tall, dark-skinned man with a round firm
chin and pencil-fine mustache and beard caught her atten-

tion. He led the discussion, which held everyone's attention—including hers.

He was roguishly handsome in a clean-cut kind of way. He had a polished businessman look, but she could tell he came from the streets. His proud nose was the most prominent feature on his face, and when he laughed that corner of the room lit up.

She turned away so fast the muffin flew off the paper plate and across the buffet. Horrified, she quickly picked up a fresh muffin and this time covered it with a napkin.

She pretended to scratch the back of her head as she glanced over her shoulder. *My God. Where did he come from?* Whoever he was, he'd just arrived. In four days she'd met or saw almost everyone who worked at the hotel, and she definitely hadn't met him.

"Here's your cup?"

Alicia thanked the waiter, and then poured herself a large cup of orange juice. She casually ascended the stairs—so as not to draw attention to herself—and caught one more sight of the man in the corner. Sexy-as-hell brother stroked his chin, and Alicia tripped up the next step. She chanted to herself, "I'm not looking for a man, don't need a man, and certainly don't want a man."

The drive across the causeway to Brunswick, Georgia was three dollars a day, which Alicia considered ridiculous, but she paid it anyway. Large cedar trees and colorful beds of azaleas in bloom covered the front yard of her aunt's two-story, A-frame house. Alicia loved the big front porch with matching white rockers. The house was comfortable, welcoming, and distinctively southern. When she knocked on the door, a teenage girl in glasses with long plats opened it and let her in. Unlike the first visit, this time the house was alive with children running from room to room. Her aunt poked her head out of the kitchen door.

"Alicia, baby, come on back here and make yo'self at home." Her attention turned to the teenager. "Tracy, make them chirren sit down and watch the television or somethin'. They's running all over the house."

Ode Simpson hugged Alicia the minute she entered the kitchen. "How you doin', baby?"

"I'm good," Alicia said as she was crushed into her aunt's ample bosom. She returned the hug in the same distant manner in which she'd hug a complete stranger. Such a warm display of affection was what Alicia had hoped for, but was ill equipped to handle. Her father hadn't been big on expressing his emotions, nor had anyone else in his family.

Ode picked up an old hand fan with a picture of Martin Luther King and the local funeral home's names on the back and fanned herself. Dressed in a blue-and-white flowery housedress, she walked back over to the stove. "I see you're babysitting today?" Alicia took a seat at the kitchen table, which doubled as a kids drawing area, where a cup of crayons sat in the middle of the table. The black-and-white, cow-themed kitchen accessories were cute in the cozy eat-in country kitchen.

"The twins is Ruth Ann's boys. I keep them everyday. But them others showin' out belong to Juanita and Sterling. The oldest in the bunch, the mousy teenager, that's Tracy, Juanita's baby girl. There's no school today so they all here until their parents pick them up after work."

"Okay." Alicia nodded. *Good God, maybe I should have come by later, after day care was over.* She smiled at her aunt thinking how different their lives were. The pitter-patter of little feet had never touched Alicia's floors. Instead, against her better judgment, she spent her mornings in the gym torturing herself. The rest of her day was usually a blur of meetings. However, during this trip, she hoped to become better acquainted with her mother's family; particularly since she wasn't close with her father's family back in Atlanta.

A small radio sat on a shelf above the sink, and Ode hummed along with the gospel station while she cooked.

"Enjoyin' ya' visit so far?" she asked, as she raised the lid and placed the apple slices into a skillet of hot grease.

"Yes, ma'am, it's really beautiful here, and everyone's so nice." Alicia stood up. "Can I help you do anything?" she asked, needing to feel useful.

Before Ode could answer, the kitchen door swung open and two little boys ran through, one screaming at the top of his lungs.

"Tracy," Ode yelled. "Come get these chirren out of here. This hot grease gonna spit at 'em." She chastised the boys. "Stop that runnin' and go sit down somewhere. Y'all know better than to show out before company."

Alicia sat back down and pulled her feet under the chair so the boys wouldn't trip over them as they ran circles around the room.

The kitchen door burst open with a loud swish, and Tracy stood there with knitted brows pointing back into the living room. She shouted at her brother and one of the twins. "Stop acting like y'all ain't got no home training and get back in here."

The boys never stopped running, but zoomed out of the kitchen back into the living room, giggling along the way.

"I said stop that runnin'," Ode yelled again. She shook her head after the door closed and replaced the lid on the apples.

Alicia forced her curt smile into something more polite. Children were an enigma to her. She'd once spent thirty minutes with her best friend's niece, explaining where rain came from. Afterwards, she'd developed a migraine.

The quiet of the kitchen returned with a gospel backdrop. "Sterling takin' care of ya' at that hotel, isn't he?" Ode asked, while washing her hands in the sink.

"I actually haven't seen much of him. I'm sure he's busy, and I've been out exploring the island a little. Are you sure I can't help you with anything?"

"Chile, you're company. Just relax, I'm almost finished. Once I feed 'em chirren they'll lie down and go to sleep."

All hail nap time.

"Juanita don't have to work this weekend, so we plan to let ya' meet the rest of the family after the wedding. You got cousins up in Beaufort and over in Savannah. I done told 'em about you and they real excited to meet Venetta's baby girl."

Alicia shared their enthusiasm, but for different reasons. She didn't know what she was more excited about, to meet them, or to hear their stories about her mother.

"Aunt Ode, I've been wanting to talk to you about my mother and Hotel Paradise."

"Is that why ya' staying there, 'cause yo' mama used to work there?" Ode turned around to stir the apples on the stove. "It ain't the best hotel on the island you know."

"Yes, but—"

"Now if ya' stayed over here, it wouldn't cost us nuttun to come visit ya'."

"Yes, ma'am. I'm sorry about that. But, that's why I rented the car all month, so I can visit with you guys. I do want to stay at Hotel Paradise because my mother worked there, but the hotel's history intrigues me as well."

Ode smiled fondly up toward the ceiling. "Yes sir, Paradise used to be a fine hotel, years ago. I saw Otis Redding there one time."

"You stayed there?"

"Naw, chile, we never had that kind of money." Ode laughed and shook her head. "They used to bring the performers in on buses. We'd get all gussied up and ride over to Hotel Paradise like we's headed to one of the fancy white hotels over there."

"Did my mom go?"

Ode's smile lost some of its enthusiasm. "Naw, that was before Willie Monroe bought the place, and yo' mama wasn't old enough to get in."

Alicia opened her mouth to ask another question, but her aunt started singing. She sung a few bars of *Sittin' on the Dock of the Bay,* and then turned to Alicia.

"Baby, what you remember about yo' mama?"

Alicia hunched her shoulders. "That she had long, thick hair, like mine." She twirled a few strands of hair around her finger in a habitual movement. "She always smelled good, and she used to bake cakes all the time. I remember her letting me lick the beaters."

"She always did have a sweet tooth. You know, ya' look just like Venetta. Ya' got her eyes, her smile—" Ode chuckled "—and all that hot long thick hair. My baby sister was beautiful." She let out a slow heavy sigh. "And she could have had anything she wanted in this world."

Alicia leaned forward resting her chin on her elbow. "But what?" she asked.

Ode's facial expression changed from that of reminiscent to a cold unexpressive stare. "But nuttin'. She left…" A beat later, Ode looked up with a broad smile. "But, we got plenty of time to talk 'bout ya' mama. Let me get these chirren fed."

A loud crash, followed by a child's screech brought Ode from the stove. She grabbed her hand fan and waved it faster as she hurried toward the kitchen door. A layer of perspiration coated her face. "Lord, what these chirren done did now?"

Alicia stood to go see what had happened, but Ode waved her back to the table.

"Ya' sit down, honey. When I come back I wants to hear all about what ya' do in Atlanta. My grandbaby wants to go to Atlanta, but I don't know. The boy ain't been away from this coast before."

Alicia sat back down, hoping the little boys were okay. She clasped her hands together in her lap, and stared at them. Dialogue about her mother had begun. If there were no more interruptions, maybe today she'd learn something significant.

Chapter 3

Darius sat around the table with Sterling and the hotel's management staff. Their morning meeting began after introductions and a southern-style breakfast. Timothy Bullock, the short, stocky hospitality manager, introduced himself first. William Wilson, the gangly maintenance supervisor, shook Darius's hand and in a husky voice spouted off his list of complaints. Sales manager Evan Bradley, showed up in a starched pink shirt and tie—the only one not in hotel uniform. After everyone sat down to eat, Gibb Underwood, the assistant general manager who worked the night shift, joined the group in a wrinkled shirt.

The waiter cleared the table, and Darius kicked things off by passing out a one-page outline of his business credentials.

"As you may already know, my knowledge of the hotel operations is limited, however, my business credentials speak for themselves. My partner and I took over a bankrupt coffee shop on Chicago's Navy Pier, and in a year's time we turned that one shop into three in the greater Chicago area. And when time permits, I help my mother with her women's specialty store. Gentlemen, in short, I know how to make money, and I plan to use that knowledge to help this hotel.

"What I'm not familiar with, I'm going to rely on my general manager, here—" he nodded at Sterling "—and his assistant—" then at Gibb "—for guidance until I get my feet on the ground. Everyone at this table is aware of the hotel's troubled financial status. I'm here to turn that around.

"Now, if you don't mind, I'd like to go around the table and have you explain what you do, and how I can help you be more successful."

Each manager explained his department's operating procedures, detailing where additional staff and improvements could be made. Timothy's passion for his team came across, while Evan didn't have a team, but explained the difficulties he faced in sales. After all the reports, Darius had a better picture of how he could help.

"Gentlemen, thank you. If you'll send me your request I'll take a look at them. The main thing I wanted to discuss this morning is the hotel's occupancy rate. Last month we were only fifty percent occupied. For an ocean-side hotel during peak season we should be full or at least 90 percent occupied. Before I sit down with Evan alone, what do you think we can do as a team to fill one hundred and twenty rooms?" Darius waited for suggestions to come flying at him, but only received puzzled stares from everyone except Gibb, who looked asleep with his eyes open.

Timothy spoke up. "I know fifty percent's pretty bad, but you have to remember we don't have fancy rooms, tennis courts, or spas, like those chain hotels. We got The Golden Isle Sons singing on Saturday nights, and the karaoke

machine in the piano bar is a hit. Sometimes we start a vol-
leyball game on the beach—the kids especially seem to like
that. But we can hardly compete with the surrounding hotels."

"Most of the tourists like to stay up the coast closer to the
historic district," Evan added.

Darius waved the waiter over for a second cup of coffee
while he listened to his managers offer up one excuse after
another. Sterling still had stress lines etched in his forehead,
which caused Darius to question his ability to handle such a
high-level position. Maybe staff changes were needed,
starting with the men at this table.

"Well…" Sterling cleared his throat. "I believe part of the
problem stems from this being an old hotel with quite a few
issues, that frankly have never been addressed. That affects
your repeat business. Occupancy *has* declined over the years.
I'm afraid this hotel may be on its last leg."

Darius chuckled and shook his head. "Nonsense, this hotel
is over forty years old, but so are numerous other buildings
on the island. What we—"

"Excuse me, sir," Sterling interrupted. "But most of the other
hotels have been saved from decay by Robinson Cedric Enterprises, who also offered to help your grandfather, but he refused."

Darius sipped his coffee and answered Sterling's snobbish
attitude with a polite smile. He didn't like being reminded of
how his grandfather almost lost the hotel to underhanded ex-
ecutives with RCE.

He set his coffee cup down. "I'm aware of RCE's offer.
They wanted to purchase Hotel Paradise—that's not what I
call an offer to help. My grandfather didn't want to sell this
property—" he looked each man in the eye so they understood
he meant business "—and gentlemen, neither do I. If by some
miracle I change my mind, you'll be the first to know. Until
then, my intentions are to bring Hotel Paradise up to par with

the other hotels on this island. I hope we can work together as a team to accomplish this. Let's do whatever it takes to fill these rooms."

Sterling stood and rubbed his palms together. "Mr. Monroe, I guess it's time to see what you've inherited. We're prepared to start the tour now."

Unaware of whether Darius had more to cover or not, Sterling ended the meeting. Darius bit his lower lip between his teeth to keep the slight irritation from his face as he stood.

After a wonderful lunch and telling her aunt what she'd been doing for the last twenty years, Alicia returned to Hotel Paradise. Unfortunately, she hadn't gotten any more information about her mother. She stopped at the front desk to see her cousin Sterling, but he was out on the property, so Alicia left a note in hopes of catching up with him later.

Once in her suite, she couldn't decide if she wanted to go for a swim, or seek out a cousin to talk to. Then a swift knock came at the door.

She opened the door to Rorie in a pair of trunks with a towel draped around his shoulder. The decision was made for her.

"That ocean is just calling me. Want to take a dip?"

"Let me grab my suit. I'm right behind you."

They pulled two lounge chairs together and kicked back in the shade before going in.

"You are coming to the party tonight, aren't you?"

"What party?" she asked, surprised. As a welcoming, the couple had already treated everyone to a party cruise.

"Sterling hooked it up so we can keep the bar open late tonight for a bachelor-slash-bachelorette party. Everyone's invited, and he promised they'd keep the drinks flowing."

She laughed. "I'll be there. Tomorrow's the big day. Are they ready?"

"As they'll ever be. Sherri's so afraid something's going to go wrong she driving everybody crazy."

"What could go wrong? Doesn't the hotel handle everything?"

"They've incorporated some special touches into the ceremony, and Sterling promised everything will go off without a hitch."

She couldn't see his eyes for his sunglasses. "You don't sound too convinced."

"That's because I for one don't believe Sterling can walk on water, like everybody else does. He's the only black general manager on the island, which is something to be proud of, but I bet you he couldn't get a general manager position in one of the other hotels."

"Rorie, why do you say that?" His smug attitude toward his cousin shocked her.

"I'm just telling it like it is. I haven't seen him in a long time, but a zebra can't change its stripes. He plays a good game, and it'll catch up with him one day."

"Sounds like somebody's jealous," she teased.

He snorted. "Hardly. I just purchased a three hundred thousand dollar townhouse in midtown Atlanta. He ain't got nothing on me."

Alicia chuckled and stood up. "Come on, let's take that dip."

After a relaxing afternoon swim, Alicia ordered a sandwich from room service, and then she showered and washed her hair.

Before she left for the party, she read a few more pages from one of her mother's journals. Or, she tried to read them. Some of the words tripped her up. *Mi glad fa see Coffee. Na want to differ with tata.* To Alicia, it looked like another language. If she didn't find out anything else during this trip, she would find someone who could decipher this stuff for her. She left the journal in the bathroom and closed the door.

The intimate piano bar with its dark burgundy upholstery had a Jamaican theme, replete with a large poster of Bob Marley. Bottle labels and advertisements for Appleton Rum hung on the walls as decoration. For a Thursday evening, the room was dead. Aside from the bartender, two tourists sat at a table in the corner. Alicia took a seat at the bar and ordered an Apple Martini.

A group of hotel employees came in and ordered drinks from the other end of the bar. Alicia didn't pay them much attention until one headed her way. As he came closer she recognized her cousin, Sterling.

"Alicia, here you are." He set his beer on the counter and gave her a musty-smelling hug. "I received your note, but you weren't in your room when I called."

She returned the embrace. "Sorry, I went for a swim. You're a pretty hard man to catch."

He sat on the stool next to her and took a couple swigs of beer. "I've got a new boss and he has me working longer hours right now. I was just on my way home for the day."

"You're not sticking around for the party tonight?"

He shook his head. "Everything for tonight's taken care of. I've been here since five o'clock this morning. I'm too pooped to party."

"Now that's what I call a long day. I totally understand."

"How's your stay been so far?"

"Just fine. Everybody's been wonderful."

"Good, good, I'm glad to hear that. I know Mama's excited to see you. She's called everyone in the family and told them about you. This is your first visit to the Islands, isn't it?"

"My second actually, but I don't remember the first time

because I was so young. I grew up thinking my mother was from New York, until my father passed away last year."

Astonished he said, "You didn't know you was Geechee?"

Wide-eyed, Alicia shook her head. "No, I didn't. Now, I read about the Gullah, or Geechee culture, but I associated it with the islands off of North and South Carolina instead of the Georgia coast."

He motioned for the bartender to bring him another beer.

"Mama-nems from St. Helena, North Carolina. She moved down here after she got married. But all the barrier islands, from North Carolina down to Florida, are full of descendants of West Africans. I'm surprised you didn't know that."

"Whatever I learned about the Gullah culture I've forgotten most of it. Don't the Gullah people have a language of their own?"

He nodded. "Only elderly people still use it. Listen and you might hear a little of it every now and then."

That would explain some of the journal entries, she thought. She didn't want to discuss the journal with Sterling, and from the way he guzzled down his beers, he already had something pressing on his mind.

However, she'd discovered Sterling was a wellspring of information. Maybe she'd try to spend more time with him.

The bartender set another bottle of beer in front of Sterling. "Would you like another drink?" Sterling asked her.

She didn't, but the longer they talked the more she learned.

"Sure, I'll have another Martini," she told the waiting bartender.

"So, Mama tells me you run your father's business in Atlanta. What type of business is it?"

"A car dealership."

He loosened the grip on the beer bottle and gave her a sideways arched-brow grin. "Nice."

"I own it, but I don't run the day-to-day operations. Not like I hear you run things around here." She didn't want the conversation in her court.

The bartender delivered her drink.

Sterling nodded and the expression on his face lengthened as he looked down into his drink. "Sometimes I feel like this is my hotel. I do everything but live here." He raised his head and looked at Alicia through the mirror behind the bar. "Mr. Monroe gave me my first job at eighteen." He turned from the mirror and looked directly at her. "I held almost every low-level position here before being promoted to management. Only Nathan, the driver, has worked here longer than I have."

"Wow, so you must know all the history of this hotel?"

"Yeah, pretty much. Now I've heard stories about the good old days, like everybody else. Back in the forties and fifties, the islands were considered a black man's paradise. A group of black businessmen built the original hotel and named it Hotel Paradise. Then the Monroes purchased the hotel, but they kept the name."

"That's more than I knew. I hope to learn all I can about the African American history of the area before I leave."

"How long did you say you're here for?"

He finished off his second beer. The bartender came by to pick up the empty bottle. Again, Sterling didn't give him much time to sit the third drink down before he picked it up.

"A couple of weeks, maybe a month. It all depends."

"On what?"

On your mother telling me what I need to know. "On how long it takes me to meet all the family and see where my mother grew up."

"Well, I think Mama's planning a cookout after this wedding to bring the family together. You should be able to meet everybody you haven't already met then."

"That's sweet of her."

"Yeah." He chuckled. "She's like that. I'll try to make it if I can. I don't normally work the weekends, but that might change. Things around here are gonna be crazy for a while."

"The new boss is kind of tough, huh?"

He frowned, shook his head, and stood up. "Nobody I can't handle. Look, I'm gonna have to run. I've missed dinner already and I like to spend a little time with the kids before they go to bed. If you need anything, just call the front desk and tell them you're my cousin. It'll be taken care of."

"Thank you Sterling. Drive carefully now."

After a quick hug Alicia watched him walk away as if he'd been drinking water all evening.

Minutes after Sterling left, the loud wedding party piled into the bar. Alicia grabbed her drink and joined Rorie and company at his table.

"Alicia, I'm so glad you didn't make me come find you—" Rorie hugged her and then looked deep into her eyes "—because you know I would have."

She kissed him on the cheek. "I know, so I saved you a trip."

A waiter brought in two huge trays of seafood appetizers, while another served glasses of rum.

Alicia didn't like to eat this late, but made an exception. Rorie, the social butterfly, talked and socialized with everyone in the room. Anyone Alicia hadn't met yet, he introduced.

An hour later, after sampling their share of appetizers and rum, the highlight of the night began—the karaoke competition.

"Okay, here's the deal," Rorie explained to everyone at the table. "Whenever we have large family gatherings we hold this contest. Monica, cousin Jean's daughter with the Pamela Anderson breasts, won last year at the family picnic and she thinks she's going to win again tonight. But I predict her reign is over."

Minutes later, he turned the music up and opened the competition.

Almost everyone in the wedding party took a turn at the microphone. Alicia laughed as the bridesmaids created a group and cried through Chaka Khan's *Through The Fire,* and then the groomsmen sang *You Should Be Mine (The Woo Woo Song).* Maurice brought the room to tears with a heartwarming, but out of tune, serenade to his bride.

The tone-deaf group delighted the hotel workers who stood in the doorway laughing.

By the time Rorie called Alicia's name, she had more than a buzz.

"Your turn, sweetheart." He handed her the mike.

With the prize bottle of Jamaican rum in sight and a welcoming cheer from the room, she took the microphone. She couldn't hold a tune, but her competition had been either too stilted or too drunk to stand up.

To her horror, *Bad Girls* by Donna Summers popped on the screen. She turned and narrowed her eyes at Rorie who grinned broadly and waved. He'd selected his favorite song for her.

Darius rested his elbows on the desk and closed the folder in front of him. With the telephone pinched between his shoulder and ear, he filed the folder away. Keith Hamilton, his business partner, had called down to update him on progress at the coffee shops.

"I don't know. I may have bitten off more than I can chew. This hotel needs a lot of work, and unfortunately the people on my management team aren't exactly go-getters."

"Man, I can't believe you're down there in the first place. You're a better man than I am. I would have just sold the place."

A northern boy born and raised in St. Paul, Minnesota, Keith loved Chicago.

"I can't do that. My father and grandfather were raised here, so I'll have to tough it out. Besides, this place is a gold mine. If I get the money to renovate like I want to, my family will be set for life."

"I hear you. If there's anything I can do from this end, just say the word. You know I've got your back, we're partners."

"Thanks. I may be giving you a call."

"Have you heard from Luke?"

Darius snorted and shook his head. "Are you kidding? I wouldn't be surprised if he wasn't in Spain or somewhere. Luke doesn't care anything about family, or this place." Since their father's death, Luke had slipped even further away from Darius.

"It's a shame, man. He should be down there helping you."

"Maybe, maybe not. Luke has a habit of getting into female trouble. I don't need that kind of drama."

"Hey, somebody's gotta give your mother a grandchild. And since you're determined to work yourself into the ground, Luke may be her only hope."

Darius turned the tarnished silver desk clock around to see the time. Children or his brother were the last things he wanted to discuss tonight. He pushed back in his chair and stretched his arms overhead.

"Well, my day started at seven a.m., and now it's almost ten p.m. My back hurts, my legs are cramped, and I need a hot shower. Guess it's time I made it back to my bachelor's pad."

Keith laughed. "It can't be that bad."

"It's not a condo on Lake Michigan, but I've got an ocean view." A quick picture of the woman he saw on the beach flashed in his head. "And some beautiful sights."

After hanging up with Keith, Darius turned out the lights and closed his office door. Only Gibb and a front desk clerk were in the hotel office when he left. Across the lobby several employees stood in the doorway of the piano bar gaping inside. They snickered and pointed their fingers enough to arouse Darius's curiosity.

He started to ignore them and head up the hill to his apartment, when he remembered Timothy raving about the karaoke machine. He changed his mind and joined the crowd at the door.

He peered over their heads and the packed room elicited a little smile from him. Crowds were good for business. Tired as hell, he craned his neck a little further to see the stage—it was empty. But, just to the right of the stage he found the object of everybody's attention.

Chapter 4

Darius watched with growing enthusiasm the woman dance in high heels atop the table; the way her curvaceous body moved. His eyes slowly worked their way up until he reached her face, and then he recognized her.

That face belonged to the hot pink bikini-wearing woman that lay on the beach outside his suite yesterday. She gyrated her hips in such a sensual way it made it difficult for him to think, breathe, or do anything else.

She shimmied her skirt up and tantalized the crowd with her legs, while she sang, "Spirit's high and the legs look hot."

Oh, hell. He had to see this. Rejuvenated suddenly, he maneuvered around the ogling men in the doorway and settled at the bar.

The spirited crowd loved her. While women cheered her on, a few tables over, a young guy's over-the-top encouragement kept the room fired up.

"Mr. Monroe, can I get you something to drink?" The bartender placed a coaster, with the hotel's name embossed on top, in front of Darius.

Darius glanced at the brawny, skewed-nosed man not remembering his name among the numerous employees he'd met in the last two days. "Sure. I'll have a Heineken, uh." He pointed at the man.

"Greg, sir."

Darius snapped his fingers as if the name had been on the tip of his tongue. "Thanks, Greg." He swung his attention back to the stage, eager to catch the rest of the show. She flirted with the crowd and then looked over at him.

They locked eyes. Every nerve ending in his body woke up. She ran a hand up the back of her hair, pulling it high atop her head. "You bad girl, you sad girl, I'm such a dirty bad girl." Then she looked away. A fire stirred deep inside him when she released her long black hair, letting it cascade around her shoulders. She ended the song with a mesmerizing and sensual kiss blown to the crowd.

Darius leaned into the bar and pointed to the crowd closest to the piano. "Who are those people?"

The bartender filled a pilsner and set it on the coaster. "A wedding party. Somebody's getting hitched tomorrow."

Alicia took a bow, and everyone in the room stood and applauded, including Darius. Men slapped high fives and yelled catcalls, while women hollered out, "You go, girl." Her personal cheerleader rushed over and helped her from the table like Alicia was a princess descending from her throne. When she threw her head back and fanned herself with her hand, Darius felt the heat.

He grabbed his beer and took a swig. Could that be the couple getting married, he asked himself?

The blonde guy picked up the microphone. "Ladies and

gents, I believe we have a winner. The new karaoke champion, and my number one bad girl, Ms. Alicia McKay." Before presenting her with the prize bottle of rum, he gave her a kiss on the cheek and a big hug. The lack of intimacy in their touch answered Darius's question.

She crossed the room, a little unsteady, back to her table amid friendly accolades.

"Maybe you should congratulate the winner, sir."

Darius took another swig of beer and arched a brow at the bartender, who smiled and tilted his head toward her table. *Why shouldn't I congratulate her? After all, I am the new owner of the hotel. It would be common courtesy.* After a brief hesitation, he said, "I think I'll do just that."

He left his beer on the counter and straightened his tie before crossing the room.

"Excuse me." He stood alongside Alicia and greeted everyone at the table with a broad smile.

"Yes." She looked up still laughing about something said before he reached the table.

Close up, her flawless caramel complexion and full lips turned him on even more. He didn't want to be disrespectful, and tried to refrain from staring, but her big brown eyes peeking out behind long curly lashes captured his heart.

"On behalf of Hotel Paradise, I'd like to congratulate you." He offered his hand before glancing over at the blond guy who didn't look so young after all.

She accepted his hand and a warm sensation jetted up his arm.

"So you represent the whole hotel?" she asked, in a loud voice over the music.

"Yes, I do." He hesitated when her blond-haired boyfriend set his drink down and gave him a guarded look. "I own the hotel. I'm Darius…Darius Monroe."

"Oh, well, thank you, Mr. Monroe. I'm Alicia." She still held on to his hand, pumping it harder now.

The minute he let go, the blond guy reached over and offered his way too soft manicured hand. "Rorie Broady. So pleased to meet you."

Darius acknowledged everyone with their bloodshot eyes and slurred speeches. They were lit. The whole table of them, he concluded. He returned his admiring gaze to Alicia. "I hope you're enjoying your stay so far?"

"Oh, I am, thank you. You have a lovely hotel."

"Okay, that's my cue to run and check on our engaged couple. Can't let them get drunk and ruin the nuptials tomorrow." Rorie turned toward the other female in the group. "Let's go put Sherrie and Maurice to bed." He turned back to Alicia and gave her another kiss on the cheek. "See you later, darling."

He stood grinning as he held his chair out and winked at Darius. "Mr. Monroe, please… Take my seat."

Darius raised his chin at Rorie after he waved good-bye and staggered off.

"Mind if I sit down a minute?" he asked, walking behind Alicia to get to the vacant seat.

"Yes." Alicia held her hand out toward the chair. "I mean no, sit down."

She pushed the half-empty glass in front of her across the table with the others. If she'd wanted him to think she wasn't drinking, it was too late.

"That was quite a performance you gave up there," he commented, as he took his seat. "Are you scheduled anywhere else so I can catch the whole act?"

She covered her face with her hands. "Oh God, I must have looked like a fool."

"Not at all. I didn't catch the competition, but you looked pretty damned good to me."

She gave him a "yeah-right" grin. "I got carried away in front of a room full of strangers, and for what? A cheap bottle of rum." She flung her finger at the bottle sitting in the center of the table and rolled her eyes.

"You know, that's some very special rum you won."

"Really?" She pulled the bottle closer and twisted her lips as she studied the label. "What's so special about it?"

"On my grandfather's first Jamaican vacation he fell in love with that stuff. He came back to Jekyll Island and started ordering it by the case. Originally, the hotel only served it during special occasions. Now that he's passed, I guess they've opened the stock." To see his grandfather's special rum being handed out like this did surprise him; but he wanted management to keep the guests happy.

"So that explains all this Jamaican stuff," she said, waving her hand around the room. "I heard your grandfather was a good man." She pointed at Darius before lowering her hand and head. "My father was a good man too, but now he's gone," she said in a slur.

Her transformation from drunk and happy to drunk and sad caught Darius by surprise. He didn't like the downcast look on her face.

"I'm sorry, was he ill?"

She nodded. "Cancer. He died last May."

Darius could tell from the pained expression on her face she still mourned his absence. "My father passed too, a couple of years ago," he offered, as a form of condolence.

"Oh, that's terrible. I wish my father hadn't died and left me." She glanced up into Darius's eyes. "It's hard being all by yourself, you know?" she said sadly.

The loneliness in her eyes tugged at his heart. He scooted his chair closer, hoping she wasn't about to cry. "Are you an only child?"

She shrugged. "As far as I know."

Now, what did that mean? She lowered her head and stared at the empty glasses on the table. Darius motioned for a waiter. He needed to cheer her up. They weren't about to have a pity party.

When the waiter approached, he had a bottle of Heineken on his tray. Darius saluted the bartender for remembering his drink. "Bring the lady a glass of water please," he instructed.

Alicia's head snapped up wide-eyed with her mouth gaped open.

"You'll thank me for it later," he said smiling. Water wouldn't sober her up, but he had to start somewhere.

He took a deep breath and changed the tone of the conversation to something more pleasant. "So, are you a bridesmaid in tomorrow's wedding?" he asked, hoping she had a friend here somewhere who could care for her.

She perked up and pointed her finger. "Always a bridesmaid, never a bride." She chuckled and cocked her head to the side while smiling at him. "I'm sorry, I've always wanted to say that. No, I'm just a guest. The bride's my cousin, I just don't know her that well."

He smiled. "So who are you here with?" he asked, concerned now from a manager's perspective.

Before she could answer, the waiter set a tall glass of ice water in front of her and asked if they wanted anything else. Alicia took a big gulp of water as Darius thanked him.

"Whew! I was thirsty," she said, holding a hand over her chest.

"Did you and Rorie come down together?" Darius probed.

She giggled and tried to rest her elbow on the table, but it slipped off the edge. "Believe it or not, that fool broke my baby doll when we were kids. I hadn't seen him since then.

I just found out yesterday he's my cousin. Maybe I should seek revenge on behalf of dolls everywhere."

"It looked like you knew him better than that to me."

She shook her head. "He's like a girlfriend. You know what I mean. He's easy to talk to, easy to get along with, just a real sweet guy." She threw her hand up and snapped her fingers. "And we both live in Atlanta."

Darius bit his bottom lip to keep from laughing. "You're a real riot you know that? Yeah, I think I understand now." Rorie was gay. "So, who *are* you here with?" he asked again.

She sat up with breasts thrust out and her arms spread like butterfly wings. "Me, myself, and I," she slurred with pride, a gleeful smile, and glassy eyes.

Oh great! With pursed lips, Darius nodded. She's alone, she's drunk, and she's beautiful. A deadly combination should the wrong guy come along.

They sat there in silence while he sipped his beer and contemplated what to do next. In her tipsy state, he wasn't comfortable leaving her there alone.

Billows of cigarette smoke drifted in their direction. She coughed and fanned it away, but Darius saw a sickening look come over her face.

"Mr. Monroe, I've enjoyed your company…but I think I'd better go now." She picked up her purse.

"Come on, I'll walk you to your room." He stood and offered his hand.

She slipped getting up, and he reached out to grab her in time to keep her from knocking over the chair. Instead of stumbling backwards, she fell forward against him.

Her long red nails landed firmly in the middle of his chest, as she looked up and asked, "So what are you…my escort for the night?"

Darius peered down into lazy brown eyes and a wicked

grin. His body weakened from her touch and the clean smell of her hair. He let go of her arm and pushed her chair back.

"I'm whatever you want me to be. As long as I get you safely to your room." He pretended to be oblivious to her flirting. Another time and under better circumstances, he'd love to tuck her into bed and crawl in next to her.

"In that case—" she stepped back and grabbed her purse and the bottle of rum from the table, waving it around by the neck "—I could use your services. Please escort me to my suite."

"Yes, ma'am." He reached for the rum afraid she'd drop it. "Here, let me carry that." He took the bottle.

Darius followed her and admired the sway of her hips as she strutted out into the quiet, empty lobby. Then he chastised himself. What on earth had he gotten himself into? He should've had Gibb, or Georgem the night security guard, escort her. He didn't need to play the knight in shining armor; but she looked so sweet he couldn't help from being chivalrous.

They strolled down the moonlit ocean path that led to her room. Beer and sheer exhaustion had caught up with him. He wanted to drop her off and then go crash. He slowed his pace to keep in step as she swayed down the pavement.

"Are you okay?" he asked, prepared to pick her up and carry her.

"I don't feel so good. I think I'm going to be sick," she slurred.

One look at her flushed face, and Darius cursed under his breath. "You'll be okay. What's your room number?" He scooped a hand under her elbow to assist in speeding her along. In high heels, she hustled to keep up with him.

"Forty-two, on the second floor."

Damn it. Darius cursed under his breath. Her room was still yards away. "We're almost there. What did you have to drink tonight anyway?" She wasn't moving fast enough despite his efforts. He shifted his arm around her waist.

"They served rum, and I had a Martini earlier. I think that's all," she said, on the verge of tears. "I'm sorry, I didn't mean to drink so—"

"Don't even worry about it." They turned down another path leading to her building. "Here we go, just a few more steps." His eyes were transfixed on her building as he willed it closer.

They finally reached her building; now he had to get her up the steps and into her suite.

"God, it's so hot out here, I'm suffocating." She fanned herself with her hand and drew a few deep breaths.

"Air conditioning is just up those steps." He prayed she could hold out. He forced himself to refrain from carrying her the rest of the way.

She lifted her legs as if they were lead blocks, and made it up three steps before she froze. Darius supported her back by placing both hands on her hips. When she didn't budge, he feared the worse.

She spun around.

His eyes widened at the sight of her bloated cheeks and closed eyes. "Oh, no," he moaned.

Chapter 5

Alicia threw up all over Darius's arm. "Oh, God. I am so sorry," she croaked.

He gasped as she stumbled past him and out onto the grass. Darius squinted and turned his head while he shook his sleeve out onto the grass. Well, this was a first. "Don't worry about it. I'll live."

"Oh, no." She turned from him, stumbling farther away, and retched again.

He ignored the cool, wet sleeve sticking to his arm and followed her onto the grass, steering her back up the stairs once she stopped retching.

Finally, they reached her suite and he fished the key from her purse. The minute he opened the door, she stormed past him and rushed into the bathroom.

After closing the door, he let out a sigh of relief. They hadn't made it in time, but he'd still safely gotten her inside. He placed her rum and her door key on top of the minifridge.

When he heard the toilet flush, he stepped over and tapped lightly on the bathroom door. "You okay in there?"

"Yeah, uh, I'll be right out."

"Take your time." He turned around and stood in the middle of the room awkwardly holding his arm away from his body. Her suite had the standard kitchenette, separate sleeping and living room, and a king-size bed. She'd added her own personal touch. A cluster of scented candles shared space with the hotel-provided clock radio on the nightstand.

Once he heard running water, he walked over to the living room sofa.

A whiff of cold air from the overhead vent made his wet shirt feel sticky and miserable against his arm. Before he could sit down, the bathroom door swung open.

Alicia appeared drooped in the doorway with a towel in her hand and an apologetic look in her eyes. He empathized with her—she couldn't be feeling too well right now.

"Mind if I use your bathroom?" he asked, holding up his wet, soiled sleeve.

Her eyebrows shot up in surprise as she bolted away from the wall, and he could see she'd momentarily forgotten she'd thrown up on him. She rushed over holding out the towel.

"What's the matter with me? Here, let me get that for you."

Before he could pull away, she set the towel on his arm. His shirt and arm clung together sending a chill through his whole body.

He looked down and grasped her wrist. "That's okay, just let me run some water over it."

She sniffled and relaxed in his hands. "I don't know what happened to me," she started to explain.

"Look, don't worry about it. It's nothing really. Why don't you sit down and let me call and get you some coffee."

She plopped down on the sofa and pressed a palm to the side of her head, then relaxed into it. "Thanks, but I don't drink coffee." After a heavy sigh, she laid back against the cushions. "Besides, room service isn't open this late, I've tried before."

He walked over to the phone. "I own the hotel, remember? Since you don't drink coffee, I'll make it tea."

She snapped her fingers and pointed them like a pistol. "That's right, you own this place. I imagine whatever Mr. Monroe wants, Mr. Monroe gets." She giggled at herself, and then closed her eyes.

He turned away and called the front desk. The night clerk answered, and Darius asked him to bring by a variety of teas.

While she rested, he stepped into the bathroom and took off his shirt and tie. The night had turned into a surreal moment for him. After seeing her on the beach yesterday he'd thought about her more than once. He thought about her dressed in a nightgown emerging from his bathroom, lying next to him on the beach in that hot pink number, or completely nude. But not once, had he ever imagined her sprawled out on the sofa drunk.

He hung his tie over the shower door and submerged his sleeve under the running water. Seconds later, a knock at the front door was followed by, "Room service."

In an effort to let her rest, he rushed out to answer the door, but a startled Alicia stumbled to her feet. She stopped, eyes widened with alarm as he crossed the room.

"Don't worry, I'll get it," he said as he passed.

"Oh…okay," she mumbled inanely and fell back onto the sofa.

He let the young desk clerk in. "Thanks, just set it down on the dresser," Darius instructed.

"I brought some chamomile and…and—" The young

man's speech stalled to a halt when he noticed Alicia sprawled out on the sofa.

Darius cleared his throat. "She got sick at that wedding party tonight."

"Yessir," he replied with a nod and set the tray down. "There's a variety here, like you requested. Can I do anything else for y'all?" he asked.

"The tea's fine, thank you."

When Darius closed the door and turned around, Alicia fixed her eyes on his chest. Why was he standing in her room half-naked?

"How do you take your tea?" he asked, glancing over at her.

She sat up and met his gaze. "Some Equal, that's all." Her eyes lowered to a tattoo above his left nipple. She walked over and stood next to him as he stirred the sweetener in her cup.

"Feel any better?" he asked smiling.

She shrugged and glanced at him without blatantly staring. "A little. But, I have a feeling tomorrow my head is going to split wide open."

He laughed, showing off his pearly whites, and her insides flipped. Alicia hadn't ever wanted a man to pull her into his arms more than she did right now. She imagined his massive arms wrapped around her body while she snuggled up to his chest.

"Come on, and sit down." With cup in hand, he motioned her back over to the sofa.

She took a deep cleansing breath before lowering herself to the sofa. "You've been so good to me tonight," she said, tucking a foot underneath her.

He smiled at her before setting the cup on the coffee table and rubbing his palms together nervously. "You might want to let it cool off a minute, then sip it."

Alicia feared he was about to leave, and she didn't want to be left alone just yet.

"Darius, thank you. You didn't have to do all this."

"Yeah, well, I thought you might need something to settle your stomach before going to bed."

"I know what would help me sleep," she giggled, barely above a whisper, and reached out to touch his chest.

His eyes followed her hand, but he didn't stop her. "What's that?" he asked in a husky voice. She traced her finger along the tiger head tattooed above his nipple.

"Come to bed with me." Surprised she'd said that out loud, she snatched her hand from his chest.

She looked up into his tawny brown, lid heavy eyes and moved in closer. His tongue parted his lips, and she leaned forward to meet him. When their lips touched, she closed her eyes and a spark of electricity ran through her body. A tingling sensation settled between her legs and turned into a throbbing ache.

She felt like she was having an out of body experience. Her mouth hungrily searched for his tongue while she caressed his nipple between her fingers. His hand came up and slid behind her head as he returned the kisses more aggressively. His warm soft lips sucked her deeper and deeper into the moment. Alicia enjoyed kissing him.

No, she *loved* kissing him.

God, she'd never been this hot for a man in all her life. He explored her mouth so expertly she never wanted him to leave her room. Their breathing grew heavier and more desperate in nature. Lightheaded and dizzy with lust, she wrapped an arm around his neck.

When she sensed him pulling away, her body screamed *no*…

Slowly he backed away, taking her hand from his neck and squeezing it. His chest rose and fell as he struggled to catch his breath. "I'd better finish cleaning my shirt," he whispered.

She met his stare, and his tongue darted across his lips, causing her to melt. The steam between them subsided, and their breathing returned to normal. He stood up.

"Drink your tea," he said, through pursed lips, and then walked into the bathroom.

She slumped back onto the sofa and took a deep calming breath. "You don't have to put it back on on my account."

He closed the bathroom door.

Darius chastised himself. She'd had her tea; it was time for him to leave. Walking her to her room had been a big mistake, and making out with her wasn't an option. He came to Jekyll Island to accomplish one thing, and she wasn't it.

He pulled his shirt from the water and squeezed out the sleeve. He grabbed a towel and looked for a place to dry it off. A red leather-bound book lay open at the corner of the vanity, so he picked it up in order to place the towel there.

He glanced down and the words "Hotel Paradise" jumped off the page at him. He flipped over to the front of the book and read the cover, which said, "My Journal." Unable to stop himself, he read a few lines.

"I've found my final resting place—Hotel Paradise. It's like no other place in the world. It's here I find peace and happiness. The only peace I've known for some time now. Without my lover, I don't know how I can go on. He's every breath I take; yet I can't be with him. And without him I don't want to live another day. I feel like the African slaves who ended their lives off these coasts centuries ago. Without their loved ones, they couldn't go on, and neither can I."

A creepy, prickly sensation ran through Darius's body. He backed into the counter and closed the book. Did she plan to kill herself?

He set the journal down and finished drying out his sleeve. His facial muscles twitched as his mind backpedaled over everything she'd said tonight. He had to admit, she did look sad, but he'd blamed that on the liquor. He shook his shirt out and looked up at himself in the mirror. What now? Should he go out and talk to her about it? He wasn't a counselor. Besides, he'd had no business reading anything in her journal.

When he walked back into the room, Alicia sat on the sofa drinking her tea. She looked better.

"Well, I'll say goodnight now so you can go to sleep."

A small smile touched her lips, and she nodded looking so feminine and innocent. He asked God to help him walk out of that room. She followed him to the door.

"If you feel sick later on, just call the front desk and ask for the manager, he'll get you medical attention if you need it." *Or call me,* he wanted to say, but didn't.

"I won't need it. I'm okay." She leaned against the minifridge by the door.

"I'll come by and check on you tomorrow."

"That won't be necessary," she said wearily.

"Uh, huh. Maybe not, but I'll be by anyway. Goodnight."

Unsure of what to do about what he'd read, he walked away with a heavier load than when he arrived. He was in way over his head in more ways than one.

Trouble stepped back under the stair rail as Darius left the building. "What the hell is he doing down here this late?" he mumbled.

Darius turned the corner, so Trouble strolled around to the beachfront of the building. All the rooms were dark, except for two. He turned to walk away when a light went out. Intrigued now, he stepped back and counted balconies. The light belonged to suite forty-two. He pitched his keys in the air playfully, before he walked away whistling.

He continued around the building until he reached the end. Positive no one spotted him, he used his key and opened the door to the maintenance room. "Let's see what Darius does best, run a hotel, or run home."

The pounding in her head grew louder and louder, even with the blanket over her head. Alicia pushed back the repulsive sound and submerged herself in her lover's arms again. Once more tasting the salty flesh of his nipples, and overcome by an urgent desire to taste the rest of him. Just as her lover laid her on her back and started kissing up her knees and thighs, another round of pounding broke through. Her body throbbed as she fought desperately to stay in the moment.

"I know you're in there, so open up."

Reluctantly, she threw the covers back and opened one eye. It was Rorie outside her door.

The head-splitting pounding returned. Unable to bear it for another minute, she pried herself from the bed and shuffled to the door.

"I'm coming, I'm coming," she chanted, as she opened the door.

"Oh my God! What happened to you?" he asked, placing a hand over his mouth.

"I'm still asleep," she said, trying to pry her other eye open. She reached up and plucked off the false eyelash and her eye sprang open.

He looked at his watch. "Uh, huh. You're still in last night's clothes too. But never fear." He held up a brown paper bag. "Since you don't have time for breakfast before the wedding, I brought you a bagel and some cream cheese."

She scrunched up her face. "That's right, the wedding is today."

He peered over her trying to see around the door. "You got somebody up in there or something?" he asked.

Had she been dreaming, or was Darius still in her bed. She looked back holding the door open a bit wider in the process. Empty. "'Fraid not," she said, turning back around.

Rorie slipped into the room. "Good. Come on, let's have breakfast and you can tell me all about last night." He strolled over to the coffee table and set his bag down. "Got any more tea?"

A strange feeling washed over her as she looked from the cup on the coffee table to the tray on her dresser. Darius had been there last night. She pulled her hair back and closed the door.

"Yeah, there's more on the tray over there." She pointed to the dresser.

"Great, I'll fix us some while you fill me in. We've got a little while before I need to get dressed." He picked up the coffeepot and headed for the bathroom.

Her mouth felt yucky and her throat scratched like sandpaper. "Nothing happened last night," she said, shuffling back over to the bed.

"Oh no?" he asked curiously.

She sat on the edge of the bed and looked around for her slippers. "After you deserted me, I came back to the room." She found her slippers and then a ponytail holder and pulled her hair back.

"Then what's this?"

Alicia turned around, and Rorie popped out of the bathroom with the coffeepot in one hand, and Darius's tie in the other.

With a smile so big it was the only thing noticeable on his face, he said, "You lying heffa! You screwed him didn't you?"

Chapter 6

Darius closed the door to his apartment and hurried up the incline to his office. He'd tossed and turned all night, unable to get Alicia off his mind. The seriousness of what he'd read in her journal bothered him; but what could he do about it?

Up ahead, Nathan the hotel driver strolled across another path. He spotted Darius and waved. Just seeing him made Darius think about his new hotel plans. A distinguished older gentleman like Nathan would lend a certain ambience to the place.

Nathan waited for Darius at the crossway. "Good to see ya' Mr. Darius. You're looking mighty fresh this morning." Nathan smiled and motioned to Darius's suit.

"Thanks, I'm just trying to look as fresh as you," Darius said with a good-hearted smile.

"Another beautiful Friday morning," Nathan said, offering his hand.

"Yes, it is. I have to admit it beats most Chicago mornings." Darius reached out and shook Nathan's hand. His grip was firm and strong like a young man's.

"Where you headed this morning?" Darius asked as they strolled the same path toward the office.

"Well, first thing, I've got to pick up a box and run it over to the convention center for Evan. Then, I reckon I'll come on back until it's time to run Sterling to the bank."

"Sterling doesn't make his own bank runs?"

"Sometimes, but I don't mind. It's part of my job."

"You know Nathan, we're starting a new campaign to increase the hotel's occupancy rate. If you have any ideas, I'd be glad to hear them. Just stop by my office anytime."

Nathan's pace slowed to a crawl. "Well, now that you mention it, back in your grandfather's early days, guests came back summer after summer. Willie Monroe took care of people. He treated them like they was family. After he slowed down and let new management run things, this place hasn't been the same. Now the focus is on saving a buck, not satisfying customers."

"I know Poppy had a way with people and he was very personable, but what did he do that was so special?" Darius asked.

"Well, for one thing, he insisted we greet repeat guests by their first names. He claimed that made them feel more like family. He also encouraged us to mingle with people traveling by themselves. If they looked bored, we'd sit down and play a game of checkers with them. Real southern hospitality stuff."

Darius nodded and picked up the pace. He'd enjoyed learning new bits and pieces about his grandfather. "I'll keep that in mind."

They approached the main building and Darius visually inspected the landscape as he did every morning. The neat lawn and bright blooming flowers always pleased him. But, the place still needed a good paint job.

The conversation with Nathan reminded him to check on Alicia, who was never too far from his mind. He decided to call her right after breakfast. No, if he had the time, he'd visit her.

When they entered through the main lobby, Nathan stopped. "Well, you have a good day now, and let me know if I can do anything for ya'."

"Good talking to you, Nathan. I meant what I said, my door's always open. I'd love to hear more stories about how Poppy ran the hotel."

"Sure thing." Nathan reached over and shook Darius's hand before walking over to the front desk.

Darius took the steps downstairs to his meeting.

Alicia closed her eyes and fell back on the pillows. She hadn't done anything wrong, yet she felt so exposed. When she opened her eyes again, cobwebs in the puckered ceiling came into view.

How could Darius have left his tie?

Rorie walked over and leaned against the dresser. "I'm right aren't I? You got busy with the owner of the damned hotel," he screamed. "Way to go, girl." He stomped his foot for effect.

She pulled the bedspread over her. "No, I didn't."

"Then how did his tie wind up in your bathroom?"

"Ugh." She threw her hands over her head. Her life wasn't an open book, especially not the embarrassing parts. She cleared the frog from her throat.

"He took it off to wipe the vomit from it." She pulled herself up into a sitting position and glared at Rorie, who stared at the tie in horror.

"The vomit?" he repeated, stretching his hand out.

"That's right," she said with a half-hearted smile. "I threw up on the man."

He dropped the tie and rubbed his hand against his jeans. "Now that's one way to get his attention," he said with a chuckle.

She rolled her eyes and adjusted her halter dress to keep her breasts from falling out. "I didn't want his attention. You shouldn't have left me with him anyway."

Rorie's chuckle rolled into a full-blown hardy laugh. "Man, I'd a given good money to see that. Just think, you had that tall fine piece of chocolate in this room, and you puked on him." He shook his head. "Tsk, tsk, what a pity."

And kissed him. She covered her face with her hands at the thought. That piece of information would forever remain private. She dropped her hands. "It didn't happen in here, it happened outside. After he helped me in, he cleaned up in the bathroom. I guess he was in such a hurry to get out of here, he forgot his tie." Embarrassed to death, she rolled over into a ball.

"My goodness, you're supposed to seduce a man like him." He picked the tie up with the tip of his finger, and carried it back into the bathroom. "Not show him what you had for dinner," he yelled, poking his head out of the bathroom.

He filled the coffeepot with water and returned to the kitchenette.

Alicia stretched out across the bed and groaned. She'd made a fool of herself yet again. She'd been lusting after Darius instead of searching for information on her mother. God, she'd never be able to face him.

Rorie yapped on. "Not to fear though, I have a PhD in the art of seduction. We'll have that man in your bed before your vacation's over."

"I didn't come down here to pick up men, or to embarrass the hell out of myself. I made a mistake last night, and it won't happen again."

Rorie strutted over and pulled the drapes wide open with one firm yank of the cord.

Sunlight hit Alicia across the face and she reached for a pillow.

"Whatever you say. But missy, we have a wedding to attend in about two hours, so get your rump up and into that bathroom." He snatched the pillow from her.

Her eyes sprang open when a slap tapped her butt.

"Let's go, little lady," he ordered.

She sprang up and spun around to see Rorie behind her…and not her father.

For just a moment, she'd flashed back to her childhood and her father trying to wake her. He'd swatted her bottom to wake her when they were about to go out with another one of his girlfriends. A Saturday morning picnic, a long drive in the country, or a leisure stroll through the mall where he purchased his *girls* gifts. She'd never wanted to go, so it always took a long time to get her out of bed. The women hadn't wanted to be bothered with her anyway. They fought for her father's attention. Alicia was always in the way.

She forced herself up while Rorie prepared two cups of tea. "Drink this and eat your bagel. Then hop in that shower and get your beautiful self down to the beach for the wedding."

"Yes, sir," she said, sitting on the sofa.

Rorie leaned against the counter with his legs crossed at the ankle, drinking his tea. Alicia looked up at him and realized she'd had two men in her room in the last twenty-four hours. So what if one was gay.

After Rorie left, she grabbed a change of underwear and moseyed into the bathroom. One look at herself in the mirror and she wanted to scream. She plucked the other eyelash off. How was she supposed to do damage control in less than two hours?

At his breakfast meeting, Darius passed out the first list of cosmetic improvements. His staff had issues with the simplest items. Each manager expressed his concern as everyone ate.

"I'm sure these minor changes can be handled with minimal impact to your daily routine. As managers, we'll just have to pitch in more."

Maintenance supervisor Will Wilson held up the list and leaned in with his forearm on the table. "I have two maintenance engineers that cover this entire property, including the surrounding grounds, and you expect us to—" he held the paper at arm's length and read off "—respond to *all* guests' maintenance calls within the hour?" He eyed Darius wearily.

Darius nodded. "Yes, what's the problem?"

"There ain't enough hours in the day. This is an old hotel, and things are always in need of repair. The best I can do is get to things within…say three hours."

Darius shook his head. "Not good enough. According to Sterling's reports—" he glanced over at Sterling who had been eyeing him keenly "—and correct me if I'm wrong Sterling, but since I've been here we've averaged about five guest complaints a day, and we aren't even full. Gentlemen, we need the repeat business. Unhappy guests won't come back. What they will do is bad-mouth us to everyone they know. So, we might need to multitask more, or hire additional staff. Whatever the case, these changes are effective Monday morning."

Will's lips set in a permanent frown as he fell back, shaking his head. "Yes, sir."

Sterling cleared his throat. "According to the budget, we don't have the money to hire another maintenance man."

Darius forced a smile. "We'll revisit the budget if it's determined we need somebody else. For now, Will can readjust the schedule and see how that works."

"The last thing I want to discuss is uniforms." He hoped he wasn't about to incite a riot.

As the waiter silently reappeared and refreshed their coffee cups all eyes stayed on Darius, some skeptical, some inviting.

"I'm not sure who decided everyone should dress the same with the only distinction between management and staff being a name tag, but beginning Monday, I'd like to see all management in suits and ties." He waited for the backlash and sullen expressions, but was mildly surprised when they didn't come. "Is everybody okay with that?"

Evan tapped a tune with his hands against the edge of the table. "I like the idea. I think a more professional look is what this hotel needs."

"Sir, your grandfather instituted that uniform policy," Sterling offered in an officious manner. "At the time, he thought it would boost morale among the employees, and it worked."

"I don't doubt my grandfather's intentions, but when you work the public areas—as I've seen you all do—and speak with guests, I want management to stand out. Changing the dress code should accomplish that."

Out of the corner of Darius's eye, he could see the front desk clerk cross the room and smelled trouble.

Timothy remarked, "I don't have a problem with the dress code either."

"Great." He stood up. "Well gentlemen, that's all I have this morning. I'll leave you in Sterling's capable hands to conclude the meeting. And Gibb, thanks for hanging in. I know you'd rather be home asleep at this hour," he said sincerely.

The night-shift manager straightened as if Darius woke him from a daydream. "No problem."

"Beginning Monday, you can continue your regular staff meetings. Thanks everyone for indulging me this week."

A tall, gangly young woman with braids approached the table and waved to get Darius's attention.

"Excuse me, Mr. Monroe." She crept closer to the table, hesitant about interrupting them.

Darius looked from her to the man that stepped up alongside her. His jaw dropped as his younger brother, Luke, stood there unshaven, and dressed like a dysfunctional rock-and-roll star.

Luke flashed a gregarious smile and threw his chin up. "What's happening?"

Darius almost fell over. What was God punishing him for now?

The two-tiered, white wedding cake, with lavender and yellow rose buds, sat in the middle of a small white table in one corner of the conference room. An ice bucket held champagne for the toast. Plates, glasses, napkins, and everything needed for the small reception was in place.

Trouble stuck out his finger and made one last circle around the cake, digging into the sour cream icing. He pinched off a rosebud and popped it in his mouth. Sweetness exploded in his mouth as he closed his eyes. The caterer had outdone herself again.

He walked over to the corner of the room and tapped the thermostat with a pair of pliers. Still not working. "That's too bad," he uttered, before shoving the pliers into his pocket.

The door to the conference room opened, and he quickly picked up a tray of glasses and plates and rushed toward the back entrance.

A local DJ backed into the room pulling a cart. "Hey, can I get a hand here?" he called out, as he yanked the cart now stuck midway through the door.

Trouble stopped and relaxed his shoulders. He couldn't turn around.

"Hey buddy, can you…"

The back door opened, and Trouble hefted the tray higher, his hand equal to his face now. A young man walked into the room.

"Say man, help that dude out," he said, as he forged through the back entrance.

"Sure." The young man ducked to keep from getting hit in the head. "Need some help?" he called out to the DJ.

Trouble hurried down the back hallway to the kitchen, and set the tray on a counter. He spoke to several people after walking through another door and back up to the hotel lobby.

Everyone had worked extra hard to show Darius how well they performed wedding ceremonies. Everybody except him; his loyalties lay elsewhere.

Chapter 7

Alicia's eyes followed Sherri to the flower-and-gauze-draped archway erected in the sand for the ceremony. Instead of a veil, Sherri wore her hair up with small cascading curls. Her simple white strapless sheath flatteringly caressed her body. Alicia loved the low V-back of the dress.

Maurice met his bride in an all-white tunic shirt and pants. The bridesmaids were stunning in soft pink dresses with apple green sashes around the waist; and the groomsmen, dressed in all white and wearing dark sunglasses, looked like musicians. Judging by the sunglasses, Alicia wasn't the only one who'd partied a bit too hard last night. The wedding party, excluding the minister, stood barefoot on the beach with the panoramic ocean view as a backdrop.

The twenty-minute ceremony included the jumping of the broom and a reciting of original poetry. By the time they were announced husband and wife, tears welled in Alicia's eyes. Weddings always filled her with so much joy. She hadn't sat through one dry-eyed yet.

After the wedding, Alicia's Aunt Ode introduced her to a few more relatives, whose names she'd never remember. Finally, Alicia mingled her way over to Rorie's mother, Sarah.

Sarah's sandalwood complexion was marred with freckles, and her grayish green eyes sparkled as she pulled Alicia in for a big hug. "Lemme tell ya', after listening to Ode all week it truly is a pleasure to see ya' for myself. Your mama and I were good friends. You look so much like her." She let go of Alicia's hand and stroked her hair. "You've got her hair that's for sure."

"Thank you. I hope we have some time to chat, I'd love to talk to you about my mother."

"Sure honey." Sarah glanced around them. "Rorie went to get my bag out of the car. I need to change into my walking shoes, but I'll be okay for a while. Come on let's go inside where it's cool."

Alicia followed Sarah and the small crowd inside for the reception. She hoped to make a brief appearance, congratulate the couple, and then make her exit. If nothing else, she had to thank them for their generosity.

The hotel conference room had been converted into a pink-and-green wonderland of wilted flowers. The heat smacked Alicia in the face the minute she crossed the threshold. Clusters of pink sweet peas, roses, and hyacinths leaned from their vases like drunks in a stupor.

Sarah sat at the first table she reached, and Alicia sat next to her.

"Whew, it's warm in here isn't it?" Sarah asked, pulling a tissue from her purse to wipe her face.

"Yes, it is." Alicia searched her purse for her invitation and handed it to Sarah.

"Thank you, baby." She fanned herself and scooted closer to the table.

"Rorie said you remember my mother bringing me down when I was younger. Did my father come with her?" Alicia inquired.

"Oh, yes. Handsome devil too. That was the only time Venetta came home. She brought you and your daddy over and we had a good old time. We sat out on the front porch and reminisced all evening. Venetta went to New York and snagged her a good fellow. He was really in love with you and your mother."

"Sounds like you two were pretty close." Alicia hesitated before continuing. "Did she ever tell you if he was my real father or not?" Alicia asked, not sure how Sarah would take her bluntness.

Sarah frowned at Alicia and stopped fanning. "Honey, of course he was your father. Why would you ask a question like that?"

"I heard a rumor that my mom was pregnant when she left the island," Alicia lied.

"Oh, no." Sarah shook her head, fanning herself faster now. "She left for New York to go to school. Almost everybody left the islands after high school back then. If yo' family had other family somewhere you went to stay with them and got you an education. That's what Venetta did too."

Except as far as Alicia could tell, her mother had never enrolled into any school.

By now, another elderly relative had taken the seat on the other side of Sarah. She also complained about the heat. "Who turned the air off?" the woman yelled to no one in particular.

Rorie appeared and dropped a blue-and-white tote bag on the floor next to his mother.

"Thank you baby." Sarah patted him on the hand and opened the bag to change shoes.

"Want a drink?" he asked, sitting next to Alicia.

She looked up as he set his tropical frozen drink next to her, and pulled out a chair. "No, thanks. If I don't see another glass of liquor for a while, it'll be fine with me."

"Oh, my bad. I guess not." He grinned and sat down. "Hey, I like what you've done with your hair. The way you put it up." He moved his finger around in a circle. "And wrapped it around in that unkept kind of way. It's working for you," he said, with a smirk on his face.

"Forget you?" she said, rolling her eyes. "It's the best I could do under the circumstances."

"Hey, I understand. You wouldn't want to upstage the bride." He leaned back, laughed, and sipped his drink.

"No, I attempted that last night, which is why I'm not sticking around here too long today."

Rorie wiped sweat from his brow, as his mother asked him to bring her a glass of water.

"Make that two," Alicia said as he walked away.

Once he was gone, Sarah reached out and touched Alicia's hand. "Honey, you just forget that. Rumors are started by wicked people with nothing else to do. There's no truth to that."

Alicia shook her head as her eyes misted over. If Sarah was right, what about what Alicia had read in her mother's journal? She'd described her belly as being swollen with his child. If that child wasn't her, then who was it?

Rorie returned with two glasses of water, and Alicia greedily drank half of hers without taking a breath. The room broke into applause as the newlyweds entered the room.

Thankfully, her exit was in sight. She turned back to Rorie. "I was thinking about you being here for a whole month with Darius, and I know what you should do," he said, taking his seat next to her.

"Oh, no. I'm afraid to hear this." She laughed and set her glass down.

"You should have yourself an island fling. Throw caution to the wind and put lust on the agenda. Make this a vacation to remember."

She laughed aloud. "Oh, it's already memorable, but there's another reason why I can't be involved with him."

Rorie shrugged. "Okay, I'm listening."

She sighed. "He reminds me too much of my father, and intimacy with him would freak me out."

"Honey, let me tell you something." Rorie leaned over and whispered in her ear. "That man is too young, too fine, and too firm to be your daddy. If you don't want him, let me have at him."

She fell back in her seat laughing, while Rorie smacked his lips.

Suddenly, a shouting match in the corner of the room caught everyone's attention. A groomsman had a hotel employee cornered, shouting about the air conditioner. Alicia spun around in time to witness the first blow to the bellhop's face.

A bridesmaid ran from the room, followed by a couple of other guests. The groom stepped in to break up the fight and accidentally caught the fist of his best man.

"Somebody call security. Get a manager," yelled several people from around the room.

Alicia jumped up, afraid if management came in she might run into Darius. Instead of following the crowd and Rorie toward the fight, she wanted to run in the opposite direction up the stairs and back to her suite. However, the two elderly women at her table couldn't run, so Alicia helped them out to a bench in the hallway, before getting out of there.

* * *

Meanwhile, if anyone had told Darius that Luke would unselfishly interrupt his budding music career to make a pit stop at Hotel Paradise, Darius wouldn't have believed it. He had expected Luke to show up after all the work was completed to claim part of his inheritance.

An Asian tour prevented Luke from flying back for their grandfather's burial. Therefore, Darius hadn't seen him since their father passed.

Darius leaned his chair back on two legs and studied his little brother's peach-fuzzed face. Luke's bohemian attire no doubt cost more than its Goodwill-inspired appearance. In his typical cool-headed manner, he strolled around the office examining anything that wasn't within eyeshot of Darius.

Continuing the conversation they'd started on the way to his office, Darius asked, "Who said I needed help?"

Luke stopped scouring the room, turned to Darius, and shrugged. "Nobody, man. But I know you. You wouldn't ask for my help even if you were drowning and I had the last life preserver."

Darius shook his head at that sarcastic wisecrack. "How long you plan to stay?"

Luke shrugged again. "As long as it takes."

Darius smirked and turned his head to look out the window. "What happened with the tour? I thought you were on the road indefinitely."

After his examination of the office, Luke settled in one of the stiff office chairs. "The tour is over. For me anyway."

At the lifeless tone of his voice, Darius snapped his head back around and lowered into his chair. "So you thought you'd come down to help me out?" he asked skeptically. "I can't believe it. And don't tell me Mom asked you to come. She wouldn't do that."

Luke narrowed his eyes and crossed his legs. "I didn't leave a great gig, or walk away from over a hundred thousand dollars because my mommy told me to."

Stupefied, Darius picked up his face from the floor. He and Luke had never been close, yet Darius understood what the money had meant to him. "Hey, forget I said that."

Luke let out a heavy sigh and popped his neck. He threw both arms in the air and clasped his hands behind his head. "I'm tired of the road anyway," he said with a smug smile. "Different hotels every week, different women every night."

Darius grunted. "Hell, you wish."

Luke shook his head. "Seriously man, it's not me anymore." He stared at Darius and lowered his arms. "And I thought my brother would understand that."

The chair squeaked when Luke stood and walked over to look out the window. "I heard you had big plans for this place." He glanced over his shoulder. "I'd like to be a part of that. I've stayed in too many hotels to count, and I've got some pretty good contacts." His gaze returned to the partial ocean view.

Luke's visit, his willingness to work, and his more grown-up attitude, all floored Darius. He looked like the same old Luke, but this was a side of him Darius hadn't seen before. The last time they worked together was when their mother opened her clothing boutique on the north side of Chicago, and that was over ten years ago.

"Some venture capitalist associates of mine are coming down in a couple of months to look over the hotel. I'm thinking along the lines of a small luxury or boutique hotel. Either way, this is a perfect location."

Luke turned from the window. "Something exclusive with lots of privacy?"

"Exactly. First class everything."

Luke whistled. "That's gonna cost you."

"I know. And it'll pay off in the long run."

Three loud knocks at the door interrupted them.

Darius's brows furrowed. "Come in."

The door swung open, and the front desk clerk stormed in breathing heavily. "Mr. Monroe, they're fighting downstairs."

Darius jumped up. "Who's fighting?" he asked, coming from behind his desk.

"People at that wedding reception. Something's wrong with the air conditioner, and I think Rodell got hit in the face."

"What!" In the wake of Luke's arrival, Darius had forgotten about the wedding. "Did you call the security guard?" he asked, following the desk clerk out of his office.

"Sir, I can't find him. I think he's gone on his lunch break."

He looked back at Luke. "Well, if you're here to help you might as well start now."

Both men hurried through the offices, following the desk clerk into the lobby.

Two angry guests met Darius. "Are you the manager? We need to see a manager."

"Yes ma'am, what's the problem?" he asked, not breaking stride as he headed for the conference room.

"My husband is down there womping your employee's butt, that's what. It's over a hundred degrees in that room, and they're standing around gawking at the thermometer like it's supposed to fix itself."

Darius grabbed the desk clerk by her arm. "Get maintenance down here and Timothy or Sterling."

She stopped in her tracks. "Sir, I can't find them either, that's why I came to get you."

He cursed under his breath. Where was his general manager? "Keep looking," he said, turning back to the irate woman. "Ma'am, we'll have everything taken care of in just a few minutes. Let's go downstairs and have a look."

Before Darius reached the stairs, Timothy came running in from the pool area with an employee behind him.

"I'm sorry sir, I'll take care of this." His little legs hurried down the steps ahead of Darius.

Darius followed him down the first set of steps. When he turned to go down the second set of split steps, he looked right into Alicia's startled eyes.

The minute she noticed him, she spun around. Her heel caught on the step, and she fell down the steps landing on her side.

"Ouch," Luke said, holding a fist to his mouth.

Darius skipped several steps until he reached the bottom where Alicia lay on her side. He pulled her dress down and reached out to help her up.

"Are you okay?" he asked.

She slowly rolled over moaning in the process.

Everyone crowded around her. "Is she okay?" Timothy asked.

Darius looked up. "I'll take care of her; you guys go ahead and handle the situation down the hall."

Timothy, his employee, Luke, and the angry bridesmaids all continued down the hall where a ruckus could be heard coming from the conference room.

Alicia sat up looking a little dazed. "Take your time," Darius said, cupping his hands under her arms to help her up.

"I'm okay," she finally said, brushing off the front of her dress. She made an effort to get up, but fell back into Darius's arms. "Oh God, my ankle. I broke my ankle," she screamed.

Chapter 8

Darius balanced Alicia in his arms as she reached down to unlock the door to her suite. Once unlocked, he kicked the door open and carried her inside.

"There on the sofa is fine," she said pointing, as he strained from carrying her all the way to her suite. Right now she wanted out of his arms and away from his hard muscles and masculine smell. She'd wrapped her arms around his neck, holding on while fighting the urge to nibble on his ear.

He passed the sofa and deposited her gently onto her bed instead. Once he released her, he stepped back and bent over to catch his breath.

He'd managed to carry all one hundred and thirty or so pounds of her all the way to her room. She was impressed, and a little embarrassed. He panted like he'd just finished a game of full-court basketball. She wasn't that heavy.

"Where's your ice bucket?" he asked, between pants, glancing around the room.

"Thank you, but I can take care of myself from here." She moved to the edge of the bed and tried to stand again. Maybe it wasn't broken, she thought. The minute her foot touched the ground, pain ripped through her foot and up her leg. She tensed and cried out.

Darius turned around at the guttural sound coming from her. "Okay, I'll leave and let you get the ice yourself."

He straightened and walked toward the door.

"Are you kidding? I broke my ankle; you can't just leave me. Get help. Call an ambulance. I need to go to the hospital."

He chuckled and walked over to her. "Wiggle your toes."

She bit her bottom lip and winced from the pain, but her toes wiggled.

"It's not broken." He reached down and gently took her legs in his hands lifting them to the bed. "You've twisted it or sprained it, but either way you'll be okay."

"How do you know?" she asked, leaning back on the bed in agony.

"Trust me, I've taken care of numerous sprains before. Now do you want to tell me where you hid the ice bucket?"

Between clenched teeth she said, "In the bathroom."

He walked into the bathroom and back out with the ice bucket in hand.

"I'll be right back," he said, stepping into the hallway.

She could have crawled under the covers and never come out. How could she have put herself in this position again? She reached down and took off her sandal, throwing it across the floor. Those damned three-inch heels were the cause of this. Her ankle had already swollen a little. Disgusted, she fell back on the bed. Why was she so successful at making a fool of herself every time this man came around?

He walked back in carrying a full ice bucket, and grabbed a hand towel from the bathroom. Alicia sat up on her elbows as he walked over to the foot of her bed.

"Show me where it hurts again," he said, lifting her leg and setting it on his lap.

She cringed and pointed to her right ankle. "Right there, on the inside. It's throbbing." Her body stiffened from the pain, but she still enjoyed the warmth of his hands on her leg. He held her leg with such gentleness it surprised her.

After making a compress, he pressed it against her ankle.

"Ew." She flinched. "That's cold."

He licked his lips and smiled. "It's ice."

"Smarty pants," she retorted.

He laughed. "You got any aspirin?"

"In the bathroom."

"Hold this," he said, getting up.

She leaned over and held the towel in place, while Darius went into the bathroom.

"What where you running from anyway?" he asked, from the bathroom.

"I wasn't running. I'd forgotten something, and I turned around to go get it, but my heel caught on your stupid steps," she lied.

"Right," he said, walking out of the bathroom. He returned with a glass of water and her bottle of Excedrin Migraine.

"You have migraine headaches?" he asked, holding up the bottle.

"Yes, and I have one right now." She held out her hand.

He shook two pills into her palm and handed her the glass of water. "Have you seen a doctor about the headaches?"

She swallowed, and then lay back on the pillow again. "I don't need to, the pills work."

The compress slid off her ankle, so Darius sat down and

gently lifted her leg in his hand, positioning her foot across his thigh. When he placed the cold, wet towel against her skin again, she tensed up.

"So, Ms. Alicia, what do you do when you're not dancing on tables or falling down stairs?"

She frowned before answering. "That's a good question. I don't know."

He gave her a sidelong glance.

"I inherited a car dealership from my father." She paused and took a deep breath. "Lately, I've been working with his partner to ensure everybody that the company will survive his death. But, that's not where I want to be. The dealership was my father's dream, not mine."

"What is it you want to do?" he asked, gently messaging the compress along her ankle.

She had a hard time concentrating with his big hands caressing her ankle. The heat radiating from his hands sent her pulse racing double time. What was she talking about?

"Uh—that's my problem. I'm interested in so many different things I can't seem to pinpoint the one thing I want to do for the rest of my life."

"Who says it has to be for the rest of your life? What did you do before your father passed?"

She smiled. "I played secretary and helped a friend set up her law practice." She laughed. "You should have seen me answering the phones and getting coffee for her important clients. I got a kick out of it."

"Sounds like you really don't have to work?"

"Of course I have to work, if I want to keep my sanity. After college I spent nine years on staff at IBM. The way I see it, I've served my corporate sentence and I'm not going back."

He laughed. "Oh, you're one of those corporate America haters."

"With a passion. I want my own business, like my father. And I'll have it someday."

He nodded and smiled. "I'm sure you will."

She laughed. "Look at us. I don't believe this."

"What's that?" he asked.

"Here we are again. You taking care of me like I'm some child."

"You hit the ground pretty hard, in case you don't remember. I'm just making sure the only thing you hurt was your ankle."

"Let's be real here. You're trying to make sure I don't sue your hotel."

He looked up in surprise. "The thought never crossed my mind. I'm here because you needed my help." He reached out and tucked the loose curl hanging alongside her face behind her ear.

The gesture served as a reminder of how bad her hair must look at the moment. "I need to get it together. I've done nothing since I've been here but make a fool of myself. Now everybody at the reception probably thinks I'm a nut."

"No, they don't," he said. "They think you're a beautiful young woman who's got it all together."

She snorted. "Looks can be deceiving."

He didn't respond, but moved his hand higher up the back of her leg. She looked down at him staring up into her eyes. He smiled and her toes curled in his hand. Then she tore her eyes away from his face, looked down at her foot, and noticed something.

She pointed to the water trickling down her ankle. "I think you're getting wet."

He looked down at the water running from her leg onto his pants. "Shoot," he said, lifting her leg and setting it on the bed before standing. He had a big wet spot on his pants, just below the crotch.

Alicia laughed and held the towel over her ankle.

He shook his head laughing. "How does it feel now?" he asked, pointing to her ankle.

She wiggled her toes. "A little numb, but it doesn't hurt as bad."

"You'll be okay," he said, placing a pillow under her leg. "Just keep it elevated."

"Thank you, and I'm sorry again for all the trouble I've caused you. I always manage to mess something up."

"What trouble?" he asked, reaching behind her and fluffing a pillow under her arms. "I've enjoyed it."

He planted a soft kiss on her forehead.

"Actually, I can't wait to see what you've got planned for tomorrow," he said, winking at her.

Alicia narrowed her eyes at him, but couldn't stop the corners of her lips from turning up.

"Now, I need to check and see how my brother's handling that reception. Call if you need anything."

He closed the door, and Alicia fell back on the bed trying to catch her breath. *God, how am I going to be able to keep my hands off that man for the whole month?*

Chapter 9

Darius walked back to his office feeling guilty as hell. He took responsibility for Alicia sitting in her room with a twisted ankle. She'd been trying to avoid him. Why, he didn't know. She certainly didn't need to.

He looked down at the wet spot on his pants and laughed. He couldn't seem to run into her without getting something on himself. What he didn't want was her death on his conscience. She'd moved her journal from the bathroom, but he had no intentions of reading anything else anyway. From now on he'd have to keep an eye on her.

When he entered his office, Evan and Sterling stood toe-to-toe in the middle of a heated discussion.

"Sterling, I sell our services—period. I shouldn't have to stick around to make sure everything goes smoothly. I'm not the general manager." Evan yanked at the gold-plated tag over the pocket of his pink shirt. "This says 'Sales.'"

Darius slammed the door to get their attention.

Startled, both heads turned toward Darius. Evan took a seat and crossed his legs. Sterling cleared his throat and pushed his glasses up his nose.

"Darius, I just wanted to let you know we moved the reception into the ballroom. Everything's fine now. Somehow the heat instead of the air was turned up, and the adjustment valve is broken. Maintenance is working to get the air conditioner back on in that room."

Darius nodded and crossed the paper-cluttered office to sit on the corner of his desk closest to Evan.

"What's this about?" he asked, gesturing between the two of them.

The piercing look Sterling gave Evan displayed no love lost.

"I was asking Evan where he was when the fight broke out," Sterling said with a smug smile.

Evan took a deep breath. "I'm not a wedding coordinator or a party planner. For the last time, I sell the services; *your* team manages them. Unless you're trying to imply something else?"

They resembled two little boys bickering on a playground, and Darius wasn't about to referee. "Where is the wedding coordinator, and why aren't we talking to her?"

Sterling released a loud sigh. "She's on vacation. That's why we all pitched in to help with today's ceremony. Somebody messed with the air conditioning."

Evan protested again, and Sterling countered by protesting even louder. The tug of war between them didn't amuse Darius the least bit.

"Gentlemen." Darius stood and moved behind his desk. "All I want to know is who's responsible for the damage today. Find out for me please."

"Yes, sir." Sterling said and turned to leave.

Evan uncrossed his legs and stood adjusting his shirtsleeves. "Darius, I dropped by to discuss something with you."

"Sure, what's up?" Darius sat down and turned his attention to Evan.

"I thought I'd check and see if you wanted to accompany me on a sales call Monday. Sterling usually rides along, but I figured you'd like to see how it works."

"Sure, who's the client?"

"The Southern Coalition of Black Female Coaches. They're preparing for their annual conference next year. I'm working with a young lady from the Brunswick chapter. She's narrowed it down to The Shores or Hotel Paradise."

Darius's eyes widened. The difference between the two hotels was like caviar to spam. "What do you think our chances are?" he asked.

Evan shrugged and hesitated before admitting, "Personally, I don't think we stand a chance in hell."

Darius smiled and nodded. "So we're the underdog?"

"Yes, sir. We always are."

"That's okay. Sometimes it can work to your advantage. I was the first African American to do business on the North Pier in Chicago. The thrill of the challenge excites me."

Evan chuckled. "I hope your magic works down here."

Darius rested his forearms on the desk and shook his head. "No magic to it, just plain old hard work. Don't take no for an answer."

Evan crossed his arms and shared a knowing smile with his boss. "Damned, we're going to land this sale. I can feel it."

"Not we. You're going to land the sale. Selling's what you do, right?"

Later that night, Sterling sat at the scuffed-up dinner table looking from his wife to their three children. His son, Allen, wanted to be a lawyer, and his daughters had their hearts set on nursing school. Although the youngest girl suffered from epilepsy, all three had excellent grades. Like any parent, he wanted them to exceed his goals in life. College cost a lot of money, and he had a plan to make sure his children attended.

However, the plans for their bright future could be ruined by the arrival of another Monroe brother.

"Papa, we're finished. Can we be excused?"

He looked into his baby girl, Sandra's, big brown eyes and smiled. Her plate was empty.

"Sure, but no television until you finish your homework."

"We finished it before dinner. Can we watch television?" Donna, his other daughter, asked.

Sterling looked over at Catherine, who smiled and gave her nod of approval.

The girls were halfway out of their seats before he could answer. "Okay, but take your plates into the kitchen."

"Yes, sir," they said in unison and scurried off.

"Papa, I'm finished too," Allen said, with his plate in hand, ready to break stride from the table. With his wire-rimmed glasses he looked as if Sterling had spit him out.

He still had food on his plate, but Sterling nodded him toward the kitchen.

After the kids left the table, Sterling sat there and pushed his food around unable to stop thinking about the latest developments at the hotel.

"What's wrong?" Catherine asked.

He shook his head. "Nothing." He didn't like to burden her with his troubles. Catherine worked part-time at a nursing home, volunteered at the kids' school, and worked at the church. Even with all her outside work, his dinner had never been late nor had his kids ever been neglected. She deserved more than his current salary could provide.

"Did you hear about the brunch?"

"Huh?" Immersed in his thoughts he didn't hear her.

"Today, at the reception, your mother announced she's having a cookout on Sunday. It'll be like a send-off brunch for Sherri and Maurice."

He removed his glasses and wiped his eyes. "I'm sorry, things were so crazy I must have missed that. Isn't Sunday our anniversary?"

"Yes, but I told her we'd be there. Since most of your family is in town for the wedding, she's invited everyone over to meet Alicia too. You can take me out another night," she said, with a big smile.

He chuckled. "I'm sure you won't let me forget."

Catherine picked up her plate and carried it into the adjoining kitchen.

"What do you make of Alicia anyway?" Sterling called out. "She shows up out of the blue, asking a lot of questions, and she doesn't know Sherri, or remember her father Sonny."

Catherine walked back into the dining room to clean off the table. "Your mother said she came to meet the family. Her visit just happened to coincide with Sherri's wedding. You're always so paranoid, Sterling. You need to cut that out. She's a sweet girl."

"I'm not paranoid. I just think the timing's funny, that's all. Did Mama tell you her father left her a car dealership?" He nibbled at his food.

"Yes, she did. And a lot of money too according to your mother."

"Maybe she's looking to purchase some real estate. Like the family land up in St. Helena." His brain kicked into overtime now as he finished his dinner. Could she have an ulterior motive for coming down?

"Your mother didn't say all that. I think all she wants to do is learn about her mother and see where she came from."

"Maybe. I guess we'll see." Sterling pushed his plate aside and stood. He kissed Catherine on the forehead and left the table.

"Where you goin'?" she asked.

"I need to make a business call."

"Don't tie up my line. Your mother should be callin' soon, she's supposed to tell me what to bring."

"I'll make it quick," he said as he walked out.

Sterling used the bedroom phone for more privacy. He locked the door in case one of the kids ran in. He dialed a familiar number.

Trouble answered the other end.

"I been waiting on you to call."

"Yeah, I got your message earlier, what's wrong?"

"I seen something Thursday night that you might be interested in."

"What's that?"

"Your boss coming out of suite forty-two at around midnight. He'd been in there a while."

Sterling's eyebrows shot up in surprise, before a smile slowly made its way to his lips. "You don't say."

"I thought you might find that useful."

"Indeed. Don't share that little piece of info with anybody else. I'll be getting back with you." He hung up and sat there for a few minutes thinking. What was Alicia doing sleeping with the enemy?

Alicia crawled into bed earlier than she had since she'd arrived at Jekyll Island. The swelling in her ankle had gone down, but the pain still kept her off her feet. She'd elevated her foot as Darius had instructed.

She still couldn't get over how she'd managed to embarrass and humiliate herself so much in less than a week.

Unfortunately, Darius had witnessed all of her catastrophes, and she'd no doubt run into him again before she left. However, with the wedding behind her, and her family leaving the hotel, she would try her best to dodge him.

The shrill sound of the telephone caught her by surprise. She looked over at the phone fearful it might be Darius. If she didn't answer, voice mail would pick up and she could call him back tomorrow. Then again, if she didn't answer, he might drop by.

She picked up the receiver on the third ring.

"Hello."

"Well, I was about to hang up and come over there to check on you," Rorie said.

Alicia sat up. "Hey, how's it going?"

"Everything's fine over here. How the hell are you doing? I heard about your fall."

"Oh, I'm okay. I twisted my ankle that's all. It's fine now." If Rorie knew about her accident, everyone knew. She wanted to crawl under the covers and hide.

"Uh, huh. Well, let me know if you need anything."

"I will, promise."

"Anyway, girl you missed all the action this afternoon."

"What happened?"

"Did you know there's another Monroe brother here? When he burst into the reception and broke up that fight, I thought Sherri's bridesmaids would pee their pants. He's just as attractive as Darius, but more thuggish, you know what I mean?"

"I think so," Alicia chuckled.

"Well, they moved everybody into another room and guess who caught the bouquet?"

"Don't tell me you caught it," she said laughing.

"Hell naw. Ruth Ann caught it, after knocking down half the women on the floor. And she knows ain't nobody going to marry her big ass."

"Why not Rorie, she's divorced? Somebody married her once."

"And just who was that? Nobody ever mentions the twins' daddy. She went off somewhere, got married, had the twins, and the man disappeared before anybody had a chance to meet him."

"I'm sure somebody met him," she said, thinking of her own father.

"Not a soul. It's like he's some big secret. And let me tell you, this family can keep secrets. Unless one of the boys needs an organ or something, we'll never know who their daddy is."

A prickling sensation ran up Alicia's spine, and she readjusted the phone to her ear. If Rorie knew about her situation, he might not have broached the subject. She cleared her throat, as someone called Rorie's name in the background.

"Hey, we're going for pizza. Do you feel like going?" he asked.

"I don't think so. I'd better rest my ankle."

"Yeah, I understand. Well, look I've got an early flight out of here tomorrow so it looks like I won't see you again until you get back to Atlanta. Of course I'll call before I leave, but be safe and don't do anything with Darius that I wouldn't do, okay?"

"Okay," she replied, laughing.

"Which, by the way, means you can get freaky as hell."

"Bye Rorie." She hung up laughing, but couldn't help thinking about the old saying, "Mama's baby and Daddy's maybe."

Chapter 10

Alicia switched from ice to heat Saturday morning, and nursed her ankle back to health. Sure-footed in a pair of black flip-flops she went to relax by the pool and watch the sun set.

A family of four and two white women who looked like they hadn't seen the sun in years sat around the pool. Alicia pulled out her mother's journal and lay back on a lounge chair. Compared to the cold air conditioner in her room, the cool ocean breeze felt wonderful.

She read over a passage describing how her mother and her lover used to meet on Saturday nights at the edge of the hotel's property. Away from watchful eyes, they sat in the sand and talked for hours.

Curious, Alicia wanted to see the area. She wanted to experience what her mother had. That was one of the reasons she came to Jekyll Island. She picked up her beach bag, tied her sarong around her waist, and set off for a stroll down the beach. The setting sun provided a beautiful backdrop for the perfect way to spend a lazy Saturday evening.

When she reached a large piece of driftwood she stopped. Surrounded by nothing but peace and quiet, she glanced back at the hotel that looked slightly smaller now. Is this the spot, she wondered? Is this where her mother and her lover pledged their undying love to one another?

"Ma'am, you can't go down there."

Startled, Alicia whipped around to see a young man standing several feet behind her in the grass with a bucket and what looked like a long stick in his hand.

"I'm sorry?" she asked.

He pointed beyond her. "If you was trying to go farther down the beach, you can't. That sign marks the end of the hotel's property."

She turned around and noticed the small sign for the first time. "Oh, I wasn't going any farther than right here. Is this okay?"

He shrugged. "Sure. But the tide'll be coming back up pretty soon."

"Thank you. I'll watch for it."

She realized now he was picking up trash from the beach. "Do you work at the hotel?" she asked.

"Yes, ma'am. I remember you, I carried your luggage to your room."

Now she recognized him. "Yes, the bellhop, I remember now. What's your name again?"

"Rodell." He came down from the marshy grass closer to her.

"I saw you working in the pool area the other day too didn't I?" Alicia asked.

He nodded. "Yeah, every morning I set all the fresh towels out."

A hard ocean breeze blew in, swirling Alicia's sarong around her hips and revealing more of her two-piece swimsuit than she would have liked at the moment. Rodell didn't miss a beat and focused on her body instead of her face. She set her beach bag down next to the driftwood and lay her towel in the sand hoping he was about to leave. Instead, he came closer.

"Are you enjoying your visit?" he asked.

"Yes, I am." She glanced around and realized they were the only ones that far down the beach. Could anybody hear her if she screamed?

Rodell set his bucket down, stretched his arms over his head, and took a deep breath. He looked innocent enough, but at over two hundred and fifty pounds standing roughly six feet tall, if he tried to overpower her she had no idea what she'd do.

"I'm sorry, I didn't mean to keep you from your work," she said, hoping he'd get the hint. The way this young man looked at her gave her the willies. She pulled out her journal.

"No problem. I need a break anyway. It's almost quitting time." He looked down at her. "How long you gonna be on the island?" he asked.

She shrugged. "A couple of weeks."

"Yeah," he laughed. "You like this place don't you?"

"It's quaint."

"It's boring." He glanced back at the hotel. "Especially this place."

"You don't like working here?"

He hiked his pants legs up and squatted down staring out into the ocean. "It's okay, but I'm in school, so I don't plan on working here the rest of my life like some of those—" he picked up a pebble from the beach and threw it out into the water "—like some of the other guys here."

"What are you majoring in?" Alicia's nervousness eased up a bit.

"Computer Science. I helped Mr. Simpson with the computer system here a couple years ago. That's how I got hired."

"That's a good field to get into." Alicia looked up and saw two other young men walking up the beach in their direction. The hairs on her arm stood up at the same time Rodell stood up.

"Well, here comes my ride." He picked up his bucket and brushed the sand from his hands.

The men stopped and waved in their direction. Alicia took a deep breath and exhaled. For a minute there she thought she'd gotten herself into another jam.

"Enjoy the sunset and don't forget about high tide," Rodell said as he walked away.

"I won't. Thank you." She kept her eyes on him and his friends until they reached the hotel. Then, she opened the journal and took a step down memory lane with her mother.

Darius stood on the deck opposite the pool staring at a father and his young son playing in the water. The father was teaching his son to swim on his back. The love between them was evident in the way they swam together. That kind of love Darius had always wanted with his father. The kind of love Luke received.

Rodell came up the steps with two other young men who were laughing and pushing him.

"Man, you know you want to hit that. You should have tried. I bet she's lonely," one of the men said.

The laughter stopped when they looked up and noticed Darius.

"Hello, Mr. Monroe," they echoed.

"Good evening fellows, getting off from work?"

"Yes, sir," they said in unison.

"Rodell, can I speak with you a moment?"

"Sure."

One of the young men patted Rodell on the shoulder. "We'll wait for you out front."

Darius leaned against the railing. "Who was that I saw you talking to out by the edge of the beach?"

"Ms. McKay. I thought she might be trying to go to the other side of the beach, so I was just making sure she saw the sign."

Darius peered up the beach, but couldn't see that far to know it was Alicia.

"She looks kind of sad too, sir." Rodell glanced down toward Darius's feet. "Too bad you don't have your beach shoes on."

"Yeah," Darius replied, pondering what he was about to do. He kept his eyes on Alicia. "What's she doing down there?"

Rodell shrugged. "Reading a book I think."

Darius turned to him. "A big red book?"

"Yeah, I think so."

Darius pulled away from the railing. "Thanks Rodell. I'll see you tomorrow." He walked away and started down the steps toward the beach.

"Yes, sir."

All Darius could think about as he stepped off the walk and onto the sand was stopping Alicia from doing something crazy. His three hundred dollar leather shoes slipped around, preventing him from walking faster.

Several people on the beach stared at him as if he'd emerged from the water fully clothed. Hadn't they seen a man walking on the beach in a suit and shoes before? He waved and smiled, which seemed to confuse them more. Some waved back, while others continued to stare. He loosened his tie.

He didn't want to be out of breath by the time he reached Alicia, so he slowed down. She was lying back holding the book up above her, reading from it. She hadn't seen or heard him approach.

"Excuse me, Miss."

She snapped the book closed and sprang up. "You scared me," she said, holding a hand over her chest and breathing hard.

"I'm sorry, but I believe I know you," Darius said, stepping closer.

She set the book next to a piece of driftwood. "No, I don't think so," she said with a smile. "You must have me mistaken with somebody else."

He smiled. He'd know that curvaceous body anywhere. Today she had on a red bikini, with a sarong tied around her hips. If she'd wanted to get his blood pressure up, she was headed in the right direction. He walked over and sat next to her in the sand.

"You resemble this young lady I carried to her room last night, but—" he reached over pretending to examine her ankle "—her ankle was broken and I wouldn't expect her to be walking around so soon."

She laughed. "Okay, you were right. I twisted it. But, it felt broken."

He brushed sand from his hands and rested his arms on his knees. "I'm sure it did. Anyway, you look fully recovered today."

"Yeah, it's fine now. Thanks for your help."

"You're welcome. But, do you *really* want to thank me?"

She cut her eyes at him, but didn't answer.

"Let me take you to dinner."

"Huh, let you take me to dinner as a way of *me* thanking *you?*" She arched her left brow at him. "How many businesses do you own?" she asked, grinning.

Darius enjoyed a hearty laugh.

"Because with logic like that, I'd like to make you an offer for one."

"A woman with a sense of humor. That's a rare, and sought after quality," he commented.

She leaned back and leered at him. "You need to get out more."

He laughed again and held up his hands. "I'm trying. But, I'd like to take you with me."

She blushed looking away from him. He could tell she wanted to say yes, but instead she shook her head.

"I don't think so."

"Why not?" he asked. "Do I have halitosis?" He held a hand to his mouth to test his breath.

She laughed and rolled her eyes at him.

"What then? I can't figure out why you'd say no. First, I let you puke on me. Then you sent me back to work yesterday with a wet spot so big everybody thought I peed my pants." She kept laughing. "And when I stand up, you know my ass is going to be wet. Not to mention, I've scuffed up a perfectly good pair of shoes to come sit in the sand with you. And you won't even have dinner with me?" *It took a big man to beg,* he told himself.

Seeing her laugh made him feel good. He leaned back placing his hands in the sand taking in the view. She had her hair up again, and the nape of her neck surrounded with little wisps of hair turned him on. He wanted to kiss her there and everywhere else. He hadn't planned to ask her out, but ever since that first kiss she'd gotten under his skin.

She'd stopped laughing and picked up her purse. She shoved the journal inside. "Darius—"

"Ah, let me warn you before you turn me down. I'm very persistent. So get ready to turn me down tomorrow, and every day after that, because I won't stop asking until you say yes."

She leaned forward to stand up.

"Let me help you." He jumped up before helping her up.

He knocked off as much sand as he could from his hands and pants.

"Turn around," she said.

He did, thinking she was about to help him.

"Yep, your ass is wet," she laughed softly and shook her head.

"Okay," He turned around facing her. "Now tell me something I don't know. Like what time I can pick you up tomorrow night?"

She turned away from him and sashayed back up the beach. "I don't remember accepting your invitation."

He followed alongside her. "You'll accept."

She stopped and propped a hand on her hip giving him the once-over. "What makes you so sure?"

He liked this spunky side of Alicia.

"You said you'll be here about a month, right?"

"Correct."

"Plan on eating most of your meals in the hotel's restaurant do you?"

She took a deep breath, raised her chin, and looked down her nose at him. "There are other restaurants on the island," she said with a shrug.

He walked slowly beside her. "And the food's equally as tasty, trust me. Jekyll Island's not known for its cuisine."

She stopped again and pulled her bag up on her shoulder. The slow appraising glance she cast in Darius's direction gave him hope. She was considering it.

"I'll be able to order something other than fish and chips?" she asked.

"This restaurant doesn't even serve fish and chips," he assured her.

She glanced out across the water for a few minutes. He didn't know what else to say to convince her, but if she said no again, he'd think of something.

"I'll have dinner with you under one condition," she said glaring at him.

His mouth twitched. "Let's hear it."

"After dinner, you never mention what I did to you again. I mean to me or anyone else."

He crossed his arms and wondered if he was about to make a promise he couldn't possibly keep. Finally, he nodded. "You've got yourself a date."

Chapter 11

Alicia arrived at the cookout early Sunday afternoon with a fruit tray in hand and a huge appetite.

No one answered the front door, so Alicia followed the music and the smell of barbecued meat to the backyard.

Two middle-aged, potbellied men stood at the huge grill talking and drinking beer. Children chased each other around the yard, reminding Alicia of her first visit. She christened the home, Ode's day care. When she entered through the gate, Tracy ran up to her.

"I remember you. What's your name?" the young girl asked.

"I'm Alicia, and you're…" She snapped her fingers pretending to have forgotten.

"I'm Tracy." She stepped back to let Alicia in.

"That's right. I remember now." Alicia smiled at the petite child who wasn't chasing her brother today. No doubt, he was in the bunch running around in the yard. "Where's Aunt Ode?"

Tracy pointed toward the house. "Nana's in the kitchen with Mama. Come on, I'll show you where to go." She tiptoed to see what Alicia held in her hand.

"Tracy!"

She jumped at the harsh sound of her name and turned around.

"Get out the way and let the woman in." One of the pot-bellied men walked over wearing long shorts and a Hawaiian-print shirt.

"You must be Alicia," he said, extending his hand.

"Yes, I am," she said, balancing the tray and shaking his hand.

"I'm Jim Porter." He reached out and pulled Tracy closer to him. "Tracy's dad. My wife Juanita is your cousin."

"Oh, yes. Were you at the wedding?" She didn't remember seeing him.

He chuckled. "No, I had to work. But believe me, I heard about it all."

Alicia smiled. "Well, it's nice to meet you."

"Let me help you with that." He took the tray and carried it up the concrete path to the back door. "Come on in. Everybody's still in the kitchen, so make yourself at home."

"Thank you." Alicia followed him glancing back at Tracy. With her lips slightly turned up, she waved.

Jim opened the back door. "Look who I found." He held the door open for Alicia.

She stepped inside the kitchen to a flurry of women all cooking or preparing dishes.

"Alicia. Here she is," Juanita called out to everyone in the room. She grabbed a towel to wipe her hands and hurried over to hug Alicia. "Come on in here."

Everyone stopped, and all eyes fell on Alicia. *This must*

be what tanked fish feel like. Her stomach fluttered as she politely smiled around the room.

"Thank you. I know this isn't much, but…" She reached back for the fruit tray. "I wanted to bring something."

"I'll set it right over here," Jim said, placing the tray in the middle of the table, and then he left the kitchen.

"You didn't have to bring anything. Come on, let me introduce you around." Juanita wrapped an arm around Alicia's shoulder.

They began at the kitchen table where Catherine and Ruth Ann sat. "You remember meeting these two broads, don't you?"

Alicia waved and smiled at the women. "Yes, I do."

"It's nice to see you again, Alicia," Catherine said, while Ruth Ann waved.

"And over here—" Juanita turned Alicia around to Sarah's freckled smiling face. "Did you meet Sarah, cousin Quincy's wife?"

The women exchanged smiles as Alicia shook her hand. "I sure did. We met at the reception."

"Yes, we suffered through that inferno together. How ya' feeling, baby?" Sarah asked.

"I'm great, and it's a beautiful day for a cookout."

Over the next few minutes, several other women traveling between the kitchen and the backyard were introduced as distant cousins and children of cousins.

The back door swung open and Sherri and Maurice paraded in. Everyone in the room fussed over the young couple, as Ode hobbled in from the dining room to join them.

Alicia prepared herself for a bone-crushing hug when Ode headed her way.

"Baby, I got somethin' for ya' don't let me forget it," Ode said, pulling Alicia into her chest.

"Yes, ma'am," Alicia uttered through restricted lungs.

"Y'all ain't got this food outside yet? What ya' doin? Runnin' ya' mouths?" Ode walked over and waved Juanita out of the way.

"Here," she pointed at Ruth Ann. "Get this stuff in bowls and get it outside. We're havin' a *cookout*, not a *cook-in*. Y'all make these chirren think we backwards or somethin'."

Within minutes, everything from the kitchen was herded out the back door and placed on the two picnic tables. Alicia wanted to sit beside Sarah, but there wasn't enough room. So, she sat at the second picnic table and Tracy sat next to her.

"Want some swamp water?" Tracy asked.

"Some what?" Alicia asked, sure she'd missed something.

Tracy laughed. "Swamp water. It's sweet tea and lemonade mixed together. It's good."

Alicia shrugged. "I'll give it a try." For some reason, Tracy had attached herself to Alicia; and to Alicia's surprise she didn't find it annoying.

Everything was so delicious Alicia ate until she couldn't eat anymore. The chef at Hotel Paradise could learn something about southern cooking from her family.

Sterling helped his mother inside. "What's wrong with your leg?" he asked, holding her arm.

"My arthritis is actin' up. I'll be okay." She walked across the kitchen to the refrigerator. "Here, look on the bottom shelf and pull out that pie."

He did as she asked. "Mama, has Alicia asked you for anything?"

"Anything like what?" Ode asked, pulling a knife from the drawer.

He set the lemon meringue pie on the counter with a thud. "I don't know—" he shrugged "—information about the family property in St. Helena, or—"

Ode shook her head. "I doubt Alicia knows anythin' about the family property. If so, she's a descendant just like y'all." She looked up at her son with a frown. "What you thinkin', that chile come to take our land? She come to get to know ya', that's all. I'll tell her about the property before she leaves, but she ain't tryin' to take nuttun' from ya'."

"Good, then maybe she can donate some back tax money," he said in a louder than normal voice.

"Boy, what's the matter with ya'? Ya' always cryin' 'bout money. That chile don't know nuttun' 'bout the property down home. She don't even know where she come from." Ode averted her eyes and made the first slice in the pie.

Sterling didn't miss a beat. "What do you mean? She's originally from New York, right?"

"I mean her people. She don't know where her people come from or anythin' 'bout our West African connection."

"I told her we were Gullah. She seemed surprised."

"See what I mean? Her daddy should have brought her down after Venetta died instead of keepin' her away from us." Ode motioned toward the counter for Sterling to hand her the cake.

"But, she had her rich daddy and his family." Sterling grabbed a piece of paper towel and helped himself to the first slice of pie.

Ode pushed the pie aside and stared down at the three-layered chocolate cake. She gripped the counter as if it held her up. "She sure did."

The back door opened.

"We've come to help with dessert," Juanita said, walking through the door with Alicia bringing up the rear.

By mid-afternoon the temperature had climbed to ninety degrees, and the backyard was scorching. If one more person hugged Alicia, she'd wring out like a wet sponge. Finally, the picnic moved inside. Alicia found Sarah in the living room talking to an elderly man whose name escaped her.

"Alicia, come have a seat," Sarah requested, patting the spot on the sofa beside her.

Alicia walked across the room and sat next to Sarah.

"Honey, you still wanting to learn more about ya' mother'?" Sarah asked, as she stroked a hand along Alicia's hair.

"Do you have a lot of memories of her?" Alicia asked. She noticed Sarah didn't have the same clip to her voice that her aunt Ode had. To Alicia, her aunt had an accent like she'd come from another country.

"We was running buddies, ya' know. We used to get into all kinds of trouble together," Sarah laughed.

"Really, like what?" Alicia asked, eager to hear anything about her mother. Sarah shared a few childhood stories depicting Alicia's mother as a prankster and practical joker. Nothing like Alicia.

"Move that stuff off the table. I want to show Alicia pictures of her mama." Ode held a large photo album in her arms.

Ruth Ann followed her and came around to clean off the table.

Alicia had wanted to ask Sarah more about her mother's crush, but her aunt Ode had momentarily put an end to that conversation. A little annoyed, Alicia leaned back into the sofa cushions chewing on her bottom lip. Her mind switched gears and she now focused on the album. She moved to the edge of the sofa eager to learn more about her mother.

Several children ran into the room and crowded around the coffee table. Ode smacked back a little hand as one reached out for the album, and then she settled next to Alicia on the sofa.

Butterflies danced in Alicia's stomach as she stared at the old tarnished album stuffed with pictures and about to burst from the seams.

Ode cleared her throat. "These pictures is from up home. Ya' mama and I was born in St. Helena, on Lady's Island."

Alicia nodded. "Sterling told me. I don't remember ever being there, although I've been told we visited once."

"That's okay, ya' was so young, but these pictures may jog ya' memory."

Alicia leaned in closer to the album, eager to step back in time for a moment. Ode flipped back the cover and an old black-and-white photograph of a man and woman standing next to a wood building was on the first page.

"That's Mama and Papa," Ode pointed out. "They's standin' outside the church in their Sunday clothes."

Alicia's hand reached out and touched the edge of the photo album. "I've never seen a picture of them before."

She stared at the photograph saying a silent hello to her grandparents. "Henry and Nancy Walker, right?"

Ode smiled and nodded. "That's right."

"They was sharp that Sunday," Sarah added.

"I think you resemble Mama Nancy," Ruth Ann told Alicia.

She nodded and stared at the bright-complexioned woman with fondness. That was her grandma. A woman she wished she'd had the pleasure of meeting.

Ode turned the page to an old cracked picture of two little girls in dresses and ankle socks. "That's me and Venetta. Ode slid the album closer to Alicia.

"Who's who?" Alicia asked, looking at two little girls in white dresses: one with a ribbon in her hair, and the other sitting in a rocking chair.

"The baby is Aunt Venetta, and that's Mama with a ribbon in her nappy head." Ruth Ann and everyone else laughed.

Alicia couldn't take her eyes off her mother. Venetta Walker had long thick plats and fat little legs. Her facial features hadn't changed much as she grew up. Her complexion was brighter than her sister's, more like their mother's, and nothing like Alicia's.

There were more going-to-church pictures. All the women wore dresses and hats, while the men had on three-piece suits; some men wore hats, and some went without.

When Alicia turned the next page, a lump formed in her throat. Her mother posed with a young man in a dark suit and hat. She wore a white ankle-length dress with an outer layer of tulle, a tulle shawl, and a pair of ballet slippers. She held a small bouquet of flowers. The tall dark-skinned young man looked like he'd just won the lottery. Was that her father?

"Who's this with Mama?" she asked.

Ode leaned forward and squinted. "That's Calvin, her prom date. He sure had a crush on ya' mama, poor thing."

Alicia took in all of Calvin's features, looking for any resemblance. "Was he her boyfriend?"

Ode and Sarah laughed.

"Lord naw," Ode said. "Papa wouldn't let us date in high school. Calvin's mama had to come to the house and ask Mama if she'd let Venetta go with him. He was a nice young man, but Venetta didn't pay much attention to him."

After Ode flipped through more school and baby pictures of other relatives, she stopped. "I need to walk—my leg's getting stiff." She struggled to stand.

The children finally lost interest and ran off to another part of the house.

Ode followed them mumbling about how age played tricks on you.

Ruth Ann took her mother's place narrating the family photos, but after a few more Simpson baby pictures Alicia lost interest. She wanted to talk more about her mother.

She leaned back on the sofa next to Sarah.

"Your mama wanted off this island so bad," Sarah said, barely above a whisper.

Alicia turned and noticed a faraway look in her eyes. "What did you say?"

"Venetta wanted to see the world. She had big dreams. Back then folks thought we was backwards, and everybody wanted to lose their Gullah dialect. Folks left the island in droves to go 'better themselves,' as they called it. Your mama wanted to be one of them."

Ruth Ann had turned the photo album around and Tracy joined her in browsing through the photographs.

"Sarah, did you see my mother right before she left the island for good?" Alicia asked.

"No, I seen her before she started working at Hotel Paradise. After high school I moved in with a cousin in Savannah to go to college. Then about ten years later, she brought you down and I seen her then. I told you about that at the reception."

"So, you didn't keep in contact with her?" Alicia asked, fishing her way around to what she really wanted to know.

Sarah crossed her arms. "No, but I know she really liked working at the hotel. You should ask Ode about it though. They corresponded a lot. I'm sure Ode saw her before she left."

Alicia wondered why her aunt hadn't told her that.

By nightfall the cookout had ended. Ode shoved a plate of food at Alicia, insisting she carry it back to the hotel.

Alicia accepted the plate and found herself alone in the kitchen with her aunt. "Aunt Ode, looking through your photo album reminded me of something I wanted to ask you."

"Oh, speaking of pictures…" Ode walked over to the counter and pulled open a drawer. She took out two old photographs and handed them to Alicia. "I want you to have those."

The old cracked black and whites were of her mother. In one photograph she stood alone, in the other a group of people were with her.

"Who are these people?" Alicia asked.

"Coworkers of hers at the hotel. She sent me that picture after she'd been workin' there 'bout a year."

Alicia held the photograph closer, looking into the faces of all the men. Did any of them look like her?

"Thank you very much, Aunt Ode. Did you see Mama before she left?"

Ode shook her head. "We talked on the phone, but I never got to see her. I'd moved to Bluffton with Fred by then."

Alicia placed the photographs in her purse. "Sounds like most of the young people left the island to attend college. I don't think Mama went to college, so do you know why she left the island?"

Ode busied herself with cleaning off the counter. "She didn't want to be no housekeeper all her life. But, I suppose only Venetta can answer that."

The rest of the family piled into the kitchen, and Alicia said goodnight after another round of hugs.

She walked down the street to her car, smiling about the pictures her aunt gave her. Then, she heard voices in the distance. Two men sat in a car parked across the street. She picked up her pace as the car door opened, and one man climbed out.

"Calling it a night?"

She couldn't see his face, but she recognized the voice, and let out a sigh of relief. "Sterling, you scared me."

He crossed the street and met her by her car door. "Sorry about that." He held a bottle of beer down at his side.

"Did you find out everything you wanted to know?" he asked, taking a swig of beer.

Alicia gave him a sidelong glance and set the plate on top of the car. "What do you mean?" she asked, while fishing her keys from her purse.

He shrugged. "You wanted to know about your mother. Did Mama tell you everything you wanted to know about her?"

"Not really." She unlocked the car door and Sterling opened it for her. She set her plate on the passenger seat. "I have a feeling there's something she doesn't want to tell me."

He nodded and took another swig. "Yeah, something like that."

Alicia started to climb into the car, but stopped and stared up at Sterling. The street light reflected off his glasses and she couldn't see his eyes. "Do you know something you'd like to tell me?"

The man sitting across the street in the car Sterling had exited rolled down his window and called out, "Man, I need to get going."

Alicia caught a glimpse of him but didn't recognize him.

"There's a lot she's not telling you, but every family has its secrets, you know." He motioned for Alicia to get into the car while he closed the door.

"What are you saying? There's some sort of secret involving my mother?" she asked, climbing in, but keeping one leg out so he couldn't close the door.

He glanced up at the house, then back at Alicia. "You'd better get going. It's late."

She looked back at Catherine standing on the front porch with her arms crossed.

He waited until Alicia pulled her leg inside and then closed the door. She rolled down her window. "Sterling, you didn't answer my question." She kept her voice even-toned.

He leaned down so that he was eye level with her. "If you

came down here to uncover some old family secrets, forget about it. Mama will probably carry them to her grave." He stood and backed away.

She hoped with all her might he was wrong.

Chapter 12

On the drive back to Jekyll Island the words "family secret" haunted Alicia. If Ruth Ann hadn't divulged the name of the father of her twins, what made Alicia think anyone would tell her who her father really was?

Monday morning after Darius's usual check of the parking lot, bathrooms, and hallways for cleanliness, he hung out behind the front desk greeting guests.

Luke walked up to the counter. "Who's your new trainee?" he asked Kamora, the young female clerk standing next to Darius.

The thin Asian woman blushed and tucked a long braid behind her ear. "You know he's not a trainee. I thought you were brothers?" she asked Luke.

Well, it didn't take long for Luke to start making his rounds, Darius thought. He had hoped Luke wouldn't be up to his old tricks; however, the young woman smiled so dreamily at Luke, Darius could only shake his head.

"Yeah, we're brothers." Luke winked at Darius.

Darius thanked Kamora for letting him shadow her for a few hours. He planned to spend time in every department to see the hotel in operation. Coming from behind the counter, he met Luke in the back office.

"Hey, where's a good place to go shopping around here? Looks like I need one of your monkey suits." Luke gestured to Darius's attire.

"A shirt and tie will do." Darius couldn't understand why Luke hadn't brought anything other than jeans if he truly intended to help out. "Call Nathan. He'll know where to take you."

"Who's Nathan? The concierge?"

"He's the hotel's driver."

Luke nodded. "Cool. How about a young lady to help me pick something out? Like that desk clerk."

Darius crossed his arms. "Same old Luke. I was afraid of that."

Luke moved his mouth, sarcastically mocking his brother. "I'm just messing with ya', chill out. Look, I came down to help, so I'll run get some office clothes and come back ready to work." He turned to walk away, then looked back over his shoulder. "Where can I find Nathan?"

After Darius gave Luke Nathan's number, he sat in his office staring at the folders on his desk. He had so many projects to work on, he didn't know where to start. Thankfully, the first phase of improvements was already underway.

The phone rang. He answered, still contemplating his next project.

"Mr. Monroe, I have a call for you from a Mr. Denton of RC Enterprises," said the hotel operator.

Darius pushed the folders in front of him aside. He'd expected this call sooner or later. "Put him through." Now he'd see what RCE planned to offer *him* for the hotel.

"Hello." A chipper voice came from the other end.

"Yes, this is Darius Monroe."

"Mr. Monroe, Mike Denton here from RC Enterprises, how are you this morning?" he asked, in a northeastern accent. To Darius he sounded like a telemarketer.

"I'm fine…thank you. What can I do for you Mr. Denton?" Darius asked, in a voice that was all business.

"First off, I want to welcome you to our little island. And when you have some time, I'd like to invite you to lunch."

"Mr. Denton, I don't believe we have anything to talk about. The hotel's not for sale." Darius kept his voice flat and monotone.

A polite laugh preceded him clearing his throat. "Mr. Monroe, you're way ahead of me. I don't believe I've made you an offer."

"No, but you made my grandfather one. And my position remains the same."

"You know, your grandfather and I were in the middle of discussions at the time of his unfortunate passing. All I wanted to do was meet the man who'd taken his place, and formally introduce myself over lunch."

Whatever Mike Denton wanted would boil down to an offer, and Darius wasn't interested.

Mike continued. "How about later in the week? I can have my secretary check your calendar."

"Sure, call my secretary. I think I can squeeze in a lunch."

Denton chuckled. "The hotel business can be very hectic I know. We'll lunch here at The Shores. I don't believe you've visited our property have you?"

"No, I haven't had the pleasure."

"Great. I'll look forward to showing you around. We'll talk soon."

"Sure thing." Darius hung up, and leaned back in his chair. He'd been warned about RCE's tactics to persuade landowners to sell. However, if the Monroes before him had held out, he could too.

Finally, makeup flawless, every strand of hair in place, and dressed in the third outfit in fifteen minutes, Alicia stood in the bathroom mirror satisfied she didn't look too eager. After all, this wasn't a date-date. She'd agreed to dinner with Darius to settle a few misfortunes, that's all. No matter how much her body disagreed with her brain, she wasn't interested in an island fling, and she planned to make that clear tonight.

The minute she walked out of the bathroom, a loud knock at the door caused her heart to leap into her throat. She took a deep breath and told herself: get a grip. Why was she nervous about this dinner? After a couple of weeks, she'd never see Darius again.

Before opening the door, she shook off her nervous jitters like a boxer about to enter the ring.

When the door opened, Darius took one look at Alicia and knew he was in trouble. He hadn't thought it possible for her to look any more beautiful, but here she stood in a short, light blue dress that hugged her in all the right places. Her full shiny lips begged to be kissed and caused his pulse to quicken. Only her high-heeled sandals were missing.

"Well, you're punctual," she mumbled in a not so welcoming tone.

"And hello to you too," he said laughing.

"I'm sorry." She rolled her eyes heavenward trying not to smile, but the corners of her lips crept up. "Good evening," she said, and then let out a quick sigh.

"That's better." Her smile sent a warming sensation to his heart, which worked its way down to his loins. "In case I don't tell you repeatedly later on, you look absolutely stunning."

"Thank you. You don't look so bad yourself."

He wanted to say, "There now, that wasn't so bad," but if he did she might change her mind and cancel dinner. So instead he asked, "Ready to go?"

She turned and walked back into the room. "I just need to grab my purse."

He admired the beautiful form of her swagger as she switched across the room and back. *Nice. Very nice.*

It took less than thirty minutes to cross the causeway from Jekyll Island over to St. Simons Island. Following Nathan's directions, Darius easily found J Mac's Restaurant and Jazz Bar on Mallery Street in the Village. With two entrances, the building took up most of the block.

Darius parked and walked around to help Alicia out. "I see you gave the high heels a rest tonight?"

She stepped out, looked down at wedged heeled sandals and shrugged. "I'm being nice to my ankles tonight. Besides, when I'm around you unforeseen things seem to happen."

He threw his head back in a hearty laugh. "Oh, I could say the same thing about you." They crossed the street and took the entrance leading into the dining room. The art-deco lighting and warm earthy colors of the room resembled dining out in Chicago.

As the hostess escorted them to a booth in a corner, several men peeked glimpses at Alicia. She definitely was a head turner. Darius held her chair out, thinking she couldn't be suicidal. He weighed the odds for and against broaching the subject, but didn't want to risk her walking out on him.

Their waiter popped over and introduced the specials of the evening, recommending a house wine.

"A glass of ice water for me, please," Alicia requested.

"Bring me a Heineken," Darius said. He skipped his usual rum and Coke, not wanting Alicia to have a flashback.

Before the waiter turned away, Alicia reached out and stopped him. "Hold on," she said. "Instead, make that an Apple Martini."

"Yes, ma'am." The waiter scribbled a note and then walked away, leaving Darius and Alicia alone again.

They sat through a brief moment of silence while Darius tried not to stare at Alicia. She was a truly beautiful woman.

"I heard the reception Friday ended on a good note. My cousin complimented the way your staff moved everything so quickly," said Alicia, breaking the quiet.

"I think we rebounded rather nicely. A couple of bruised egos, some ruined food, and an air conditioning bill, but everyone still had a good time."

"It must be hard running a hotel."

"Your cousin, Sterling, sees to most of the day-to-day business. I spend most of my time working on renovation plans."

The waiter returned with their drinks. "Here we go folks, a Martini for the lady, and a Heineken for you, sir." He clasped his hands together and flashed a friendly smile. "I'll be right back to take your orders. I have a group over there in a big hurry to leave, if you don't mind?"

"Take your time." Darius waved him off.

Alicia took a sip of her martini. "When do you plan to start renovating?"

"We started with a few small improvements today. I'm hoping to land some major investors to completely remake the hotel. You've been there for a week now, tell me what you think."

She shrugged and wondered how much of the truth he wanted. "Well, for starters it's nice and clean."

"Stop right there." He held his hands up in a gesture of surrender. "See, that's not the first thing I want to come to mind when you think of Hotel Paradise. The name alone suggests a more prestigious hotel. When guests walk into the lobby I want them to feel as if they've stepped into paradise."

"A black man's paradise. Isn't that how the original owners referred to the hotel?"

He smiled and crossed his arms. "I'm impressed. You know a little history about the hotel."

She shrugged and held up her fingers measuring an inch. "About this much. I know your grandfather's father purchased it from the original owners—a group of black businessmen back in the 1950s."

"So you're a history buff?" he asked.

"Not really. I'm just interested in history involving the islands. My mother's from St. Helena, North Carolina."

"So you're Geechee?"

She nodded. "Geechee or Gullah. I guess they're one and the same. I don't really know a lot about the Gullah culture, but I'm learning."

"Growing up, your parents didn't bring you down every summer and show you where they used to play and the long roads they walked for miles to get to school, et cetera, et cetera?" he asked with a laugh.

"Sounds like you've heard that speech a lot."

"Hundreds of times. I can recite them in my sleep. My family's not Gullah though; they moved into the area years after slavery. My grandfather and my father grew up here."

"No, I was spared those speeches. After my mother passed, I think my father forgot about St. Helena and my family here. He never even told me about them. We traveled a lot, but he was originally from California, so that's where we spent most of our summers."

"Is that what you meant earlier when you said you didn't know your family so well?"

"Yep. My father was so busy managing his business and his women that he never mentioned them."

Darius gave a highbrow nod. "And he never remarried?"

She laughed. "I'm sure he couldn't make up his mind which one to marry. Don't get me wrong, my father was a wonderful man. He gave me everything a girl could ask for. At sixteen he purchased my first car. After college, he paid for me to tour Europe with some friends. Every winter he took me to the slopes, and he didn't even ski. I saw the Eiffel Tower before I knew what it was. He showed me the world, with one girlfriend or another tagging along each trip."

"You sound bitter."

The corners of her lips turned up. "For a time I was, but I like to think I've matured beyond that stage. I'm sure he was fulfilling some fantasy he had about giving his child everything he didn't have."

Darius leaned back and crossed his arms. "Sounds like a charmed life to me."

"It was. I don't mean to sound ungrateful, but there are just some things children need other than trips." God, she was running her mouth too much. Darius didn't need to know all her business.

Saved by the bell. The waiter finally reappeared and took their dinner orders. So far, the seafood Alicia had eaten on the island registered five on a scale from one to ten. She hoped the food at J Mac's would measure up to the standards she'd hoped for.

"Yeah, I know what you mean." Darius stared off across the room for a minute. "My childhood wasn't quite that charmed, but it wasn't bad. Of course, the only traveling we did was to come down here and visit my grandfather. An MBA was the only thing my old man wanted from me, and I got it. He didn't care what I wanted to do. I think he knew even when my brother and I were in high school that one day one of us would have to take over the hotel."

"You and your brother have MBA's?" she asked.

Darius shook his head. "I got the MBA, while Luke quit school, joined a band, and traveled around the world."

"Now, you sound bitter," she stated.

"I was in Chicago working all day and cramming for exams all night; he was eating sushi in Japan or drinking vodka in Germany. Why would I be bitter?" he asked, sarcastically. "About once a month I took my horn down to Cisco's, a small jazz spot on the south side, and joined a jam session."

"What kind of horn do you play?" she asked, intrigued. Not only was he good-looking, he was also a musician; and Alicia, like most women she knew, had a thing for musicians.

"The saxophone, but I haven't played in years."

She crossed her legs. The saxophone was her favorite, and the sexiest of all instruments. "Did you belong to a band too?"

"I joined a couple different bands up until I started graduate school. No time for a band, though, if you're serious about your studies."

"Sounds like your father groomed you instead of your brother to take over the business."

"Forced is more like it." Darius leaned back and finished his beer.

Okay, bitter may not have been a strong enough word. And Alicia thought she had issues.

The waiter returned carrying a large tray with what smelled and looked like the best food Alicia had seen all week.

Sterling held the door open for Catherine who'd fussed all the way to the restaurant. He was supposed to have picked her up at six-thirty for their anniversary dinner. However, he didn't get off work until seven. He'd hoped by the time he entered the house she would have changed her mind, but just like a woman, she'd stood in the kitchen dressed up and tapping her foot against the floor. She'd made reservations for seven. She was pissed.

J Mac's was her choice, not his. He never liked a dimly lit restaurant where you couldn't see your food. The skinny waiter in all black with blond hair looked like a character from a vampire movie. He walked them through the restaurant and to a table in the back. Sterling hated when white folks did that. He wasn't sitting in the back of anybody's restaurant. Just as he opened his mouth to demand another table, he caught sight of something that surprised the hell out of him. He closed his mouth.

Chapter 13

Still standing, Sterling could see Darius and Alicia sitting in a booth smiling at each other like two love struck teenagers.

"What is it?" Catherine asked.

"Nothing." He sat down before she had a chance to stand up and see for herself.

"Oh, I thought you were going to say you didn't like this table. You know how picky you can be."

"No, it's perfect. Let's just order something to eat." He didn't want Catherine to see Alicia. If she did, she wouldn't be able to resist saying hello.

So Darius was making a move on Alicia, and he'd been in town less than a week. Sterling had to hand it to him, he moved fast. If something developed between them, he had to find a way to benefit from it. Darius had what he wanted—the hotel. Alicia had what he needed—money.

* * *

Alicia's fish was excellent, the Martini was wonderful, and the company wasn't bad either. She had planned to put Darius in his place tonight, but she quickly forgot about that. Throughout the meal, he'd amused her with humorous childhood stories and fond memories of Jekyll Island.

"Sounds like you and your brother were busy getting into trouble whenever you could," she said.

"I like to refer to them as adventures," he said with a smile.

"I bet your mother didn't see it that way."

"No, and neither did the slim black belt that was her constant companion. But my Poppy…that's what we called our grandfather. He was the greatest. He fed our adventures when we were down here. He used to give us little odd jobs around the hotel. Instead of working, we'd run from building to building knocking on doors."

"I bet the staff was glad to see you guys go home."

"Probably so. I came down every summer until the tenth grade."

The more they talked, the more Alicia enjoyed herself. Darius had been a perfect gentleman. They were enjoying a delicious meal together, and the jazz band next door added to the evening.

"Do you still plan on staying with us the rest of the month?" he asked.

She took a deep breath, no longer looking forward to returning to her empty, lonely hotel room tonight. "Right now, yes, but I don't know. I might change my plans."

He gave a nonchalant nod as the conversation halted. Alicia could envision the wheels turning in his head trying to think of something to fill the silence. He nibbled on his bottom lip, looking pensive all of a sudden.

"I know you're not married, but there has to be somebody in Atlanta scratching at the bits waiting for you to return."

"Scratching at the bits?" she repeated laughing. "Now there's a term I haven't heard before."

He grinned and shrugged. "Well, is it true?"

The intensity of his gaze sent a chill through her body. She glanced down at the crumbs on her plate before meeting his gaze. "No, there's nobody waiting for me. Nobody that matters anyway." Her last disastrous relationship didn't count.

He leaned forward holding her gaze. "I want to take you somewhere tomorrow."

She smiled and shook her head. "I thought this was a one date deal?"

"Then we won't call it a date. Did you happen to bring any sneakers down with you?"

"Yeah, but aren't you too busy at the hotel to go playing tour guide?"

His grin was slow to appear, but absolutely mesmerizing to her senses. "Some things a man's never too busy for."

The lobby was filled with guests heading downstairs for lunch as Alicia picked up a parasailing brochure from a small table next to the concierge desk advertising. There was no way in hell she'd try that sport, but it did look interesting.

"I'm game if you are."

She turned around half-expecting to find Darius. Instead the familiar clean-shaven face with a devilish, handsome smile belonged to his brother, Luke.

"Oh no," she responded holding up the brochure. "I'm just killing time and waiting for someone. I don't parasail."

He reached over and picked up another brochure. "Neither do I, so it's something we can learn together."

Alicia took a step back, taking in this man in all his cockiness. His resemblance to Darius was striking. "I don't think so. If I die, I prefer it not be with a stranger."

He laughed. "Cute, I like that," he said, holding out his hand. "I'm Luke."

"I'm Alicia," she responded, returning the handshake. Although she'd only caught a glimpse of him while lying at the bottom of the stairs a few days ago, she remembered him.

"Alicia." He let the name roll around off his tongue. "That's a pretty name."

"Thank you." Was Darius's brother hitting on her?

He set the brochure on the table. "Are you looking for something to get into this evening?"

She shook her head. "Not particularly. Why? Are you the concierge?"

Luke glanced down and read the sign on the desk. He turned back around and adjusted his suit jacket. "Yes, I am. Can I make you reservations somewhere? Or perhaps you'd like a private tour of the island?"

What a charmer. It must run in the family, she thought.

A middle-aged woman walked up to the desk behind him and took a seat. "Hello, can I help you?"

Alicia turned to Luke, smiling.

He hunched his shoulders. "Okay, so I'm not the concierge, but that private tour can still be arranged." He gestured toward the front entrance. "My car's right outside."

Alicia crossed her arms. "Nice try, but I'll pass."

He shrugged and turned to the woman now behind the desk. "I tried to get you some business, sorry."

"Mr. Monroe, don't tell me we've got you working the concierge desk?" Sterling asked jokingly as he joined them.

Although Alicia could hardly wait to sit down and talk to Sterling about his "family secret" comment, she didn't want to appear too eager, so she dropped her arms and let them hang at her side.

"I'm helping out wherever I can, Sterling—" Luke gestured back at the woman at the desk "—but, I believe this pretty lady's got everything covered."

The woman grinned from ear to ear.

Sterling patted Alicia on the arm before glancing at his watch. "Sorry I'm late. I grabbed one last phone call, and you know how that is."

Alicia smiled and nodded in agreement.

"Mr. Monroe." Sterling turned to Luke. "My cousin and I were about to grab some lunch, would you like to join us?"

Alicia's eyes grew to the size of saucers. *Please say no,* she said to herself, waiting on Luke to respond. She glanced away in case he looked to see whether she wanted him to join them. She had personal issues to discuss with Sterling that she couldn't bring up if Luke joined them.

"You know, with me and my brother running around here, addressing me as Mr. Monroe might get confusing, so please call me Luke. And I'm gonna have to pass on that lunch, I'm on the way to meet my brother for lunch now. But—" he clasped his hands together and tilted his head toward Alicia "—I'll take a rain check."

She didn't have an opportunity to respond before Sterling did. "Sure, we'll look forward to it."

Luke's smile faded as he regarded Sterling with an appraising glance. He said good-bye, shoved a hand in his pocket, and walked away. Alicia could foresee trouble brewing between those two.

"So where would you like to go?" Sterling asked.

"Some place where we can have a private conversation."

He nodded and took off his glasses, cleaning the lenses

with his tie. After wiping off every speck of dust, he turned around and asked the concierge for something.

Alicia crossed her arms again. She hoped he wasn't going to try and worm his way out of this conversation. She could see Luke standing at the front desk looking back at them.

Sterling handed her several sheets of paper stapled together. "Look through this menu guide and let me know what looks good to you." He replaced his glasses.

Alicia leafed through the four-page guide, uninterested in where they ate, only wanting to get him away from the hotel and any distractions.

"I think I know what you want to talk about," he said, as they left the building.

"Good," she responded.

"I don't know if I have the answers you want, but I'm sure we'll be able to work something out."

Meanwhile, Darius sat in his office, starving and waiting for Luke. After a long morning of overseeing the various hotel improvements, he found himself trapped in his office by a nervous-looking hospitality manager.

Timothy uncrossed his legs and moved to the edge of his seat. "Mr. Monroe, I know you haven't had time to look at them proposals, but I wanted you to know that for years I've tried to bring other performers in from time to time. But every proposal I submit gets shot down."

The proposals had been sitting on Darius's desk for two days now. He glanced at them, and then up at Timothy's clasped hands and at the nervous way in which he twirled his thumbs. "Who shoots you down?"

"Your grandfather, Sterling, both of 'em. I kept trying to tell 'em what the guest surveys say about our entertainment, but they never listened to me. People wants to party a little, and the Golden Isle Sons don't play the Top Forty."

Darius took a deep breath. He'd missed the band's performance Saturday night. "Can I get a look at those surveys?"

Timothy stopped his nervous twitching and reached down into his briefcase. He surprised Darius by pulling out a fat folder and sliding it across the desk.

"Here's some of 'em. I have more in my office." Darius opened the folder and scanned the responses.

"You can see the unfavorable responses to the band. Folks want to dance on weekends."

The written comments section requested more up-to-date music, dancing, and overall better entertainment. The dates on the surveys were all within a two-year period.

"If the band's been getting this type of feedback, then why hasn't something been done about it?" Darius asked.

"We got a five-year contract with 'em that can't be broken. I'm stuck with 'em, and that's pretty much my yearly entertainment budget."

"Why is all the budget being spent on one band?" Darius asked with a frown.

Timothy's chest rose and fell as he sat back with a sigh. "I don't know. Sterling was the hospitality manager when that contract was negotiated. He signed them up for five straight years, and I think he wants to keep them on. No matter what."

Darius shook his head perplexed. "What kind of…deal did they work out?"

Timothy crossed his legs and resumed his nervous thumb dance. "I haven't been able to find out. Only the general manager has access to the contracts. But, I was hoping you'd look into it."

Darius gave Timothy a knowing smile and closed the folder. "I'll pull the contract and see what I can do."

"Thank you, sir. And, if you don't mind, can I ask that you not mention my name when discussing this with Sterling?"

"Of course," Darius agreed, as Timothy stood and shook his hand. Was he afraid of Sterling, Darius wondered?

By the time Timothy left, Darius's stomach had started to emit a loud grumble. He reached over and picked up the phone as his office door opened, and Luke strode in.

"I was just about to call you," Darius said, hanging up.

"I ran into your general manager in the lobby," Luke said with a smirk.

In dress slacks, a white shirt, and a tie, Luke looked more like the owner of the hotel now, instead of a member of some band.

"Sterling's an interesting man."

Luke took a seat across from Darius's desk and pushed back until the chair tilted on two legs. "He did invite me to lunch though, with my new friend, Alicia."

At the mention of her name, Darius's throat tightened. What did he mean by *new friend?* He set the folder down. "Alicia who? Where did you meet her?" he asked, in rapid succession.

Luke gestured toward the door. "In the lobby a few minutes ago. I didn't get her last name, but man I'm sure you've seen her around. Long hair, bomb body, sexy legs—"

"I get the picture. I know who you're talking about." Something about his little brother describing Alicia annoyed Darius. He didn't think Luke had much respect for women. Years of touring and being on the road had ruined his appreciation for a good woman. Darius couldn't stand to hear him reduce her to body parts.

"Yeah well, that's what I'm missing out on, so come on, let's go grab some food."

"Look, I'm starving, but before we go I need you to do something for me."

Luke let the chair roll forward. "That's why I'm here."

Darius tossed the folder across his desk. "Start with that. Our entertainment needs an upgrade."

Luke took the folder and flipped through the contents.

"Ask Sterling for a copy of the contract," Darius said standing up. "I need you to tell me how we can get out of it."

Luke kept reading as he stood up. "Now this is right up my alley."

"I thought so." But where was he going to work? "Hey, I'm sorry there's not another desk or office, but we'll put one in somewhere. Until then, feel free to use this office whenever you need to."

"Don't worry about it. For now, I can work from my suite. I'm in room forty-four. It's big enough to hold meetings or whatever else."

Darius blinked; surprised to learn that Luke's room was two doors down from Alicia's. He didn't know if he should be concerned about that or not. However, given his brother had only a brief history with any woman, he figured it was okay. For the moment, he decided not to dwell on it.

Darius came from behind his desk. "I'm starved, let's grab some lunch."

Chapter 14

Sterling sat across from Alicia and drank a beer, content to talk about everything but their family. She'd picked out a small café in the historic district for lunch, and was happy to find an end table on the patio. They had all the privacy they needed. Now, if she could only change the subject.

"…That's why I'm positive William's about to quit. And I think Luke is after my job. When the air conditioner went out, instead of waiting until I returned from the bank, he—"

"Sterling!" Frustrated that he wouldn't shut up about the hotel, Alicia ran a hand across her forehead. "I'm sorry, I know I asked how things were going, but I really wanted to talk about something else."

He looked surprised. "Oh, that's right." He bit into his turkey sandwich and chewed.

"Yeah, well—" Alicia tucked an annoying strand of hair behind her ear "—after the cookout, you said there was a lot

Aunt Ode wasn't telling me. And something about family secrets."

He set his sandwich down. "Let me ask you something. Exactly why are you here?"

Stunned by the bluntness of his question, she blinked back whatever guilty look might be on her face and tried not to look surprised.

"To see you guys," she said, nonchalantly and crossed her arms. "You already know that."

"No, I mean why are you *really* here? What is it about the family that you want to know? Like I said, I may not have the answers, but maybe we can help each other."

Her body immediately stiffened. What did he want from her? She relaxed her arms as she formed her lips to tell a lie. "Okay, what I haven't told anyone is that I don't remember my mother. That's why I've been asking all the questions. I'll do anything to learn more about her. But, nobody seems to want to talk about her."

He responded with a slow nod of his head.

"If you've heard something about my mother, or can tell me why aunt Ode won't talk about her, I'd appreciate you telling me." She pulled her chair closer to the table.

He removed his glasses and cleaned the lenses with the corner of his napkin. A stall tactic of his she'd picked up on.

"I don't remember Aunt Venetta, and I can't imagine what it feels like not to remember your mother; but I have heard a few things over the years that led me to believe Mama's not telling you something."

"What?"

He shrugged. "I think Aunt Venetta was like the black sheep of the family. Mama called her a wild child. Whenever she gets mad at Ruth Ann, she tells her she's just like her aunt Venetta." He glanced away and took another swig of beer.

Alicia remembered what Rorie had said about no one in the family knowing the father of Ruth Ann's boys. Had her mother been the same way, and no one knew who the father of her baby was?

"Sterling, I'll tell you what I really need to know."

His back straightened and his left brow rose. "What's that?"

Her heart pounded against her chest. If Sterling was the big man in the family like Rorie insinuated, she should be able to trust him. Besides, he had said they could help each other.

"I need to know who my mother went to stay with in New York, and why."

"Why not ask Mama?"

"Because, I don't think she'd tell me. You see, I found some papers that suggest she might have been pregnant when she arrived in New York, but I can't be sure."

"Pregnant?" he asked.

She shrugged. "I'm not sure."

"So that's what you want?"

"I need to know if I'm a family secret."

Darius had exchanged his work clothes for a pair of khakis and a Chicago Bulls T-shirt. Alicia had on the same white skirt and top she'd worn since lunch. As agreed, she met him after dinner by the pool.

He tapped the flashlight against his open palm until a beam of light shot out across the dark sand.

"Are you sure we need that?" Alicia asked, pointing at his flashlight and then toward the moon.

The half-moon illuminated the sky. "We'll need it." He shined the light at her feet smiling at her blue-and-white cross trainers. "Good, you've got your sneakers on."

Alicia pointed one foot out in front of her. "They're my running shoes, I just haven't been running lately."

Darius reached out for her hand. "Give me your hand, these steps can be slippery."

Her hand disappeared as his long fingers wrapped around it. His palm was warm, and his grip firm. Beads of perspiration clung to Alicia's forehead, although a gentle breeze blew in off the ocean.

He shined the light down the steps ahead of them. Darius hadn't let go of her hand as they stepped out onto the cool sand. Another flashlight glowed in the distance farther down the shoreline.

"Can I ask what we're doing out here?" she asked.

"I want to show you something. Hopefully, anyway." He fanned the flashlight in a left-to-right motion in front of them as they strolled down the beach.

She followed him wondering what the hell they were looking for. Silently, he kept walking.

After about two minutes, she couldn't stand it any longer. "Okay, I give up. What are you doing?"

He let go of her hand, and stooped down shining his light on something stuck in the sand. A discarded plastic cup had caught his attention.

"Are we on some type of a treasure hunt or something?" she finally asked.

He stood and aimed the flashlight up toward the grass, then continued the stroll. Alicia fell in step beside him. This time, clasping her hands behind her back.

"Have you ever heard of loggerhead turtles?" Darius asked.

"I don't think so."

"No, well, this island is their nesting area. I took a little jog out here early this morning and saw some tracks in the sand. They come ashore to lay eggs around this time of year." His light fanned across the sand.

"Huh, have you ever seen one?" she asked intrigued.

"A long time ago. Poppy brought us out one night and we saw this giant reptile making its nightly trek up the beach. At least, that's how he explained it."

She chuckled. "I bet your summers here were great. I've only seen turtles at the aquarium. Oh, and I saw one at a pet shop once."

He laughed. "It's real peaceful out here at night. You can think and clear your head if you need to." He shot her a glance.

"Yeah, I suppose," she murmured.

A rustling sound caught their attention, and Darius stopped.

"Did you hear that?" he whispered.

"Yeah," Alicia stepped closer to him. "What was it?"

He aimed the light toward the grass, and caught the long skinny tail of something as it shot through the bushes.

"Whoa!" he stepped back, and almost knocked her down.

"Ouch," Alicia jumped as Darius reached back for her apologizing.

"I'm sorry, did I hurt you?"

"No, I'm fine. That looked like a rat," she said, gripping Darius's arm.

He grabbed her hand and backed farther away from the grass, while shining the light over the bushes. "I hate rats."

"So do I. Does the hotel have rats?" she asked.

"None that I've seen. But I'm going to have maintenance look around; maybe set some traps."

"We had rats in the basement of our apartment in New York. We used to throw rocks at them."

"So the big city girl's not afraid of rats?" He turned to her smiling.

"Oh, I'm afraid of them. I've lived in Atlanta most of my life, with no rats. They give me the creeps."

"Well, I haven't had to deal with any, and I don't want to. I came out here to have a peaceful walk, not to chase rats."

He took her hand again as they continued their stroll along the beach, still looking for turtles.

"Don't worry, if they come after us, all we have to do is jump in the water; rats can't swim."

Darius laughed. "Then that makes two of us."

"No way. Don't tell me you can't swim?"

He shook his head. "Never learned. I grew up in the city with no pool or access to one."

"But you're from Chicago, what about Lake Michigan?"

"I've been on the lake on a boat, but never set foot in the water."

"And your father or grandfather didn't teach you how to swim?"

He grunted. "Are you kidding? They were too busy arguing all the damned time."

"What about your brother? Can he swim?"

"Like a fish. And I have no idea where he learned. He just jumped in one day and started swimming."

"He's a natural," she stated.

"So, what's it like growing up an only child and not having to worry about sibling rivalry?"

"Lonely," she said somberly.

"No one to fight with, huh."

"Did you and your brother fight a lot?"

The light ambling in the distance was closing in on them.

"Like cats and dogs, and over any and everything. The only time we weren't fighting is when one of us got into a fight with somebody else. Then we kicked butt together."

She laughed. "Sounds like that happened often."

"I grew up on the south side of Chicago. We had fights for dessert."

Alicia kept laughing. Whoever was coming up the beach toward them shined a light in her face, momentarily blinding her. She stopped.

"Who the hell is that?" Darius grumbled, holding his hand up to shield the light.

The stream of light ran down the beach and out toward the water. Whoever it was was closer now, and Alicia could see a man in faded jeans, a baseball cap, and a Hotel Paradise name badge.

"Oh, I'm sorry, Mr. Monroe, is that you?" The night security guard met them.

"Yeah, George. It's me. What are you doing out here?"

"Sir, I was just patrolling the beach. I checks it 'bout this time every night." George squinted his already narrow eyes to see who was with Darius. "Good evening, ma'am."

The scrawny man with hollow cheeks and crooked teeth smiled at Alicia. "Hello," she said politely. For a moment, she thought they were about to be mugged on the beach. And with nothing but a five-dollar bill in her pocket, the thief would probably have killed her.

"Well, you folks be careful now, it's getting late." He aimed his light ahead of him now and continued down the beach.

"Okay George. Thanks." Darius looked over his shoulder as George walked away. Then he turned to Alicia.

"Creepy," she whispered.

"That's only the second time I've seen that man since I've been here. This must be where he spends most of his time. Patrolling the beach," Darius noted in a soft-spoken voice.

Alicia laughed. "And I've never seen him."

"He's right though, it is getting late. I guess what I saw wasn't a turtle track after all. Come on, I'll walk you back to your room."

Darius held out his arm and wrapped it around Alicia's

shoulders. His flashlight, aimed in front of them, followed George's tracks back up the beach.

The sheer surprise of his arm sliding around her shoulder caused her stomach muscles to clench. Her body sent out a distress signal to her brain. She needed willpower in a hurry. With his arm around her, they strolled back up the beach in silence.

Slowly, Darius stopped and turned her to face him. She met his gaze, and then lost what little ounce of willpower she built up. He had nice shoulders and a broad chest. The Bulls T-shirt showed off strong, hard arms that slid around her waist. She'd already checked out his tight sexy butt in the khakis. He was tall, athletic, handsome, and standing entirely too close to resist.

She threw caution to the wind, and stood on her tiptoes pressing her lips against his. Goose bumps sprang up as the warm firmness of his lips met hers. He pulled her closer and slid his hand up the small of her back, pressing her against his hard body.

She closed her eyes. Her heart pounded against her chest as she pushed her tongue between his lips. He willingly let her explore, touch, and taste his hot, soft mouth. She shivered as his fingers traced little circles along her back. She lowered her feet and finally pulled back from his mouth. She'd only wanted a quick taste of him, but he wouldn't hear of it.

"Uh-uh, Alicia," he said, in a voice so croaky she hardly recognized it as his.

He tilted his head and brought his mouth down over hers in a kiss so hot and demanding, it ignited a fire deep within her. Her arms rose from her sides and wrapped around his neck. *Oh God, what I've been missing.* Her whole body quivered.

Her knees weakened.

His tongue probed with more urgency, sending her into a

tizzy. She'd stepped over an unforeseen line drawn in the sand with Darius. Things between them would never be the same. She tightened her grip around his neck.

Their bodies pressed up against one another so hard she could feel his racing heart beat. By no means did it outrun her own. Her breasts smashed up against his chest, where her hard nipples experienced a thrilling sensation of their own. Suddenly, she became all too aware of how this was affecting him.

His budding erection probed at her stomach. Seconds later, he pulled his mouth away and looked down at her trembling body.

"What are we doing out here?" she asked softly, between ragged breaths.

"Kissing," he whispered, as his lips found hers again. This time he nipped at her lower lip before sucking it into his mouth.

"Wait." She lowered her arms and placed a hand against his chest. She needed to breathe and think. For someone who'd never had a one-night stand and had been celibate for the last two years, what was she thinking?

Darius gripped her hips and looked down into her eyes. He'd taken a step back.

"I'm sorry," she whispered. "But I'm not looking for a relationship right now, and I don't know if I can handle anything else." A quick island fling sounded exciting, but in theory she didn't think she could do it.

His eyes closed. He let out a hard breath and lowered his forehead to hers. "I never expected to run into anyone like you here." His breathing returned to normal, as his head rose. "Forgive me for stepping out of line. I don't want to run you away; I just want to get to know you." He removed his hands from her hips.

A twinge of guilt shot through her. She hadn't meant to be

hot one minute, then cold the next. If Darius wasn't so handsome, with such a fine, hard body, she could have resisted him. "I'm the one that kissed you," she admitted.

He shifted the flashlight around and shined it away from them. She was right, she had kissed him, and for the second time. One quality he didn't like in a woman was a tease. He hoped Alicia wasn't like that.

"Tell you what. We'll just take things slow and no more teasing. As temping as it might be."

Speechless for probably the first time in her life, she nodded in agreement.

On the stroll back up the beach Darius fanned his flashlight hoping to see at least one turtle.

As they approached the steps leading back to the hotel, they saw someone sitting on the top step. The man stood as Darius shinned his light in that direction.

"Y'all taking a late night stroll?" Gibb asked, puffing on a cigarette.

Alicia walked up the steps before Darius, who stopped to shake Gibb's hand. "Yeah, nice out isn't it?"

"Yessir. Nice night for a…stroll along the beach." Gibb nodded and smiled at Alicia.

"Y'all didn't see George out there did you?" he asked in his lazy drawl.

"As a matter of fact we did. He came back this way before we did though. You didn't see him?"

"No sir. I stepped out here for a smoke break hoping to catch him."

"Is something wrong?" Darius asked.

Gibb frowned and shook his head. "Naw, everything's okay. George kind of disappears sometimes until it's about time to go home."

"Well, let me know if you need anything."

* * *

Darius walked Alicia to her room, and she felt like a sixteen year old coming home from her first date. The only thing missing was her father peeking out the window. She opened the door to her suite and turned on the light, and then turned back to Darius.

"Want to come in?" She couldn't believe she'd extended the offer after what had just transpired on the beach.

He licked his lips and leaned in to plant another soft, wet kiss on the lips that tasted like her lip-gloss.

"I'd better not, it's late. But, why don't you have breakfast with me in the morning?"

She leaned against the door and tilted her head up at him. "What time do you eat breakfast?"

He turned his lips up. "Hum, usually around seven."

"In the morning?" she asked, pushing away from the door.

He laughed. "Okay, if that's too early for you, how about eight?"

"Make it eight-thirty and we've got a date."

He smiled down at her. "Okay, eight-thirty."

"Goodnight." Alicia grabbed the door to close it.

"Oh—" Darius reached out to stop her "—by the way, I have breakfast in my apartment, not the dining room. It's opposite this building, on the end, you can't miss it. See you in the morning."

Her jaw dropped.

Chapter 15

Alicia fell across the bed face first and screamed into her pillow. Ten p.m. on Jekyll Island might as well have been two a.m. and she'd invited Darius into her room. And for what? Sex, what else? God, she wanted that man. She'd practically attacked him on the beach, and then pulled back like a big tease.

But, wasn't two years of celibacy long enough? *What* was she holding out for? *Whom* was she holding out for?

She sat up and pulled her top over her head. She had no business getting involved with Darius. In a few more weeks she'd be leaving Jekyll Island, going back to Atlanta and her single-in-the-city lifestyle. If she played her cards right, she might land a date or two before the end of summer.

She wiggled out of her skirt. Then again, maybe she'd spend the rest of the summer at the dealership pretending to be interested.

She walked into the bathroom and slipped into her robe. Looking in the mirror, she brushed her hair back and blushed at herself like a schoolgirl. That's what Darius did to her. He made her feel like a teenager.

Then, she dropped her hands as she remembered something. She couldn't have breakfast with Darius tomorrow!

The next morning, Darius took the liberty of ordering the hotel's signature big southern breakfast with eggs, sausage, grits and fried green tomatoes. For Alicia, he added a special request of Belgian waffles with strawberries and fresh squeezed juice.

While he waited, he cleared files and newspapers from the sofa. Housekeeping kept the room clean, but Darius was the king of clutter. He closed his laptop, which sat open on his desk where he'd spent the early hours of the morning answering e-mail from Keith regarding The Coffee Spot. He didn't plan on doing any work for the next hour or so while he entertained his beautiful guest. A knock at the door prompted him to glance at his watch: 8:20.

Darius opened the door to two young men carrying trays full of food. He let them in and picked up the phone to call the guest of honor.

Thirty minutes later, disappointed that Alicia hadn't shown up or called, Darius sat back and finished his breakfast—alone. He convinced himself that something important came up. Something so important she couldn't pick up the phone to call him. Whatever the case, he didn't have time to sit around crying over it; he had a hotel to run.

Trouble had missed his calling in life. He should have been a football player. Interception was his specialty. He pulled a folded piece of paper from his pocket and threw it in a passing garbage can.

His favorite desk clerk wasn't working this morning, although she'd been scheduled to. He crossed the grounds and walked up to the suites at the end of the building. He stood between suite forty-two and forty-four dangling the master key with a crafty smile.

By ten a.m., room service had cleared all traces of breakfast from Darius's room. He caught up with his daily routine of walking through the hotel before settling down to look into the next project.

Before lunch, he called Alicia again, but there was still no answer. Then he walked out to check the front desk himself for any messages. He couldn't believe she'd just left him hanging with no explanation.

He opened the door and walked over to Kamora. She was leaning against the counter talking to Rodell. The young man straightened at the sight of Darius and pretended to be asking for information.

Darius smiled. He'd already noticed Rodell's interest in the young woman. "Kamora."

She straightened up and turned around. "Yes, sir?"

"Were there any messages left out here for me today?"

She looked around the counter, then up at Darius. "No, sir."

"Have you been here all morning?" he asked.

"Yes, but Robby worked this morning too. He's gone to help Mr. Simpson with something right now. If he took a message, it would be right here—" she pointed to a space next to the computer on the counter "—but, there's nothing."

Rodell had backed away from the counter, but hadn't walked away. The phone rang and Kamora answered it. Darius walked around her to the end of the counter.

"Rodell, come here a minute." Darius waved him back over.

"Yes, sir."

Darius had asked the young man to call him by his first name, but Rodell insisted on *sir*. "Have you seen Ms. McKay lately?"

"Ms. McKay?" Rodell's eyebrows shot up. "No, sir, I haven't."

"Well, I need a huge favor. Look the hotel over and let me know if you find her, or anyone who can tell you where she's gone. Once you find her, keep an eye on her for me every day until she checks out later this month."

Rodell nodded, but gave Darius a strange look.

"I'm concerned something might happen to her. I'll tell you more later, but can you do that for me?" Darius asked.

"Sure, sir. I'll look for her right now and call you when I find her."

On the short walk back to his office, Darius remembered something. Her journal. He remembered what he'd read and hoped to God she hadn't done something crazy.

He rushed from his office down the beach path toward her room. His heart pounded faster and faster keeping in time with his steps. Once he reached the building, he took the stairs two at a time.

He took a minute to catch his breath and then knocked. The second time, he banged harder. "Damn it, Alicia, where are you?"

The squeaky sound of a door opening and a woman's giggle grabbed his attention. Was that Alicia's laugh? If so, she was coming out of Luke's room. Darius stepped back frowning and looked two doors down.

After leaving a note for Darius asking for a rain check, Alicia had climbed into the back seat of Juanita's SUV ready for the three-hour drive to St. Helena. She'd expected to see her aunt Ode in the passenger seat; but Juanita explained that Ode's arthritis had flared up and she couldn't handle the ride. Instead, Ruth Ann had joined them.

Beside Alicia, Tracy danced in her seat with a pair of headphones on. Alicia didn't know why the child wasn't in school.

Disappointed that she wouldn't be able to learn anything new from her aunt, Alicia sat back at least happy that her cousins hadn't brought all their children for the ride.

"So, Alicia—" Ruth Ann twisted around facing the back seat "—Mama said you don't remember your trip to St. Helena?"

"No, I don't. I'm afraid I was too young. Although, I suppose I might remember something."

"There's not much to see anyway," Ruth Ann added.

"Yes, there is," Juanita corrected her. "We'll stop at the Penn Center. It's a museum full of history on the Gullah culture. Then we'll grab some lunch at Gullah Grub. It's a small, local restaurant with great food."

Ruth Ann jumped in. "Then, get ready to sit on the porch and listen to some stuffy old stories," she said, looking back at Alicia.

"Don't listen to her." Juanita looked at Alicia through the rearview mirror. "Telling stories through folklore and song is how we keep our Gullah culture alive. We'll be staying with Bessie, cousin Quincy's mother. She still lives in their family home. You'll enjoy it; just don't expect hotel accommodations."

Ruth Ann turned around and readjusted the radio, turning it from the gospel station of Juanita's choice to one with hip-hop traveling music, as she referred to it.

Three hours later, they crossed the bridge to Lady's Island and drove into St. Helena, North Carolina. As they traveled the two-lane road, many of the old houses looked familiar. But they resembled houses Alicia could have seen in and around Atlanta.

By now, Tracy had shed her earphones and was peering out the window.

"Nana used to go to church here. She said her old boyfriend still lives here," Tracy said.

Because of the volume on the radio, the ladies in the front seat couldn't hear, but Alicia responded with, "who was that?"

Tracy shrugged. "I don't know. Nana just said she left her old beau in St. Helena. Aunt Ruth said beau means boyfriend." Her eyes sparkled as she said the word *boyfriend*.

Alicia nodded. "Uh, huh. And does Miss Tracy have a boyfriend?"

Tracy looked from her mother to her aunt before looking at Alicia and nodding. Then she motioned for Alicia to come closer.

She bent her head down and Tracy whispered in her ear. "His name's Michael, and he goes to my school."

Alicia's mouth formed an O shape, and she winked and shook her head to assure Tracy her secret was safe with her. Alicia held a finger over her lips and gave the child a conspirator's smile.

"Well, here we are," Juanita said, as they drove down another two-lane country road.

Alicia listened to Juanita and Ruth Ann's brief history lessons on the Low Country area until they pulled up to the Penn Center—the first school built in the south for the education of blacks.

Juanita drove around to the parking lot, and everyone climbed out.

"This is where Mama Nancy went to school," Ruth Ann volunteered.

"It is?" Alicia asked, surprised. No one had mentioned that before. Excitement and curiosity built up inside her as they walked in. She'd learned more than she'd ever expected to, and it excited her.

Once inside the York W. Baily Museum, they were greeted by Charles, an eighty-seven-year-old former student and proud volunteer.

Alicia spent over three hours touring the exhibits, watching a film, and browsing the bookstore. She purchased several books to help her understand the Gullah and West African connection.

Darius stepped back and waited for whomever to show herself. A young woman in a pink tube top and a pair of white short shorts sashayed out of Luke's room into the hallway. Darius shook his head, and let out a sigh of relief. He hadn't actually expected Alicia to be in his brother's room, but Luke had a way with women that Darius didn't quite understand.

Darius hadn't seen this young woman before. He didn't think she worked at the hotel. When Luke noticed him, his face grew serious. What little faith Darius had in Luke being sincere about helping with the hotel went out the window.

The young lady shook Luke's hand and walked away.

Darius entered the suite behind her.

"Before you say anything, I'm auditioning new singers." Luke closed the door behind them.

Darius cut his eyes at Luke. "In your room?"

"It's my office," he said, pointing to the papers scattered about the desk and coffee table.

"Nice try. But do you know how sleazy this looks?" Darius walked over to see the view from there.

Luke shrugged. "I've auditioned in a hotel room before. What's wrong with it?"

Darius shook his head. "We have an empty conference room in the lower level of the lobby. Why don't you hold your auditions there from now on?"

Luke nodded. "Yes, sir, whatever you say." He straightened the papers and pictures in his office.

The condescending tone of Luke's voice made the hair on Darius's arm stand up. "Don't do that. I'm not your father."

"Yeah," Luke rubbed his nose and cleared his throat. "You could have fooled me."

Darius closed his eyes for a brief second and bit his lip. He didn't want to argue with Luke. Why couldn't they work together without all the drama?

Luke dropped the papers into a neat stack on his desk. "Look, I didn't come down here to fight with you. You asked me to work on the entertainment and that's what I'm doing. I'll move the auditions to the conference room, no problem."

"Good, and get together with Timothy. He's the manager in charge of entertainment and I think you guys should work together."

"What does he know about music?" Luke asked.

"He knows something you don't—this area." Darius crossed the room and headed for the door. "Any luck with the Golden Isle Sons contract?"

Luke snapped his fingers. "Yeah, I'm still working on that. I'll have it resolved by tomorrow. Kind of got caught up in the auditions."

Darius pointed to the unmade, ruffled bed. "No more *auditions* in here, I'm running a respectable hotel."

Luke arched a brow. "Oh, now that was low."

Alicia hadn't expected hotel accommodations, but she had hoped for air conditioning. Cousin Bessie lived in an ancient white house with a worn-out, screened-in front porch and comfortable patio furniture that had seen better days. In the living room window, a large fan circulated warm air in the eighty-degree weather.

Bessie, a full-figured woman with large breasts and a pair of oversized glasses, greeted everyone with a hug and a kiss. "How oonah da do?" She translated when she hugged Alicia. "How you doing, honey?"

Alicia returned the hug with a smile. "I'm fine, thank you." She liked how the Gullah people had a language of their own, and wished she knew more about it.

Bessie took care of her father—ninety-one-year-old Mr. Billy, as everybody called him. Later that evening, the girls sat around the kitchen table listening to Mr. Billy tell old family stories while Bessie cooked.

Mr. Billy's Gullah accent was more pronounced than Alicia's aunt Ode's accent. She could hardly understand what he said.

"Mi remember de li gal," he said, pointing to Alicia. Bessie had mentioned Venetta, telling Alicia how she remembered her mother being a rambunctious little girl.

Alicia sat attentively, listening to the ramblings of an old man. She didn't know if he remembered her or her mother. Sitting right beside Alicia, Tracy hung on Mr. Billy's every word.

One minute he said something muddled, the next he seemed in complete control of his faculties.

"But you got your pappy coloring," Mr. Billy added, pointing at Alicia.

She glanced from Juanita to Ruth Ann to see if either one of them heard the old man. They hadn't; they were too busy talking to Bessie. Mr. Billy rambled on, not seeming to care if anyone listened to him or not. But Alicia understood every word this time.

"Did you know my father?" Alicia asked, leaning over with her elbow on her leg and chin in hand.

Mr. Billy grabbed a few more peanuts and kept rambling, never answering her question. She didn't know what to conclude from the musings of this old man.

After a restful night's sleep, Alicia woke up and almost forgot where she was. She'd shared a room with Ruth Ann and slept like a baby on the comfortable twin bed.

Mr. Billy sat on the front porch in his rocking chair, as they prepared to leave. Following everyone else's lead, Alicia gave Mr. Billy a hug and a kiss good-bye. As she walked down the steps, he shouted out.

"Coffee. Da's we used fa call your daddy, mi thinks so."

Alice looked at Juanita, who shrugged.

"Okay Mr. Billy, you have a nice day now," Juanita called out as they piled into the car.

Alicia climbed in the backseat and looked out the window at Mr. Billy. He sat there rocking away, talking as Bessie waved good-bye. Did he really know her father? Or, did he have her mixed up with somebody else? Bessie had said he suffered a stroke five years ago. His mind came and went.

On the ride back to Jekyll Island, Alicia wrote down the name Mr. Billy had shouted out. Maybe it meant something, maybe it didn't.

Back at the hotel, Sterling supervised the gardeners and hired landscapers who laid new sod and planted flowers and trees around the front of the hotel. Better curb appeal was part of Darius's hotel makeover.

Sterling's morning had started off on a bad note. Before ten, he'd fired two housekeepers. According to Timothy, they were stealing from guest rooms.

He finally took a break from the heat to place a few phone

calls. He'd have to replace the housekeepers as soon as possible. Minutes later, he looked up from his desk at Luke standing in the doorway.

Luke tapped on the door and walked in at the same time. "I hope I'm not disturbing anything?"

"Not at all. What can I do for you?" Sterling asked, putting on his best fake smile. He didn't like this arrogant little Monroe, but he hadn't figured out how to get rid of him yet.

Luke took a seat. "I need to get a copy of the Golden Isle Sons contract. Darius says you have the contracts."

Sterling swallowed hard. "I uh, I'll have to look for that contract and get back to you."

"You don't have a copy here in your office?" Luke asked.

Sterling yanked open the file drawer next to his desk. He pulled out a folder labeled Golden Isle Sons and opened it face up on his desk.

Luke looked down at the empty folder, then back up at Sterling. "You don't have the contract."

"Seems like I don't, but as I said, I can get you a copy."

"Today?" Luke asked, standing up.

"I'll ask my secretary and have a copy run up to your suite." Sterling didn't like the look in Luke's eyes, or anything else about him.

"Thanks, if I'm not in, just have them slip it under the door."

"Yes, sir."

After Luke cleared the hallway, Sterling replaced the bogus folder and slammed the drawer closed. Things were about to get ugly.

Chapter 16

Darius had tossed and turned all night wondering where Alicia was. He told himself, she'd probably spent the night with someone in her family, but he wish he knew that for sure.

Forced to move on with the running of his hotel, Darius found Sterling out front.

"Darius, what do you think about the paint job?" Sterling asked, when Darius joined him.

Darius surveyed the building and nodded his approval. "Nice job. No more large chunks of paint falling off the wall." Sterling had assured him everything was on schedule and progressing nicely.

"The painters should be finished by the end of the week. Nothing like a good coat of paint to restore the place back to its original beauty."

"Yep, how are all the other changes coming along? Any more complaints I need to know about?" Darius hadn't been to one of Sterling's management meetings all week and had been spared the bickering and complaining.

"If you're talking about William, no. Maintenance had been answering guest complaints immediately. Which is something he told me they'd never be able to do. Of course, the main building has had to wait for repairs, but the guests are all being serviced without us having to hire someone else."

"So William's pitching in?"

"He is, but between you and me, I think he's about to quit."

Darius shook his head. "What's wrong? Is he afraid of a little work?"

"He's asked for a raise twice, and I can't give it to him. No room in the budget."

Darius pulled the car keys from his pocket. "Well I hope we don't lose him, but you're right, we can't afford the raise. You're doing great work Sterling. I appreciate everything."

"You're welcome, sir."

"I've got a business luncheon, but I should be back in a couple of hours. If anyone's looking for me, I can be reached at The Shores or on my cell phone."

"The Shores," Sterling repeated.

"Yep, but don't worry, whatever RCE's selling, I'm not buying. I'm glad you've got everything under control around here. Let me know if you need anything."

"I'll do that."

In hindsight, Darius thought he probably never should of mentioned The Shores to Sterling. RCE's main office sat in the lobby of the grand resort. Darius's presence there no doubt made his general manager wonder about the future of Hotel Paradise.

Darius sat across the table from Mike Denton, a burly white man in his early fifties with a friendly smile and a grip tight enough to break a bone.

For lunch the restaurant served a seafood buffet that included fresh fruits, cheeses, and a choice of breads. Darius hadn't seen a spread like this anywhere else on the island. They ate off china with real silverware and stemware. No ordinary table settings at The Shores.

"Mr. Monroe, as I said over the phone, your grandfather and I had been discussing the future of Hotel Paradise. Great man, Willie Monroe, he held onto that hotel through some very difficult times. Too bad neither one of his boys came back to run the place; it probably wouldn't have fallen on such hard times if one had."

Mike Denton popped a peeled shrimp in his mouth and discarded the shell.

The cheap shot at his father pissed Darius off. "The hotel's just fine. As a matter of fact, we're in the process of renovating."

"So I've heard." Mike wiped his hands on a linen napkin and pointed at Darius's plate. "Eat, you haven't touched your food."

Mike's fat stubby fingers tore through another piece of shrimp, almost causing Darius to lose his appetite. But he forced himself to eat.

After several minutes of eating and drinking, Mike leaned back in his seat. "Darius, I didn't invite you here to insult you. You know as well as I do that RCE's interested in acquiring Hotel Paradise. We made an offer to your grandfather, and we're prepared to make another offer to you."

Darius wiped his mouth and listened up. The meal was over, time to be seduced.

"You're a smart businessman. I'm well aware of your coffee shops and your real estate. Your businesses are worth about a million. I'm sure you have no intentions of relocating from Chicago to the island to run the hotel. And I believe your brother's a touring musician."

Not surprised that RCE had done its homework, Darius crossed his arms and waited for the offer.

"You see. RCE wants to help you out. As you know, we've purchased numerous pieces of beachfront property on the island. But money's not the issue here and we understand that." Mike leaned forward, elbows on the table, and clasped his fingers together.

"The hotel's been in your family for generations, and your father's children are the only heirs. You don't have to carry on that burden. RCE is prepared to make an all-cash offer of $1.9 million for Hotel Paradise."

Darius's eyes narrowed. The offer was obscene, and he had to admit, enticing.

Mike continued. "We'll even keep your staff on. Of course, a few changes will have to be made."

Biting his lip to squelch the urge to laugh, Darius shook his head and grinned.

"I'm flattered by the offer. And like you, I've done my homework too. Hotel Paradise has great potential for a patient investor, and will eventually be worth triple your offer. Thanks for wanting to help us out, but frankly, I'm not interested."

Mike pressed his tongue against his cheek and nodded with a smile. "I'll tell you what, why don't you discuss it with your family. I'll go back to my boss and let him know you're not interested—" he threw his hands up in a helpless gesture "—who knows, maybe he'll come back with a serious offer."

Darius pushed his plate away and erased all traces of a smile from his face. "Thanks for lunch, but this is about the only thing RCE has to offer me. The hotel is not for sale."

Somehow during the ride back from St. Helena, Alicia had agreed to let Tracy spend the evening with her. They changed into bathing suits, grabbed a couple of lounge chairs, and found a perfect spot on the beach.

She looked over at Tracy sitting next to her in a flowery two-piece bathing suit with a book in her lap and her sunglasses on. The child was turning into a mini Alicia. She never thought she'd admit it, but she enjoyed the company. In some ways, Tracy reminded her of herself at that age. She looked lonely and starved for attention. No doubt her bad little brothers snared all the attention in their house.

"Are you hungry yet?" Alicia asked.

"Are you?" Tracy countered.

Alicia smiled. "No, but I will be in a little while."

"Me too. Can I swim before we eat?" Tracy asked, getting up.

"Sure, let's have some fun before dinner." Alicia grabbed one of the body boards stored on the beach and followed Tracy into the water. The women played around in the water until Tracy begged to ride a pedal boat. Alicia finally gave in once she promised not to go too far.

The sunset ended their afternoon fun, so they returned to Alicia's room to shower and change for dinner.

The weekend brought more guests into the hotel, so the restaurant was buzzing with waiters and waitresses scurrying through the room filling orders.

Alicia looked up from her menu as Darius stalked across the room with a piercing look in his eyes. Her throat went dry. She hadn't seen him in two days and whether it made sense or not, she'd missed him. The site of him maneuvering around people and chairs to reach her excited her.

"What happened to you," he asked, as he reached the table. He hadn't even noticed Tracy was sitting there.

"Excuse me?" Alicia asked, surprised by his icy tone.

He pulled over a vacant chair. "I've been trying to find you every since you missed breakfast yesterday, what happened?"

"You didn't get my note?" she asked.

"What note?" he challenged.

She blinked. "I left a note with the front desk asking for a rain check. I'd forgotten my cousin was taking me to St. Helena on a little overnight excursion. I called your room, but the line was busy."

Darius sat back and let out a slow breath. He finally noticed Tracy and gave a polite smile. Then he turned back to Alicia. "I was on my computer, and the room only has one line. Anyway, I didn't get the note; who did you leave it with?"

She shrugged. "I didn't get his name, but he said he'd make sure you got it. I'm sorry."

Darius nodded. "I'm just glad you're okay." He chuckled. "All sorts of things ran through my head." He looked over at Tracy again. "Who's this little lady?"

"This is my cousin, Tracy Porter," Alicia said, introducing her.

Darius held out his hand, and Tracy blushed into her menu. "Nice to meet you, Tracy."

"Hi," she said shyly, taking his hand.

"Ladies, I'll leave you to your dinner. I just wanted to make sure you were all right." He stood up and moved the chair back. "Alicia, why don't you give me a call when you get a moment."

She smiled up at him. "Sure."

He waved at Tracy before walking away. The view of him leaving was as appealing as his approach.

"Is that your boyfriend?" Tracy asked.

Alicia laughed. "No, why? Do you think he's cute?"

Tracy nodded. "He's handsome. Like Michael at my school."

Alicia agreed with Tracy, but he had something Tracy's Michael most likely didn't—sex appeal.

Someone had stopped Darius to talk as he was on his way

out. Afterwards, he glanced back over his shoulder at Alicia. They locked eyes. Her body temperature rose in succession with her rapid heartbeat. He winked and a small smile touched his lips. She bit the inside of her lip in an effort to keep from blushing. But, it didn't work. He left the room while she blushed into her dinner menu.

"And for you ma'am?"

She looked up, and to her surprise the waiter stood there with a pad and pencil waiting for her order. Where had he come from?

Running late again, Sterling pulled into the parking lot of Shiloh Baptist Church and killed the engine. He pulled his tie off and threw it in the back seat, then hurried through the small parking lot and up to the back door of the church.

Catherine sat behind a small table that impersonated a desk, and held a finger up at Sterling when he walked in, indicating she'd be ready in a minute. And he'd hurried to get there, he told himself.

"I'll be out in the hallway," he said, stepping back out.

Two silver-haired women chatted at the end of the hall. Darius recognized them as Mrs. Maus and Mrs. Kirby, two of his mother's friends from the island. The bowlegged one, Mrs. Maus, left when her son came in to pick her up. He waved down the hall when he spotted Sterling.

When Mrs. Kirby turned around, Sterling walked toward her. Since he had some time to kill, he walked down the hall to say hello.

"Sterling, I thought that was you. Ya' know I don't see too good these days. How ya' doin' this evenin'?" she asked from her seat on a bench in the lobby.

"I'm fine, Mrs. Kirby." He spoke loudly, remembering the

old woman couldn't hear too well either. He joined her on the bench. "Waiting for your granddaughter?"

"Yes, she'll be here directly. She started workin' over at that Clarion Hotel this week."

"So I heard. I could have gotten her on at Hotel Paradise."

"I told her that. Yes, I told her to check with ya'," she replied, between clucking false teeth. "Ya' cousin from Atlanta's stayin' over there with ya', isn't she?"

Surprised she was even aware whom Alicia was, he responded, "Yes, Alicia. Did my mom mention her?"

"She sure did. I don't recall her name, but I remember her mother, Venetta."

"It's Alicia McKay. You remember her mother?" he asked, with raised brows.

"Oh, yes. I worked for Dr. Bailey over home. I was his nurse."

"Is that so?" Sterling asked, looking down the hall to make sure Catherine wasn't on her way.

"He was the Walkers' family doctor." She laughed. "Actually, Dr. Bailey was the only doctor in St. Helena, you know. If a midwife didn't deliver your baby, Dr. Bailey did."

"Did he deliver my aunt Venetta's baby?" he asked, hoping to hit pay dirt.

"Aw, naw honey. Single, unmarried women didn't have babies like they do now. At least not one of Henry Walker's daughters." She shook her head and let out a tired sigh. "It's a shame the way young women's having babies now."

"So she didn't have the baby?" Or, had she had an abortion, he wondered?

"Oh, she had her baby, but she didn't have it here. Once Dr. Bailey told her parents she was pregnant, they sent her to New York to stay with some of their kinfolks. She had the baby up there."

"Oh, really?" Sterling's voice raised a pitch.

"Beautiful woman she was. Venetta kept Henry busy chasing the boys away," she said with a chuckle.

The door to the office opened, and Catherine walked out.

"Mrs. Kirby, do you happen to know who the father of her baby was?"

The old woman looked up at him and shook her head.

Catherine reached the end of the hall and only had to step across the massive lobby now. Sterling clenched his fist and held his breath. *Hurry up old woman.*

"She never would tell anybody. But I suspect it was one of the young men over at Hotel Paradise. She spent so much time over there."

"Mrs. Kirby, how was your Bible study this evening?" Catherine asked, as she stepped up to them.

"Ah baby, it was wonderful. Associate Pastor Barnes is gonna make a fine minister one day."

Sterling stood up and kissed Catherine on the cheek.

"Honey, if your granddaughter doesn't get here soon, do you want me and Sterling to run you home?" Catherine asked.

Sterling grasped Catherine by the arm. "Did you forget we're not going straight home?" He fished for something to say, when the front doors of the church opened.

"There's my granddaughter now."

A young woman walked in and Sterling breathed a sigh of relief. On the way to the car Catherine questioned him.

"Where is it I forgot we were going, Sterling?"

He opened her car door and looked over at her. "Home."

Alicia woke Friday morning with the energy of a rambunctious child. After freshening up, she pulled back the curtains and welcomed the bright morning sun. She opened the sliding doors and walked out onto the balcony. As if the ocean called her name, she leaned over the rail and inhaled the fresh, un-polluted air.

"Good morning, neighbor," a masculine voice called out.

Alicia looked around, and two patios over was Luke in a pair of jeans, with no shirt or shoes. He leaned against the rail with a mug in his hand.

"Good morning to you too," she replied.

He moved over to the side of the patio facing her. "Did you enjoy your lunch the other day?"

"Yes, I did. Thank you. How about you?" she asked, noticing his tattooed chest and forearms.

He shrugged. "I had lunch with my brother. The company wasn't as interesting, or as beautiful."

"Well thank you."

"Hey, don't forget you owe me a rain check on lunch."

"Sterling and I owe you that rain check," she corrected him.

"If you don't mind, we can leave him behind. I see enough of him everyday."

Alicia laughed.

"I'd like to get to know the young lady who's got my cool-headed brother all twisted up."

Pleasantly surprised, she crossed her arms and gave a little bob of her head. "I don't know about that."

"Oh, yes. You see, Darius and I have this love-hate relationship going on. And when I mentioned that I'd met you the other day, I thought he was going to blow a gasket."

Alicia's interest peaked, and she stepped over to the side of the rail facing his patio. "Now why would he do that?" she asked.

"I'd say because he wants to keep you all to himself." He set his mug down on the patio table and looked her over. "But, what do you say I cash in on that rain check over lunch today, and we can talk about it?"

Her phone began ringing. "Sorry, not today." She gestured toward the ringing phone. "I'd better get that."

"Then you have a nice day, until I see you again."

"Sure, you too." She hurried inside and snatched up the phone, yelling hello before whoever it was could hang up.

"Tell that man to get out of your bed, your cousin's on the phone."

"Rorie!" Alicia laughed, happy to hear his regal voice. "How the hell are you? Did you make it home okay?"

"I'm fabulous. Back in the nine-to-five rut, but still fabulous. How is everything going down there? Have you seen Darius lately?"

"It's kind of hard not to. Believe it or not, he talked me into dinner the other night." Glad to have someone to discuss Darius with, she told Rorie about their dinner date.

"Now that's what I'm talking about," he yelled into the phone. "Have you jumped his bones yet, girl?" He laughed into the phone.

"You are so crude. I'm a lady, I'm not going to jump his bones." Which is why she'd invited him in for a booty call the other night, she chastised herself.

"Oh hell, don't give me that, even ladies get horny."

Cradling the phone, she fell back on the bed. "Boy, I'm not having this conversation with you."

"Hey, if you still need lessons in seduction just let me know, baby. We can work it out over the phone."

"I do need something from you, but not that." She sat up and pushed a pillow in her back.

"Anything babe."

She took a deep breath. "Remember when we talked about Ruth Ann and her twins' daddy?"

"The secret daddy, yeah, what about it?"

She let out a long slow breath. "Well, I was wondering what other family secrets you know about?"

"Enough to write a book, honey, but none of them should concern you. Why?"

"Sterling mentioned something about family secrets at the cookout that you missed Sunday."

"Hold up, don't tell me you're listening to Sterling? The man's got that family eating out of his hands. They think he knows everything because he manages that hotel. He didn't try to tell you who the father was did he?"

"No, he just said the family had a lot of secrets, and I was wondering what they were."

"Honey, what family doesn't have secrets? I bet you didn't know that Darius's uncle was supposed to be running that hotel. He was next in line, not Darius's father."

"How do you know that?"

"Last week, I heard two different stories. One, that he committed suicide. Another, that he's in a mental institution. Either way, that's a Monroe family secret. Old man Monroe never talked about him according to an old guy I met at the hotel. What I'm trying to say, is even the Monroe family has secrets."

"Yeah, I guess so."

"Just do me a favor, and don't listen to everything Sterling says. He means well, but the man's got issues."

"I've noticed he drinks a lot."

"Like a fish. But all them country folks do that. Look, enough about him. What I want to know is how you're going to seduce Darius."

"Aaaaaahh," she groaned.

Chapter 17

What started out as a good day only got better. By sunset, Alicia found herself sitting at a small, decorated table for two in the middle of the hotel's lush garden. Huge live oaks, dripping with Spanish moss and beautiful plants and flowers in bloom surrounded her.

A waiter stepped forward and refilled her wineglass.

"I still can't believe you did all this," Alicia said, glancing around at the beautiful table setting.

"All I did was show up. I asked my staff to prepare dinner in the garden and—" Darius held up his hands "—this is what they came up with."

"It's beautiful." *And romantic*, she wanted to say but didn't. She was impressed by the simple black-and-white table setting, all white pillar candles, and touches of greenery. "I had no idea you were going to spring this on me at the end of the garden tour."

He winked at her. "It's called the element of surprise. I hope you like surprises?"

"I do." She couldn't stop looking around at the array of colors and smells. "Everything is so alive and beautiful. I know I already said that, but I guess I'm blown away."

"Thank you. This is one facet of the property I'd like to keep intact. I want to duplicate this setting in the new lobby," he shared with her.

"It's very peaceful," she observed.

Their personal waiter appeared with two fresh salads.

"Everybody needs a little peace and quiet every now and then. How was your visit to St. Helena?" Darius asked, picking up his fork.

"It was nice. Real laid-back."

"More so than here?" he asked with a chuckle.

"Yeah, I think so. It was a different kind of quiet. Have you ever been there?" Alicia picked up her fork and tasted her salad.

He shook his head. "Afraid not, but maybe I'll get up there sometime before I leave. I've heard about the island before. You have family there, right?"

She nodded. "Uh-huh. I've met so many relatives in the last two weeks. I know I won't remember them all. You have family in this area too don't you?"

"I used to. A few relatives moved down and worked at the hotel some years back, but they've all moved away. That's why after my grandmother passed, Poppy sold his house and moved into the hotel. This place was his home."

"Your father wasn't an only child was he?" She remembered what Rorie had said about his uncle, but didn't want to come out and ask about it.

"He had a brother. My Uncle James. Unfortunately, he couldn't take care of himself, let alone Poppy. He was an alcoholic."

"Was?"

"Yeah, he died ten years ago from cirrhosis of the liver. About six months before his death, he moved in with my parents, and they took care of him until he passed."

"Did your grandfather ever come see him?"

Darius shook his head and leaned back in the seat. "Are you kidding? And leave all this." He held his arms open wide. "He gave up on my uncle a long time ago. I guess you can say they had a love-hate relationship. Poppy hated when Uncle James drank, but that's the only way James could stand to be around the old man."

"Wow, that's sad."

"You know—" Darius pointed his fork at Alicia "—you're the only person I've ever told that."

His voice sounded lifeless and distant as he finished his salad. Alicia teared up a little. She pushed her salad aside and the waiter reappeared with the main course; salmon, baby carrots, and potatoes.

Darius looked away as if he was waiting for the waiter to leave. She could tell he had more on his mind that he needed to unload. She responded with a smile, hoping he'd continue.

"People say it's a shame that one of the Monroe boys didn't come back to run the hotel; but the truth of the matter is they never could have as long as Poppy was here."

"But I've heard nothing but good things about your grandfather."

"He was a wonderful man to everybody except his own sons. The one thing my father picked up from him is the same thing that ran my father away. He was a control freak. My father rebelled and left a couple of years after high school. By then, Uncle James was already established in Chicago where my father joined him."

"I know my cousin Sterling thinks the world of your grandfather." Alicia started on her salmon and Darius followed suit.

"According to my father, Sterling was the kind of son my poppy always wanted, but never had. Sterling let the old man control his career. Poppy even paid for Sterling's hotel training. I'm sure Sterling doesn't know that I'm aware of that, but it's true."

"I didn't know that." She nibbled at her food while talking. "Since his sons weren't coming back, do you think he was grooming Sterling to one day take over the hotel?

Darius sighed heavily. "It seemed like it, but a few weeks before he passed we had a long conversation. He practically begged me not to let the hotel leave the family's hands."

"That's amazing that he'd beg you to keep it, but couldn't work with his own sons."

"I don't think he would have ever admitted it, but he was hurt that they didn't want to stay on the island and live like he had. I promised him I'd take over and keep the place open."

"So, you're moving here to live in the hotel like your grandfather?"

"I never promised that. I'll be here for a couple of months at the most. Then, I'll come back from time to time to oversee the renovations. I'll probably hire a management firm."

"Oh, I thought this was going to become home for you," she said, in a teasing voice.

"I'm not sure I could live here any more than my father could. I'm thinking I'll be back in Chicago in time for winter."

"Burrr." She hugged herself and shook, insinuating how cold it was in Chicago.

"I see you've experienced Chicago in the winter before?"

"Once, and I won't make that mistake twice."

"Then, I guess that means I'll have to come see you."

Alicia stopped her fork in mid-air; startled by the way he managed to turn things around. "In Atlanta?" she asked.

He nodded. "Sure. I get down that way every now and then. You did say you weren't seeing anyone right?"

She lowered her fork. "True, but what about you? Don't tell me you're a single, hard-working man with nobody to go home to." A man like Darius Monroe wasn't single. At least if he lived in Atlanta he wouldn't be, Alicia thought. He had everything going for him.

He smiled. "It's sad, but true. I don't have time for much but work and my boys these days."

Her face fell. "Boys? As in more than one?" she asked with raised brows.

"Yep. I mentor a group from the local boys' club."

Relieved, she smiled. "That's wonderful. What do you do with them?" If she wasn't already impressed with this man, he'd added another gold star in his favor.

"I teach them basic business skills. Every now and then, I let one work in the coffee shop for a day to see what it's like."

"I wish I could do something like that. I volunteered a couple of times in college, but didn't keep it up." Darius was everything Alicia wanted to be. He didn't just appear to have it all together; he had it all together.

"I started with the boys' club when I was in college. Over the years, I've done everything from supervised camping trips to having boys shadow me for a day."

"That's very commendable of you. You're a good son. I bet your father would be proud."

Instead of smiling and holding his chin up like a proud man should, he lowered his head and looked off into the gardens. "Yeah," he said somberly.

"You don't think so?" she asked reluctantly.

He raised his head and gave her a I'd-rather-not-dwell-on-it look before saying, "My father cared about business, not volunteering."

"Okay, so you're stepping in here where he should have. He'd be proud of that, wouldn't he?"

He tilted his head and replied, "I'd like to think so."

The waiter crept up to the table and lit the candles as the sun disappeared over the marsh. Alicia, feeling a little melancholy, looked off into the orange glow of the sky.

"My father wouldn't be too proud of me right now," she murmured.

"Of course he would. You came here to find your family."

"Oh, I don't mean about that. It's the dealership he'd be disappointed about. I'm just not interested in running the business. After he passed, I tried. I went in there every day and worked with his sales team…but my heart wasn't in it."

"When he was living, did he ever talk to you about taking over the business?"

She snickered and pointed at herself. "What, Smoky talk to *me* about business? His business? That never happened."

"Your father's name was Smoky?"

She shrugged and laughed. "No, actually it was Steven McKay, but everybody called him Smoky because he had smoky brown eyes. Anyway, I worked as an intern at the dealership after I received my Bachelor's degree, but he never groomed me to take over. Besides, he was too young to even think about that."

"So what are you going to do with the business?"

She took a deep breath. "I'm thinking of selling to his partner. He's prepared to buy me out. I just have to make up my mind. He's a very nice man who's taught me a lot about the business. Unfortunately though, selling cars just doesn't excite me like it did my father."

"What does excite you?"

Besides you? she wanted to say when he licked his lips. She'd developed an infatuation with his lips and the seductive way his tongue darted out—ever so smoothly touching the top and then the bottom lip before sliding back into his mouth. The twinkle in his eye as he sat staring across the table at her made her blush.

"Well, I've always dreamed of opening my own spa."

"You like massages?" he asked, his voice deeper now.

"Of course, but I want to do more than massages. A girlfriend and I spent a week out in Arizona last year, and the spa experience was unbelievable. My girlfriend's a certified nutritionist who has her own business in Atlanta."

"Sounds like you know exactly what you want to do, so why aren't you doing it?"

She hunched her shoulders. "I don't know, fear I guess."

"Of failure or success?"

She laughed. "Why would I be afraid of success?"

He wrinkled his nose. "Plenty of people are afraid of success. You had a very successful father, and it sounds like that success took him away from you. Maybe you're afraid the same thing will happen to you when you have children."

She shook her head. "I'd never ignore my kids like that. No matter how successful my business turned out, I'd find the time for them. Private time with just me and them."

After finishing off his dinner, Darius pushed his chair back. "Well, with your father's genes I doubt you'd be a failure at anything you do. I want a world-class spa here in the new hotel too. With all the latest treatments and gadgets."

Maybe that's why she was floundering around with no direction, Alicia wondered. Maybe she didn't have her father's genes. Whatever Smoky set out to do, he did it—swiftly and successfully. "Study long, and you study wrong." She remembered him telling her that often.

"I hope you enjoyed your meal?" he asked after she set her fork down.

Alicia picked up her napkin and wiped her mouth. "I did. It was wonderful, thank you."

"If you're finished, I have a special dessert planned." He pushed up from his chair.

"You're kidding! I'm stuffed, I don't think I have room for dessert."

He walked over and held out his hand to help her up. "Come on. You'll have room for this dessert, trust me."

She set her napkin on the table and took his hand.

They walked through the garden following a well-lit path that led to the lobby.

"Where are we going?" she asked.

Darius smiled down at her. "You'll see."

He let go of her hand when he opened the side door to the lobby. Once inside, she followed him into the piano bar. No karaoke tonight. A young man sat behind the piano accompanied by a saxophonist playing soft, romantic music.

Two couples had already started slow dancing to the music. Darius turned to Alicia, took her hand, and led her to the small dance floor. He gave the musicians a cursory nod before turning around to face her.

He pulled her into his arms, slid his hands around her waist, and started moving to the music. No words were spoken as they found their rhythm. Her body fit into his like the missing piece to a jigsaw puzzle. His big, strong hands wrapped around her body, holding her tight, sent shivers down her spine. She could feel his warm breath against her neck relaxing her body.

Her arms found their way around his neck, and he pulled her even closer against his warm body. She obeyed the swaying of his hips, keeping her pelvis pressed firmly against him. With her head resting against his chest, she inhaled the intoxicating scent of his cologne. Being in his arms felt like the most perfect place for her.

The heat from his body moved through her chest and down between her legs, arousing sensations that had been dormant for years. His thigh pressing between her legs was the only thing that kept her legs from trembling. The sensual saxophone music only added to an already blissful evening.

From the corner of her eye, she could see two women standing in the doorway staring at them. Hotel employees no doubt, staring at Darius not her. On numerous occasions she'd seen the admiring way they looked at him when he walked by. She wasn't the only one admiring him.

This was the perfect end to a perfect meal.

The musicians played a more up-tempo tune next, and Alicia turned to leave the floor, but Darius grabbed her hand.

"Don't tell me you're tired?" he asked, pulling her back onto the dance floor.

"No, but I'm not exactly Ginger Rogers."

"I've seen you dance on a table top before, have you forgotten? You'd give Ginger a run for her money. Now, show me what you got."

She laughed and tried not to embarrass herself too much. Darius, on the other hand, could dance. When the band broke for a short intermission, they took a seat. Darius signaled a waiter over.

"Would you like something to drink?" he asked Alicia.

Not wanting to repeat their first meeting, she ordered a soda.

"So you can dance, but you can't swim?" she asked.

He smiled. "When you're a musician and hanging around clubs so much you pick up a thing or two."

"Huh, I bet. And I'm sure you got picked up a lot too."

He laughed. "Not quite."

A silence fell over the table as they listened to the piped-in music while waiting for the musicians to return. Alicia hadn't enjoyed a man's company this much in a long time. It felt so good when he held her, she almost wanted to cry. Her father was the last man to truly hug her.

"You know, you've talked about your father a lot tonight, but what about your mother. Is she from this area too?" Alicia asked, just to have something to talk about.

He nodded. "She's from Florida. If my dad had left the island right after high school, like most of the islanders, they never would have met. He didn't meet her until his junior year, she was an incoming freshman."

"Did he stick around to help your grandfather a while?"

"Yeah, but actually he fell in love with a girl from the island and couldn't make himself leave."

Alicia smiled. "That's sweet."

Darius chuckled. "Yeah, but she eventually broke his heart when she left the island. A few months later, he enrolled in Loyola University in Chicago."

"Well that's sad, but cute since that's where he met your mom."

"She said it was love at first sight. Do you believe in that?"

Alicia shrugged. "Why not? I guess anything's possible, if you know what you want. Do you believe in it?"

He gave her something between a nod and a shrug, not fully committing to either. "I didn't at the time she told me that story, but I'm kind of changing my mind."

"Oh yeah. Have you ever been in love?" she inquired.

"Once. And you?" he retorted.

"Oh, but he doesn't want to talk about it," she said jokingly.

"There's nothing to talk about. I fell in love, she didn't. She moved on to bigger and better things."

"Just like that, huh? Cut and dry."

"Nothing's ever quite that simple. And don't you try to dodge the question either. Have you ever been in love?"

She shook her head. "I don't think so. I thought I was in love once, but now that I look back on it…it was nothing more than a simple crush."

"When did you come to that realization?"

"Recently actually."

As he started the next set, the piano player thanked everyone for sticking around. Darius stood up and took Alicia's hand.

"Can I have this dance?"

Just when Alicia took his hand, convinced she was about to have a summer fling, loud screams from the lobby broke everything up. A child was missing.

Minutes later, the child was found in another guest's room. However, the scare ended their perfect night.

Afterwards, Darius walked Alicia back to her room.

"Thank you for a wonderful dinner and dancing tonight."

"You're very welcome. I'm glad you enjoyed it, and I'm sorry it got cut short."

"That's okay. You're the owner, you always have to be on the job."

"I hope I'll get to see you tomorrow?"

"I'll be here," she replied.

He leaned forward and planted a quick goodnight kiss on her forehead. Seconds later he was gone, and she stood in the mirror and wondered why she hadn't invited him in tonight.

She grabbed a bottle of water from the minifridge to cool herself off. She undressed and jumped into bed. As usual, she grabbed her mother's journal to read a few pages and remind herself why she'd given up a month of her life to spend here. The page she opened began: *A day in paradise.*

She'd stumbled upon the day her mother realized she was

in love with a man who could never be hers. She described him as tall, dark, and delicious, a perfect gentleman in every way.

So much about this man was on the page, but not enough to know who he was. She never mentioned his name. Only that he was her first love and she wanted to spend the rest of her life with him.

Alicia closed the book, and then closed her eyes.

Chapter 18

Saturday morning on his way to the hotel's small excuse for a gym, Darius noticed something on the patio of the piano bar that interested him. Luke and Timothy sat huddled at a table in the corner. Darius delayed his workout for a minute to catch them before they left.

When he walked out onto the patio, Timothy stopped talking and sat up as if he didn't want Darius to know what they were discussing.

"Hey, bro. Headed for the gym?" Luke asked, reaching up to shake hands as they often did.

"Yeah, I thought I'd grab a quick workout."

"How'd you like the guys last night?"

"Nice. Where'd you find them?"

"At this little spot in Brunswick. We're discussing something long-term. I'll let you know about it."

"Well, before they finished their set last night the crowd had nearly doubled. Almost made me wish I had my sax."

Luke smiled fondly at Darius standing over their table. "I'm glad to hear that."

"Almost, I said. So, how's it going with the Golden Isle Sons?" Darius asked Luke and Timothy.

Timothy clasped his hands together and waited for Luke to answer.

"Sterling is still looking for the contract. When I stopped by, he pulled out an empty folder. He's supposed to have his secretary print me a copy, but I'm still waiting."

Darius looked at Timothy who was awfully quiet. "What's going on?"

Timothy held his hands up as if to say he had no clue. "Beats me. We just got the one secretary for the whole office, and I know she's swamped. But the original contract should be filed away."

"Is Sterling working today?" Darius asked.

"No, he's off weekends."

"That's okay," Luke spoke up. "I made a phone call. I'll have a copy of the contract tonight when the band shows up." He leaned back in his chair and glanced up at Darius. "Don't worry about it, we've got it taken care of."

The Golden Isle Sons did their best to capture the oldies-but-goodies sound, but their best wasn't good enough in Darius's opinion. Dressed in glitzy suits, the quartet made little effort to rouse the six or seven guests in attendance for the Saturday night performance. One heavy set, middle-aged white woman would have disagreed with Darius however; since she was the only one on the dance floor. Darius had stepped into the ballroom to check out the band, and Gibb, on his way to a smoke break, joined him.

All in their mid-fifties, the band's cover of MC Hammer's *Can't Touch This* couldn't touch it. Darius glanced over at Gibb. He made a helpless gesture and shook his head.

"They're here every Saturday night, right?" Darius asked.

"Uh-huh, each and every Saturday night," Gibb stressed. "Some nights are better than others though. Darius, if you've got a minute I'd like to talk to you about something," Gibb continued.

"Sure, let's grab a seat." Darius sat at one of the numerous empty tables in front of them.

"Sir, I'm gonna have to let George go. I've talked to him about his disappearing on the job, but he keeps doing it. I told Sterling, and I thought I'd mention it to you since so many people were let go this week."

Darius had lost two employees in one week and hadn't backfilled the positions yet. Staffing was becoming a concern. "How long will it take to find a replacement?"

"I know somebody that can start next week."

Darius arched a brow. "And you've given George sufficient warnings?"

"Yes, sir."

"Then do what you have to, but make sure all the hiring procedures are followed. Get somebody else in here quickly. What do you think George does when he disappears?"

Gibb pulled a cigarette out and tapped the filter against the table. "I smelled liquor on his breath one time, if 'in I had to guess, I'd say he's somewhere sleepin' it off. Last night, a guest reported a man standin' on the beach takin' a piss. I'm sure it was George."

Darius laughed. "Okay, let him go."

The band switched from MC Hammer to Elton John. Darius cringed. "Gibb, let me ask you something?" Gibb glanced at him attentively. "When my grandfather was here, a group of employees tried to get him to sell the hotel to RCE. Do you have any idea who on staff was involved?"

Gibb sat up straight and crossed his arms. His features

grimaced as he shook his head. "Naw, I—I—don't know nothing about that," he mumbled and then hunched his shoulders. "Musta been some folks on day shift, or maybe they're gone. Before old man Monroe passed, a few folks quit, I do know that."

His sleepy-eyed face drooped as he cleared his throat.

Darius gave Gibb a slow, appraising glance. Could he be talking to one of the co-conspirators now?

"Well, if you hear anything from the night shift crew, I'd appreciate you sharing it with me."

Gibb nodded. "Sure thing." He glanced at his watch. "I bess be goin', it's about time to make my rounds. Enjoy your entertainment." He winked at Darius and stood.

"Yeah, I'm about to call it quits myself," Darius said standing. "Have a good night."

"I will, sir."

Darius waited for the band to take a break and made his way to the side of the stage. He introduced himself and lied about how much he enjoyed the set. The bandleader greeted him with a big smile, and said he remembered talking to him. Confused, Darius concluded he remembered the name Monroe and had gotten him mixed up with Luke. He didn't bother to correct him.

Darius had wanted to spend time with Alicia on Sunday; however she'd spent the day with her family. Instead, he worked most of the day, but she was never far from his mind. Over the course of the week he'd gotten to know her better, and she didn't appear to be suicidal. She'd been sometimes cheerful, sometimes sad, but never suicidal. If only he could get another look at her journal.

By the time Monday morning rolled around, he fought the urge to go over and knock on her door. Instead, he picked up the phone and called. She answered on the third ring, sounding anything but cheerful.

"Hey, what's wrong, you don't sound too good this morning?"

"Nothing...I'm fine. How are you?"

He detected a hitch in her voice and knew something was wrong. "I'm good. My meeting this morning was cancelled, so I thought I'd see if you wanted to meet me for breakfast."

"At your place?" she asked, sounding skeptical.

"No, in the dining room," he replied. She sounded a bit short-tempered. He hadn't realized how much he looked forward to seeing her until he heard her voice.

She sighed. "I'm really not up to it this morning if you don't mind."

"How did things go at your aunt's yesterday?"

"Just fine. Darius, I'll have to call you back later. I need to lie down right now."

"Sure. I'll check on you later."

"Okay."

He hung up and a knot constricted in his throat. The sound of her quavering voice sent a sickening wave through his body. Something was wrong. He didn't know if stopping by was a good idea or not. He had to admit that when he first met her he was mainly concerned about her killing herself on his property, but now he cared about Alicia and wanted to see her happy. Somehow, he had to check on her.

Meanwhile, Sterling hung up the phone after calling the front desk and paging Rodell. He picked the phone back up and dialed Alicia's number for the second time after getting a busy signal earlier. In between, his mother had called to chastise him for discussing things with Alicia he knew nothing about. She also told him she'd talked to Alicia about their family property.

Alicia finally picked up, but didn't sound her usual self.

"Sterling, I don't really feel like talking right now, what can I do for you?"

"I'm sorry your visit yesterday wasn't a pleasant one."

"So you heard. I guess news travels fast in small towns."

"I'm afraid so. Don't worry though; I've been talking to some people, and if you're free for lunch I think you'd be interested in hearing what I've learned."

"What time?" she asked.

"How's one o'clock in the dining room?"

"I'll be there," she confirmed.

He hung up whistling his favorite tune, just as a knock came at his door.

"Come in," he called out while picking up a manila envelope sitting on the corner of his desk.

Rodell walked in chipper-eyed and ready to go to work. That's what Sterling liked about the young man, he always seemed eager to please. He worked hard and had Sterling's complete trust.

"Yes, sir. Did you need me to do something?"

Sterling stood and came from behind his desk meeting Rodell midway across the floor. "Rodell, I need you to run this envelope over to Luke Monroe's suite. Do you know where that is?"

He nodded.

"Good." Rodell turned around and Sterling gave him an affectionate slap on the back while leading him to the door. "Now, if he's not there, just slide it under the door. Before you go though, I need one more thing."

Rodell tucked the envelope under his arm and waited.

His office door was still open, so Sterling glanced behind

them to make sure no one was standing in the hallway. "Stop by Darius's office. I believe you'll find an envelope on his desk about the same size as this one. I need you to bring that back here. It'll be from The Golden Isle Sons, or it may say Melvin Miller on the return. That envelope contains some old information that he doesn't need to see."

The young man had a confused look on his face, but took a few slow steps until he reached the doorway. Then he turned around. "Do you want me to bring that envelope back here before I drop this other one off?" He held up the envelope for Luke.

"No, no, deliver that one first, and then come back to Darius's office. He'll be out of the office this morning. But, don't let anyone see you in his office. Now, this is strictly between you and me."

Rodell nodded.

"I'd get it myself, but I'm about to go into the managers' meeting. Bring it back and leave it on my desk."

Still looking confused, Rodell left the office. Sterling closed his door and headed downstairs for his meeting.

Darius never locked his office door, but he'd always pulled it shut. This morning the door was cracked. He pushed it the rest of the way open. Standing with his back to him was Rodell looking for something on his desk.

"Can I help you find something?" Darius asked.

The young man jumped and spun around at the sound of Darius's voice. His eyes widened as a nervous laugh escaped his lips. "Uh-uh, I was looking for…the tide report. Kamora said she thought somebody laid it on your desk by mistake."

Darius crossed the room not taking his eyes from the young man. Nothing of value was in his office, but he didn't like employees snooping around. "I never get the tide reports," he commented, pulling out his chair and surveying the top of his desk. Everything looked as he'd left it yesterday.

Rodell turned around facing Darius. "That's why she sent me in looking for it. She said it was a mistake and it belongs at the front desk." He tilted his head and bit his lip. "I guess with so many people getting fired and things nobody wants to make a mistake. I was just trying to grab it before you came in." He looked down at Darius's desk. "But I don't see it, so I guess maybe it's in Sterling's office." He turned to leave. "Sorry, I'll go check his office."

"Hold on a minute." Darius sat down and gestured for Rodell to take a seat.

Looking like a stiff piece of wood, the young man sat down. Darius could see the fear of being fired in his eyes.

"I need to ask you something."

"Yes, sir."

"You've been watching Ms. McKay for me haven't you?"

He bobbed his head, not sure if he wanted to nod or shake it. "Kind of, sir. I couldn't find her yesterday."

"From now on, whenever a long time period goes by and you don't see her, let me know. She's not feeling well this morning, so I need you to keep an eye on her and let me know if she leaves the property. Consider her your assignment from now on, until she leaves."

"But sir, I have to deliver the luggage."

"Oh, I understand that. I have other people keeping an eye on her as well. Until she leaves, it'll be our job to make sure she's okay."

Rodell looked puzzled as he scratched his cheek and slouched a little. "Is she sick or something?"

"Nothing like that." Darius unlocked his desk drawer. "I'm just concerned that she might try to do something to harm herself. And we don't want anything like that to happen here at the hotel."

The assuring nod Rodell gave didn't register in his eyes.

"I'm not asking you to babysit her, just keep an eye out for her and let me know whenever she leaves. Can you do that for me?"

"Oh, yes sir. She's a nice lady. I'd hate to see anything happen to her."

"Thank you," Darius responded with a smile.

Chapter 19

Alicia found a table in the back corner of the dining room and waited for Sterling. Disappointed and upset over the way her cousins had cornered her on Sunday, she wanted to go home. She hadn't even known her mother was from the islands, let alone that she needed to pay a share of the property taxes.

Sterling finally came darting across the room in a light brown suit that looked like it could have belonged to his little brother, if he'd had one. He exchanged greetings with several servers and stopped to chat with guests before he made it to the table.

"Sorry, I always seem to be running late, but I had a house-keeping disaster to settle." He pushed his glasses up his nose and looked Alicia over. "It's not easy running this place you know," he continued. "I swear that Luke Monroe is out to get me and I don't know why. I haven't done anything to him."

Alicia let him vent before interrupting him. He looked more stressed than she felt.

"You know, I believe he's trying to undermine everything I've done here. And Darius plans to tear the hotel down and build a boutique hotel for rich white folks."

"That's not what he told me," she stated. "He's fighting to keep the hotel in his family's hands."

Sterling's expression was sullen as he arched a brow. "Trust me, he's bringing investors in here who'll throw a lot of money at this place and he'll clear the existing staff out and bring in all new people. That'll be the end of Hotel Paradise as we know it," he said smugly.

"Sterling, I think you've got it all wrong. I don't think he plans to get rid of anybody here; all he talks about is building the hotel up," she argued.

He looked at her as if she'd let him in on a big inside secret. "He discusses his plans for the hotel with you?" he asked. The question was laced with suspicious undertones.

She suddenly wished she hadn't opened her mouth. "No, of course not. But he did say he wanted to renovate the hotel and make it comparable with the others on the island." Her relationship, or whatever she had with Darius, was none of Sterling's business.

Sterling nodded and motioned over the waitress who'd been waiting for his signal. "Well, whatever his plans are, you can bet they won't include me," he alleged.

They placed their lunch orders.

"So, what did you want to talk about?" she asked, not wanting to appear too eager for whatever morsel of information he had.

"I placed some calls and got a few people to talk. It looks like you were right."

Her heartbeat accelerated and she arched a brow waiting for him to continue. "I was right about what?" she asked sharply.

He leaned in, placing both forearms on the table. "You said

you believed your mother was pregnant when she left the island—and she was."

"Who told you that?" she demanded. Was he playing with her emotions, knowing how much this information meant to her?

"Never mind about that. It's true. I got it from a reliable source. She was sent away because she was pregnant."

Alicia chewed on her dry, cracked bottom lip and stared probingly into Sterling's eyes. Would he lie to her? They were family, but she'd known him less than a month. She looked down and pulled her hands apart, placing them palms down on the edge of the table. Wringing her hands was a nervous habit she didn't want to start.

"Who was the father?" she asked as her heart hammered against her chest.

He shrugged. "I don't know. That's as much as I could find out. I'm still working on who she went to stay with." He leaned back into his seat. "So, maybe you aren't an only child after all."

She pushed back from the table and rested her back against the chair. "I'm an only child," she said, releasing a heavy sigh.

His eyes narrowed as he leaned in, once again searching her face. "You think she was pregnant with *you* when she left?"

Now that it looked like her worse fear might be coming true, she couldn't speak. She nodded.

"Damn," Sterling murmured.

Luke finished off a mediocre fish sandwich with fries and pushed the plate aside. The interaction between Sterling and Alicia across the room had captured his attention. The plate of food in front of her hadn't been touched. All the gesturing and the whispering between them didn't look like pleasant family talk. The woman looked upset.

Luke had never trusted Sterling.

"Would you like to hear me sing now?" asked the young woman sitting across from Luke.

He pushed away from the table. "Sure, let's step across the hall into the conference room. I've got everything set up for auditions there." If he had to audition every woman in Glynn County he would, until he found the female lead for the house band he dreamed of putting together.

Finally finding her voice, Alicia told Sterling, "That's why I need to talk to the family she went to stay with. I have no idea who they were, or if they're still alive. Maybe they can tell me if she had the baby or not. I believe she met the man I called my father a few months after arriving in New York."

Sterling placed an elbow on the table and covered his mouth with his hand. "So, he might not be your real father?" he pondered.

She nodded again. "Yeah."

He shifted in his seat. "That is *if* you are the baby in question. If not, maybe you have a sister or brother somewhere. But they wouldn't be entitled to your father's car dealership or whatever other money he left you?"

Alicia's jaw dropped, and she let out a hard sigh. Lately, all conversations with her family revolved around money.

"I mean *if* there was another child. That answers any questions you have about being your father's legal heir," he pressed on.

"No matter what I find out, I'm his legal heir," she confirmed.

"Good. Because with a little money you can find out anything about anyone, if you know the right people to ask."

"And I suppose you do?"

He smiled. "Of course I do." He pushed back in his seat and crossed his legs. "What you have to do is determine how much it's worth to you."

After a disappointing lunch, Alicia spent the rest of the afternoon sitting on her balcony looking out into the ocean. The hypnotic waves calmed her shattered nerves and almost put her to sleep.

"Hey Rapunzel, want to let down your hair?"

She lowered her feet from the railing and looked down at Darius standing in the middle of the lawn and looking up at her. The site of him woke her from that near-sleep buzz and put a smile on her face.

"I'm afraid it's not long, or strong enough."

"Then you want to open the door?"

She smiled. "Come on up." The time she'd spent with Darius lately was the only thing that made her feel good. She opened the door and leaned against the doorway as he came up the stairs.

Dressed in a gray suit and looking dapper as usual, he stopped in front of her and planted a soft kiss on her forehead. "Feeling any better?"

She shook her head, and he walked in. After closing the door she grabbed a cold bottle of water from the minifridge and offered it to him.

"Thanks, it must be ninety degrees out today." He loosened his tie.

"Yeah, but the breeze coming off the ocean is wonderful." She walked over to the sofa and sat down. He followed her.

"So why aren't you down at the beach instead of holed up in here?" he asked, opening his water and taking a drink.

She tucked a foot under her and shrugged. "I'm just not in the mood today."

"This morning you had me thinking I'd done something to you the way you cut me off."

"I'm sorry. I woke up in a bad mood."

"Anything I can help with?" he asked sincerely.

"No." She frowned down into her lap. Still slightly upset about yesterday, a well of tears formed in her eyes.

Darius set his water on the coffee table and twisted in his seat to face her. She held her head up trying to blink the tears back, but a few slid down her cheek.

He reached out and placed a hand on her cheek, turning her to face him. "Hey, what's wrong?"

She pulled away from him embarrassed for acting like a child. How could she have let family she hardly knew hurt her feelings the way they had? She set her water on the table and wiped the tears away.

"Maybe spending so much time around here was a mistake," she said between her tears. "I should have left after the wedding."

He wiped at her tears with his thumb. "What are you talking about? Have I done something to hurt you?" he pleaded.

She shook her head. "It's not you. It's my family. I forced myself on them and it wasn't fair. They probably resent me for it. I bet that's why they attacked me yesterday." The tears kept flowing no matter how much she blinked them back.

"What? Who attacked you?"

She leaned forward resting her elbows on her thighs. "Not physically, but they came at me talking about property taxes they've been paying all these years that I should start helping with. I don't know anything about any property." Her trickle of tears turned into a snivel.

He gently massaged her back. "Did you tell them about your father's money?"

"I told my aunt, and I guess she told everyone else. It just hurts, you know. I'd hoped to develop a good relationship with them."

"I'd be lying if I said I understood. I'm not very close to my relatives, but I do know what it feels like to have someone you want to love you, not give you that love you're seeking."

Through her tears she could see the sincerity in his eyes. He could make her feel all better, if she'd let him.

Alicia couldn't control the sniveling as a full-blown crying spell took over. Darius was there to pull her into his chest and comfort her.

"I just don't want to be alone anymore," she admitted.

"What about your father's family?" he asked.

She wanted to pull back and not mess up his shirt, but being in his embrace felt so wonderful she couldn't move. "We're not that close. Most of them live in California, and I only get out there once or twice a year."

He hugged her tighter now and through her tears Alicia could hear him whispering in her ear. "It'll be all right."

But would it?

Her crying turned into sniffling, as she pulled away from his embrace. She stood and walked over to a box of tissues on the counter.

"I never know if I'm doing the right thing or not. I had such a hard time making up my mind to come here, and now I think I did the wrong thing." She blew her nose.

Darius walked over to her. "Don't say that. If you hadn't come we would have never met." He reached out and twirled his finger around a strand of hair that had come loose from the knot she'd created at the nape of her neck.

"You'd probably have been better off not meeting me. I've been a mess ever since I've been here, and I'm not normally like this."

He used both hands and undid the knot, letting her hair cascade around her shoulders. Her breath hitched in her throat. She felt a tingling sensation when his hands landed on her shoulders.

His hand moved up her shoulder to cup the nape of her neck. "I can't think of anything I'd rather do than spend time with you."

A smile tipped the corners of her mouth. He simply stared down at her for a moment without speaking, his eyes tracing every inch of her face until she turned away. Her gaze landed on the bed, and wicked, nasty thoughts ran through her mind. She wanted him naked in her bed.

"But I can't stay," he added. "I have another meeting. I just wanted to drop by and check on you." He wiped the last lone tear from her face and kissed her on the forehead.

She forced herself to suck it up. *Stop whimpering like a baby and pull yourself together,* she told herself. "Thanks for stopping by."

"Can I see you later?"

"You know, this is getting dangerous. I don't think that's such a good idea." As much as she wanted this man, she had to be sensible about the situation.

"I know—you're not ready for a relationship. I just want to keep you company, that's all."

She grinned. "Sure that's all."

He smiled and slowly slid his hands down her arms. "I'll call you when my meeting's over."

After saying good-bye, Alicia returned to her seat on the balcony. His presence had perked her up, if only the lower half of her anatomy, but she wasn't as depressed as before he arrived. She could talk to Darius, and she needed that right now. However, if she didn't leave the island soon, she'd be giving in to her two-year vow of celibacy.

Walking past her room for the second time today was that same bellhop she kept running into. At first she couldn't remember his name, but when he waved at her it came to her, Rodell.

Chapter 20

To lift her spirits Alicia resorted to her old standby—shopping. First, she returned to some of the unique shops in the Historic district and picked up a few gifts. Then, she wound up in the island's sole shopping mall where she managed to find a cute pair of shoes and purse to match. Jekyll Island didn't have much to offer in the way of shopping, but the trip cheered her up.

On the way back to her room she ran into Luke coming out of the recreation office in a pair of trunks and a T-shirt.

"Working hard are we?" Alicia asked, as he stepped out of the office.

He lowered his sunglasses and smiled. Not the same charismatic smile he'd given her before, but it registered as a smile. "Just checking out the pedal boats." He glanced down at her bags and then up at her face.

She'd slowed down to talk to him. He closed the door and

joined her. "I see you found something on this island worth buying?" He pointed at her bags.

She shrugged. "A woman can always find something when she goes shopping."

He reached out for the bags. "Here, let me carry those for you. I'm headed your way."

"Uh, sure." She released the bags.

"I hope you enjoyed the jazz set I arranged Friday night?"

"Oh, that was your doing? I enjoyed it very much, so I guess I should say thank you."

"You're welcome. Music is what I do. Having a piano bar with nobody to play the piano is a crime."

He lost his smile and took on a more serious look. "I need to ask you something. How well do you know Sterling?"

She blinked. "He's my cousin, but I don't know him very well. Why?"

Luke's pace slowed. "I'm just asking. I saw you guys at lunch the other day and you looked a little upset."

She shrugged. "Oh, it was nothing."

"Family business?" he assumed.

"Yeah, you know how that is," she replied with a little laugh.

He picked up his pace. "I've also noticed that you've been spending a lot of time with Darius."

"We've spent some time together. I wouldn't call it a lot, he's busy with the hotel."

"Not too busy to get sidetracked by a beautiful woman." His tone was harsh and flat.

Unable to get her mind around what was happening, Alicia shook her head. "Thank you. I think." She laughed.

"That was a compliment wasn't it?" she asked, turning to him.

He smiled. "Of course." They'd reached their building and he motioned for her to go up ahead of him.

Alicia wasn't at all fooled by his plastic smile, but she wasn't sure what she'd done to deserve it. At the top of the steps she turned to him. "Do you have a problem with me spending time with your brother?"

He shook his head. "I'm just not sure that he has the time to give you right now. The renovation of this hotel is important to him, to me, and to my family."

"I'm sure it is, but isn't that for him to decide?" She stopped in front of her door and fished the key from her purse. She didn't like Luke's tone. Sterling had said Luke was out for his job, now what did he want from her?

"Somebody on staff here tried to get my grandfather to sell the hotel, and I believe that same person has been undermining the integrity and financial structure of this hotel ever since. I think that somebody is your cousin."

Alicia opened her door then turned back to him. She snatched her bags back. "You don't like him do you?"

He gave a vague gesture. "Not really. He's not a very trustworthy man, and you've been spending a lot of time with him. It looks like you guys are up to something to me."

"I don't know what you're talking about, but I'm not my cousin. And I'm not up to anything." She put her bags down inside and yanked her purse from her shoulder.

"Maybe not." He stepped back and winked at her. "Only time will tell."

Alicia closed the door as he turned away. *What the hell was that all about?* she wondered.

The next day, Darius pulled all the stops trying to cheer up her mood. Alicia hadn't played miniature golf since college, but he insisted on taking her. Darius, on the other hand, was an old pro. He downplayed his skills and allowed her to win a game.

That evening, they headed across the causeway and down

to the Brunswick Landing Marina. The Emerald Princess awaited them for a night full of music, dancing, and gambling. The ship was the smallest floating casino Alicia had ever been on.

Throughout the evening, Alicia tried her luck at everything from the roulette wheel to blackjack, not having luck anywhere.

"I think these machines are rigged," she told Darius.

"They must be if you can't win." He walked behind her and wrapped an arm around her shoulder.

A touch here, a hug there. His public displays of affection proved he wasn't put off by her previous proclamations of not wanting a relationship. His willingness to sit and listen as she poured her heart out showed true generosity. Why he chose to spend the day with her instead of at the hotel surprised her, but she wasn't complaining. She'd already made up her mind about him and purchased some condoms at the drugstore should the opportunity arise. And she hoped like hell it would.

"Let me play this last dollar," she said, dropping a coin into the slot and pulling the one arm bandit.

Lucky seven... Lucky seven... Nothing.

"The story of my life," Alicia sighed, and leaned back into his chest. "Almost, but not quite."

Something poked her in the back and she jumped, looking over her shoulder. "What's that?"

Darius reached down and unclipped his cell phone from his belt. "My phone, sorry. Here, can you put this in your purse? I turned it off for the evening."

"What if you get an important call?" she asked, taking the phone.

"Nothing's more important than what I'm doing right now." He grasped her shoulders and led her away from the slot machines toward the bar.

Little comments like that kept a smile on her face. He

always said the right things. Unlike Alicia, who was so inde-
cisive she missed the boat half the time.

"I can never get lucky," she remarked, referring to the slot
machine. They took a seat at the bar, and Darius ordered drinks.

"Some people would say you were born lucky."

"I know, but they only see the outside, the material stuff;
they don't know what's inside me, what I want but can't
have."

After her glass of wine and his beer arrived, Darius took
her by the hand and led the way from the gaming level to the
observation deck.

The orange glow of the setting sun absolutely took Alicia's
breath away. It looked like she could row out to it if she
wanted to. They strolled along the deck leading toward the
dance floor.

Darius stopped short and, leaning against the rail, looked
out into the ocean. She stood beside him stirring her drink.

"What is it you want, but can't have?" He turned his head
toward her, biting his bottom lip.

Alicia rested her forearms against the rail and looked down
into her drink. "You really want to know?" she asked. Darius
had shown genuine concern and interest in everything she
said.

"Of course."

Alicia took a deep breath. "More time with my mother. You
were lucky to have grown up with both parents. I'd give
anything to spend more time with my mother. Even my
father's money can't buy me that."

He gave her a sympathetic smile. "If I could, trust me, I'd
make that happen for you. It must have been difficult growing
up without your mother and her love. There's no substitute
for a mother, no matter how many women your father sub-
jected you to in order to find one."

Alicia had told him all about her father's girlfriends, but she'd never considered he was looking for someone to replace her mother.

"I spent more time with my mother growing up than my dad. The bond between mother and child is special. But, I'm sure your father did what he thought was best."

"As hard as he tried, he could never fill that void left by my mother's death."

"What did she die of?" he asked.

"Breast cancer."

The door burst open, and a string of drunken young people staggered onto the observation desk. The group passed Alicia and Darius and headed for the dance floor.

Darius nursed his drink. "I'm sorry you lost your mother. You can have mine if you want her, but let me warn you she's a handful."

Alicia laughed as he lightened up the moment. "You haven't told me very much about your mother."

He shrugged. "She's a feisty, petite woman whose life is wrapped up in her store and her customers. I don't think she's taken a vacation since she opened the store."

"Do you see her often?"

"About once a week, or every other week if I'm busy."

A waitress came along and Darius set his drink on her tray. A breeze came over the rail blowing Alicia's hair into her face. She pulled it back, tucking a handful behind her ear, and noticed the inviting way Darius was looking at her. Her heart soared.

He reached over and touched her arm, letting his hand travel down to her palm. She opened her hand and let his fingers weave between hers. She smiled up at him and his eyes softened.

A longing for him had been building ever since their first walk on the beach. She hadn't wanted to admit it, but she'd wanted him even then.

"You know, you're petty lucky too," she commented.

"Oh yeah. How so?"

"Look at what your father did for you."

He laughed and pulled his hand back. "What, leave me that old hotel?"

"No, I'd say you owe your business success to your father."

Darius turned around, leaning against the rail with his side. "How did you come to that conclusion?"

"It's obvious he saw the business potential in you at a young age and steered you in the right direction. Now you're a successful business owner. Look at what you did for your mother's business and what you plan to do for the hotel. You're creating a family legacy."

"Is that what he was doing?" Darius studied Alicia.

"Uh-huh." She ignored the skeptical look Darius gave her. Maybe he couldn't see what his father had done for him, but she could. "I've met your brother, and I don't think he could do what you're doing. I bet he doesn't have the business sense."

"If he applied himself, he could. He's just more interested in music and women."

"And you're not?"

"Oh, I'm interested in women all right. One woman in particular." He reached out for her hand and brought it to his lips. He placed a soft, gentle kiss in the palm of her hand that made her toes curl.

"I'll be glad when this boat docks," he said.

"Why?" she asked.

"I've got something I want to show you," he said with a wink.

Kamora sniffed. The lobby of Hotel Paradise was a non-smoking area, but somebody somewhere had lit up. Gibb, her boss, was standing on the other side of the lobby talking to Sterling. They'd smell it soon enough.

A few minutes later, the smell became more prominent. Now, however, it didn't smell like cigarette smoke. Gibb and Sterling had walked out to the front of the hotel and she couldn't leave the front desk. She picked up the phone to call the kitchen. No one answered. She rang the hotel operator and asked her to put her through. Still no answer.

She sniffed again. Something was burning. Fire! She left the front desk and ran out to the front of the building. When she came running back with Sterling and Gibb, two kitchen workers had run upstairs into the lobby.

"Mr. Simpson—" one of the young men yelled "—the kitchen's on fire."

"I'll call the fire department," Kamora yelled.

"Let us check it out first," Gibb said, following the men downstairs.

The front desk phone was ringing off the hook. Kamora returned to her job and answered the calls. Several guests smelled the smoke as well. She hung up and wondered when the alarm would go off.

Darius stood behind Alicia with his arms wrapped around her as the ship headed back to dock. Standing under the starlit sky, he looked out into the ocean, feeling like a young woman in love. She hadn't known this man a month, yet she had strong feelings for him.

He bent his head and kissed her along the neck, tugging her earlobe. Her body was on fire. She wanted his lips to kiss her all over her body. Pressed against him, the rise and fall of his chest warmed her insides. His body was exactly what she needed. Those little nasty fantasies of hers surfaced again and she rested her head against his chest and closed her eyes.

In this daydream, they are so overcome with desire for one another they aren't able to make it to her room. She lies bare-

breasted on the beach while Darius plants sensual kisses from
her forehead down to her breasts. He circles her nipples with
his tongue before taking each breast into his mouth and
feasting. He kisses and licks his way down to her stomach.

She arches her back in response to the tingling sensation
running through her body. His tongue plays with her navel
and then stops at the waistband of her pants. But only long
enough to unbutton and discard it. Her stomach muscles
tighten. The waves crashing against the beach behind them
drown out her soft moans. He spreads her legs and kisses the
inside of her thighs. Her breath catches in her throat.

Suddenly, her daydream came to an end. Darius twisted her
around, his soft eyes looking into hers. "Why are you so
quiet?" he asked.

She smiled. "I was just daydreaming."

"About what?" he asked, turning her back around and
squeezing her tighter.

She melted into his arms. "Oh, nothing."

Back on shore, it took Darius no time to get to the hotel.
He bypassed the lobby and drove down the private driveway
that led to his apartment.

He wasn't ready for the evening to end, and he hoped
Alicia wasn't either. He offered her a nightcap and turned the
radio on. The "Quiet Storm," a night full of slow jams played
on the radio. She walked around his apartment nodding and
smiling. Housekeeping had made him look good.

"So what is it you wanted me to see?" she asked, placing
a hand on her hip.

He came around and met her on the other side of the sofa.
Her hand slid off her hip. He pulled her purse from her shoulder
and pitched it on the sofa. All evening he'd enjoyed the view
of her back in that halter top. He didn't think he could stand

another moment of not holding her in his arms. He took her face between his hands and looked long and hard into her eyes seeing a beautiful woman full of life. All she needed was love.

"You're killing me, you know that?" he declared, in a voice so unlike his he almost didn't recognize it.

"How so?" she asked, her breathing louder now.

He bent down and took her mouth like the starved man that he was. The sweet taste of Alicia's mouth stirred something deep inside him that surfaced every time she was around. A whiff of her perfume, the sight of her hair blowing in the wind, or the sound of her giggle, all made him want to get next to her in more ways than one. He wanted her and not just for tonight.

He'd dreamed of removing her clothes slowly, savoring every inch of what he knew to be her curvaceous, beautiful brown body. His desire to have her soft skin against him ignited a flame inside his body.

When he released her soft, tender lips to catch his breath, her eyes remained closed. He smiled. "Stay with me tonight?"

Her eyes flew open.

Chapter 21

Those precious four words scared the hell out of Alicia. She'd wanted this moment, she'd dreamed it up; but now that the opportunity presented itself she feared she'd chicken out.

"I can't," she said, reaching up to grasp his wrist, and pulling his hands away from her face.

His hands stopped at her shoulders and caressed them slowly. "Why not?"

Yeah, why the hell not? This is your chance at that summer fling. You'd already made up your mind once. But something had happened. She still wanted Darius; but she didn't want him to consider her a one-night stand.

Sweat broke out on her forehead like she was having an early menopause attack. She backed away. "Is the air on in here?" she asked. Fanning herself, she walked toward the patio door.

Darius followed her and opened the sliding glass door. She

stepped out and grasped her shoulders, taking a deep cleansing breath. Her pulse raced a mile a minute.

Here I go, doubting myself again. This has got to stop. When she first laid eyes on Darius she'd called him "sexy as hell." And now "sexy as hell" wanted her, and that scared her to death.

He strolled up behind her and placed one finger at a time on her shoulder and whispered in her ear. "I'm still waiting for an answer."

"I'm scared," she admitted.

"Of what? Certainly not of me," he said after a beat. "I won't hurt you."

She turned around to face him. "Of what you'd think of me if I did stay."

He grinned. "I'd think you feel the same way about me that I feel about you. That for tonight at least, you had pity on a lonely man that longs to have your warm body next to his."

She gave him a you've-got-to-be-kidding grin. "You want pity sex?"

He studied her face for a moment and then the corners of his lips turned up. "Never. Alicia, I think you want me just as much as I want you. But, I wouldn't think any less of you if you asked me to walk you to your room right now."

If she wanted to back out, he'd opened the door for her. But she wasn't crazy. She responded by wrapping her arms around his neck and giving him a kiss that let him know she didn't want to leave.

In the background, *Do Me Baby* by Prince came on the radio. As if the song triggered something lying dormant within her, she came alive.

Suddenly desperate for the warmth of his mouth and the sheer comfort of being held, she pushed her tongue into his mouth with a forcefulness she didn't know she possessed. If she could have, she would have climbed up his body. A fire raged inside her.

In return, Darius took control of the kiss. His soft, hot tongue stroked hers, filling her mouth. His hands slid down her hips and around her bottom. He filled his hands and squeezed until he lifted her into his arms.

Alicia wrapped her legs around his waist without removing her lips from his hot, wet mouth. She clung to him and held on for dear life.

With her wrapped around him, he made his way into the bedroom. He bent over the bed gently, placed her on her back, and came down on top of her.

Alicia shivered in response to his hard body and enormous erection pressed against her. His hand found its way under her top searing her flesh as it traveled up to stroke her erect nipple. Then he rolled over giving his hand better access to her as he untied the material holding up her halter top, and kissed his way down her neck. She bit her bottom lip trying her best to silence the moans escaping from her lips. She wanted him in the worst way now. No second thoughts, no doubts, nothing stood in her way now.

"Damn, Alicia," he whispered, in a low husky voice. "God, I want you so bad." A second later, he stood over her, yanking his shirt over his head and kicking off his shoes. She rose on her elbows admiring his well-defined, six-pack abs and the patch of soft black hair on his chest.

He reached out for her hand and pulled her up to a sitting position. He discarded her top, tossing it in a chair behind him. Reaching out his hands, he cupped her breasts.

She reached out and tugged at his belt, wanting desperately to see what she was in store for. He unzipped and dropped his pants, then kicked them across the room. In boxers that fit his firm, hard thighs and hugged his bulging erection, he stood there staring down at her. The rise and fall of his chest brought her to her feet.

With her breasts pressed against his chest, she captured his lips once again. His hands settled around her waist holding her slightly away from him. Then he unhooked her pants and eased them over her hips. Alicia stepped back and wiggled the rest of the way out of them. Darius sat her on the bed and first unfastened the ankle strap on her heels. He held her foot in the palm of his hand and kissed the inside of her ankle sending tiny shivers up her leg.

In nothing but a purple thong, she lay on the bed looking up at him and trembling. "Nice," he said, licking his lips.

His searing gaze swept over her body as she took her feet and tugged at his boxers. He slid his hands beneath the waistband and pulled the boxers over his hips and his erection, until they lay at his feet. He stepped out of them, and she gasped.

"Better than nice," she said with a smile. *Try enormous.* His body came down and he braced himself over her, leaving mere inches between them. His kisses started at her lips while one hand caressed her breasts. At his touch, Alicia arched her back and moaned in frustration. She wanted his touch, but she wanted it faster and harder. She wanted to feel him inside of her.

He removed his hand from her breast and replaced it with his mouth. The minute his wet tongue touched her nipple, she moaned from sheer ecstasy. He sucked one breast with his hot, soft mouth, and she drifted off into never-never land. She closed her eyes and bit her lip so hard she thought she might draw blood.

When his hand moved down between her legs, stroking the fabric of her thong, she wanted to explode. She wanted those damned panties out of the way. With her free hand she reached down and pulled at the fabric. He released her breast and gripped the small strip of lace between her legs, tugging at it until it clung around her ankle. As he pushed her panties past her feet to the floor with one hand, she felt him tremble.

When his big hands came back up, he caressed the soft folds between her legs. Unable to contain herself she screamed his name. "Darius. Oh, God."

At that moment, he took her other breast into his mouth and sucked and licked until she all but crawled on her back. He pressed her legs open and stroked his fingers between the lips of her vagina, reaching the tiny bud that caused her to cry out, "Wait."

Darius pushed up on both hands, his pupils dilated as he stared down at her. "God, don't tell me you're having second thoughts *now*," he pleaded, trying to catch his breath.

She shook her head and whispered, "I've got a condom in my purse."

He slowly lowered himself to one elbow laughing. "What are you doing walking around with condoms in your purse?" he asked, smiling down at her.

She shrugged. *Jesus, I hope he doesn't think I'm a slut.* "I guess I was kind of hoping and praying," she admitted with a nervous laugh.

He got up off the bed and pulled open the nightstand drawer. Turning around with a condom in his hand he said, "I was hoping and praying too." He winked and smiled suggestively. "We'll save yours for later."

When he rolled over on his back, she took the package from him and ripped it open. Slowly, she rolled it down his shaft, feeling his massiveness between her hands. He closed his eyes and groaned as her fingers closed around him. He flipped over on top of her, his eyes dark and smoldering as he whispered in her ear, "You're so beautiful."

She opened her mouth to respond but he covered it with

his, and in one quick thrust he dove deep inside her. She wrapped herself around him and silently screamed, *Hallelujah for summer flings.*

Alicia and Darius walked hand in hand up the path from his apartment, then down another path to hers. Two years of pent-up sexual tension had exploded from her at such a rate that she was just now coming down.

Darius raised her hand to his lips and planted big wet sloppy kisses on the back of her hand and wrist.

"Darius, what if somebody sees you?" she said, glancing around them half expecting to see someone else out there at two in the morning.

"So what if they do," he replied between kisses.

"You're the owner of the hotel," she said, incredulously fighting off the urge to giggle out loud.

He released her hand and pulled her into his arms. "Let's see what they think of this." He bent her over, and smothered her with kisses.

Call her a slut, but she wanted him again. Standing out in the open with balconies on one side and the ocean on the other, they held each other lips locked.

"Well if that isn't cute."

Darius released Alicia's mouth and looked up. Before she turned around she recognized the voice. It was Luke. What the hell could he be doing out at this time of morning? Darius loosened his arms around her enough for her to turn around and look right into Luke's face.

"I'm glad we could amuse you," Darius replied, holding Alicia tighter.

"Yeah, well I've got some amusing information for you. A couple thousand dollars worth of amusement."

"What are you talkin' about?" Darius loosened his hold on her.

"I tried to call you, but I couldn't get through. Where's your cell phone?"

Alicia pulled the phone from her purse and placed it in Darius's outstretched hand.

"What the hell happened?" he asked, while turning on his phone.

"We had a small fire this evening."

Darius's eyes widened in alarm. "Was anybody hurt?"

"Nope. It was a small grease fire in the kitchen."

A frown creased Darius's forehead as he listened to his messages.

The slow scrutinizing stare Luke gave Alicia hit her right in the gut. He didn't like her, but for the life of her, she couldn't figure out what she'd done to him.

"Have you talked to Sterling this afternoon?" he asked Alicia.

"No, I haven't. Why?"

"Just checking to see if you knew or heard anything."

"I'm afraid I don't keep tabs on him," she said.

Darius clicked his phone closed and clipped it to his belt. "Gibb said everything's taken care of. How bad was it?"

"I checked it out. It wasn't too bad. According to Kamora, the kitchen extinguishers were empty. We're lucky the whole place didn't burn down."

"How did it happen?"

"You'll have to ask Sterling. When I came back, everything was over. I tried calling him, but like you, he wouldn't answer his cell phone."

Alicia felt Luke's eyes on her again.

"I can't believe the extinguishers didn't work, they've been checked recently," Darius commented.

"Well, we'll be serving a limited breakfast in the morning." Luke walked around them. "I'll see you in your office first thing tomorrow. You might want to stop and talk to Gibb on the way back. That is, if you'll be heading back anytime soon."

Darius gave Luke a cold stare. "I'll stop by right after I walk Alicia to her door."

"Well, enjoy yourselves," Luke said walking ahead of them.

Darius took Alicia by the hand and started up the path to her room.

"What a way to end an otherwise perfect night, huh?" he said, smiling down at her.

"Not the perfect ending I'd hoped for. But, it was still like a day in Paradise." She looked down at his hand holding hers and smiled.

Luke burst into Darius's office the next morning carrying a gold envelope. "I need to talk to you about something."

Still annoyed with the way Luke spoke to Alicia last night, Darius didn't care to hear anything he had to say. "I'm busy." He concentrated on the open file in front of him.

"Yeah, but we need to discuss this." Luke took a seat across from Darius's desk and proceeded to open the envelope.

Frustrated, Darius stopped reading. He studied his little brother a moment before closing his folder.

"Where do you get off talking to Alicia like you did last night?" he asked, unable to keep the anger from his voice.

Frozen, Luke looked up moving only his eyeballs as he cut from Darius back to the papers in his hand. "She's Sterling's cousin and I—"

"I know you don't like Sterling, and I don't care about that. The next time you disrespect Alicia, be prepared to get your ass kicked."

Luke smiled. He slid the papers back into the envelope and closed it. "You've been dying to do just that. And it doesn't have anything to do with Alicia."

"What the hell are you talking about?"

"Admit it, man—" Luke threw his hands up "—you're pissed off at me. You always have been." He dropped his hands and reared back in his seat. "You were just waiting on any opportunity to call me out. And me trying to warn you about your little girlfriend and her cousin's it."

"Warn me!" Darius exploded, then laughed. "About what?"

Luke let out a heavy sigh and sat up. "About them plotting to take the hotel."

Darius shot up. "Have you lost your mind?" He emerged from behind his desk to stand a few feet from his brother. "The woman came down for a wedding. Who's she plotting with? RCE? Maybe she's an inside spy or something," he huffed.

"She might be for all I know. I see she's got your nose wide open." Luke stood up and snatched the envelope from Darius's desk.

"And not you. Is that what bothers you? She told me about your rain check for lunch."

Luke laughed and shook his head. "Man, she's not even my type. Too much meat on them bones," he said, staring into his brother's eyes.

A spasm of irritation crossed Darius face as he held back the urge to stomp the silly smile from Luke's face. Instead, he shot him a warning look and took his seat again. "I don't think we should be working together," he muttered bitterly.

"That's too bad, because I'm not going anywhere. We're going to have to face the past sometime, so we might as well get it over with."

Luke crossed his arms and took a stance looking down at Darius with raised brows. "I know you don't want to talk about it, but I'm tired of being treated like a second-class citizen by you. You'd think I robbed you of your life or something. Do you want to trade lives? You run around the world to make a buck, and I'll stay put for a while." Luke scratched at his chin as he paced across Darius's office. "The man's dead. I can't go back and fix what he did, and neither can you."

Two women passing by slowed and peered into the office. Luke walked over and slammed the door.

The noise shook Darius from his dazed state. Whether he wanted to or not, they had to settle this here and now. "Is that really why you came down? To talk about our father?" He rose from his chair and came around his desk again. "Because you seem more interested in bedding the front desk clerk than working on any of the renovation plans. But forget about that. Let's talk about him. Let's talk about the special relationship you two had that didn't include me. Who was treated like a second-class citizen growing up?"

After blinking back a moment of surprise, Luke sighed and looked down at the envelope in his hand. "I know you're bitter, but it's displaced anger. We're brothers. I never excluded you from anything."

"For years, he had me wondering if I was really his son or not. Do you know how that felt? While I was studying, you guys went fishing, discovered new music, and even jammed together."

Luke shook his head. "Come on man, he's dead. Get over it. I'm sure he'd be sorry if he knew how you felt."

"He knew how I felt. I made sure he did."

Luke shoved the envelope under his arm. "So this isn't about my music career?"

Darius waved the question off with a peremptory gesture. "I didn't want a career in music. Not really. All I wanted was a relationship with my father."

Chapter 22

No longer wanting to have this discussion, Luke stood staring at Darius when someone knocked at the door. The hurt and pain on his brother's face bothered him. Why hadn't he ever told him all this before?

Darius turned around and peered out the window. Luke set the envelope down on Darius's desk and opened the door. Sterling walked in.

"Darius, you wanted to see me?" he asked.

Luke walked out and closed the door.

Alicia sat across the kitchen table from her aunt Ode determined this time to leave with some sort of an answer. She'd shared her conversation with Sterling with her aunt.

"I know now that she was pregnant. Sterling found out for me."

Not looking the least bit surprised, Ode continued cooking,

but gave Alicia a cursory glance over her shoulder. "What else did he tell you?"

"That's all, but you could have told me that. Aunt Ode, I've been here for about three weeks trying to talk to you about my mother. All I've been able to get out of you are stories about your childhood in St. Helena."

Ode whirled around pointing a fork at Alicia. "Yo' mama left from around here when she was seventeen. All I got are childhood memories."

Not to be deterred by a deadly fork, Alicia bit back. "But how come I had to learn from Sterling that she was pregnant? I could be that baby."

Ode set the fork down with so much force that it rattled. Alicia jumped in her seat. With Ode's unyielding jaw set and in a strained voice she said, "Ya' have a good life. Ya' better off than most, and now ya' know where ya' come from. Do ya' need to know more than that?"

Ode turned away with a pained expression on her face, but the answer was, yes. Alicia did need to know more than that.

Alicia stood up, and in a voice void of emotion said, "I'll be going home on Sunday. I just came by to thank you for the pictures and everything else."

Ode wiped her hands on a towel and with a big smile made her way to the kitchen table. "Honey, whatcha talkin' 'bout." She lowered herself into the chair next to Alicia. "I thought you was gonna stay until the end of the month?"

Muscles tensed in Alicia's neck as she lowered her gaze to the floor. She couldn't handle another round of this.

Ode reached out and took Alicia's hand in hers and squeezed it. "I loved ya' mama. And I wouldn't do nuttun' to hurt ya'." In a proud voice she continued. "Venetta had big dreams. She wanted everythin'. And when she wanted somethin', she went after it and got it. She wanted to learn a good trade and move to the mainland, and that's what she did."

The emotion in Ode's voice tugged at Alicia's heartstrings. But that still didn't tell her what she needed to know. She was more than convinced now that her aunt would never tell her more than she already knew.

Alicia stood up, easing her hand from her aunt's. "Aunt Ode, I'll try to stop by one more time before I leave, but I'm leaving Sunday," she said in a voice as cold as death.

Her aunt held on to the kitchen table as she pushed herself up, and with a drawn face and outstretched arms embraced her niece.

Darius spent most of Wednesday going over the hotel's renovation plans and working the kitchen repair into the budget. He'd finally picked up the gold envelope Luke left for him and pulled out the contract. Luke had compared the contract given to him by the Golden Isle Sons to the one Sterling gave him and had highlighted the inconsistencies. Darius had begun to look over the contract when a soft tap on his office door interrupted him.

"Come in."

The door opened slowly, and Alicia stood there in a berry-colored halter dress with locks of long black hair lying around her shoulders. His breath caught in his throat.

She strode in, closing the door behind her. The beach bag on her shoulder slid off and hit the floor.

He pushed the papers aside and sat up, leaning back in his seat. The sight of her brought a smile to his face and a yearning to his loins.

"I'm on my way to the beach, want to join me?"

He pushed his chair back and motioned for her to come to him.

She stared him down as she walked around his desk.

He swiveled his chair around to face her and patted his lap. "Come sit right here."

Her eyes danced and she smiled wickedly as she sashayed up to him, straddling him, and planting a soft kiss on his lips. What was it about this woman that he couldn't get enough of, he thought?

She wrapped her arms around his neck, and he slid his hands up her thighs cupping her butt cheeks to position her higher on his lap.

"Miss me?" she asked.

"Like hell. I'm still crying because you didn't stay the night." He eased down in his seat and positioned her crotch directly over his swelling erection. That's exactly where he wanted her.

She whispered in his ear, "Come to the beach with me."

"Baby, I wish I could, but I have a meeting this afternoon." She pouted as he fingered his way up from her thighs to her waist, rocking her into him. Her skin was so soft to the touch, he needed to feel her closer to him. Skin to skin.

She opened her mouth to say something, but he couldn't help himself and silenced her by placing his mouth over hers, sucking her beautiful lips. She smelled as fresh and sweet as she had last night.

Memories of her naked and spent in his bed put a smile on his face. He released her mouth as she tugged his shirt up and out of his pants. "What are you doing?" he asked, laughing.

"What time is your meeting?" She ran her hands under his shirt and up his chest.

With his chest on fire, he glanced down at the paperweight clock on his desk. "Four o'clock."

She glanced over at the clock. "Good, we've got twenty minutes." She'd loosened his tie and unbuttoned his shirt. Then the phone rang.

If he hadn't been waiting on an important call, he would have let it ring, but he had to answer it.

He took Alicia's hands in his. "Hold on, I need to get this." He leaned over and picked up the phone.

"Timothy, what you got?" This was the call he'd been waiting for.

That name was all Alicia needed to hear. She rebuttoned Darius's shirt and removed herself from his lap.

"What time is he coming?" Darius said into the phone while standing and tucking his shirt back into his pants. He winked at Alicia and mouthed, "I'm sorry."

She threw up a hand and walked over and sat down in the chair across from his desk. In the time she had left on the island, she'd planned to leave Darius Monroe with something he'd never forget.

After overhearing his part of the conversation, it sounded like he was going to be busy for the rest of the afternoon. By the time he hung up, he had only five minutes before his four o'clock meeting.

He came around his desk and sat on the corner. "And just what were you trying to do Ms. McKay, seduce me?"

"Oh, I would have, if that phone hadn't rung," she said, uncrossing her legs and standing up. She positioned herself between his legs.

He wrapped his arms around her waist and pulled her closer to him. "Do you realize this is my office, and somebody could have caught us?"

"Yes." She traced a finger along his lips before he sucked it into his mouth. Her whole body tingled. "But, that's a chance *we* were willing to take."

He released her finger. "You're my kind of woman all right. I'll tell you what, why don't you plan on having dinner with me tonight?"

If she stuck to her guns and left Sunday like she had told her aunt she was going to, then she had to have him once more before she returned to Atlanta and to her life of celibacy.

"Dinner at your place I presume?"

He winked. "Where else? You did enjoy your visit last night didn't you?" he asked with a wicked smile.

"Yes, sir, and I'll be holding my breath until tonight."

He brought his mouth down to meet hers for their most toe-curling, sensual kiss to date.

Later that night, Alicia walked out of Darius's bathroom and crossed his modest bedroom, which had all white bedding. She hadn't paid much attention to the bedroom the night before; she'd been too busy trying to get into his pants. The whitewashed furniture gave the room an old, lived-in feel. She guessed it originated from his grandfather's home since it didn't match anything else in the hotel.

When she walked into the living room, Darius had fixed himself a drink and walked out onto the balcony looking out at the ocean. She stood in the doorway quietly watching him.

"Know what you smell like?" he asked, without turning around.

She stepped out to join him. "What's that?"

He turned to face her with a lopsided grin on his face. "My mother's flower bed."

"So, you know a little something about flowers too?"

He shrugged and chuckled. "Not the least bit, but she has some beautiful flowers in the yard that bloom every spring and smell like perfume. When I smell you, that's what I'm reminded of."

"Are you saying I make you homesick?"

He shook his head. "No, I'm saying you're beautiful and you smell wonderful."

She stepped closer to him. "Thank you. So next spring when the flowers bloom, will you think of me?"

He pulled her next to him. "I think of you practically every minute of every day. I saw you for the first time walking along the beach in that pink bikini, and I haven't been able to get you out of my mind since."

"And I thought it was my table dance that turned you on," she said, giving him a bump with her hip.

He set his drink on the patio table and backed against the rail with her between his legs. His eyes studied every line and detail of her beautiful face before he leaned in and kissed the tip of her nose. "Ms. McKay, everything about you turns me on."

A few minutes later, in nothing but her red silk bikini panties and a pair of high-heeled red strap sandals, Alicia sat on the sofa looking up at Darius.

It was a crime a body like his ever had to be covered in clothes. His broad shoulders and muscular six-pack abs were slowly revealed as he shed his shirt. He threw it on the sofa, and his upper body muscles flexed in the process. Alicia's eyes roamed over his hairy chest down to his navel that peeked out as he unfastened his pants.

His pants slid down his legs revealing an enormous erection underneath his boxers. After kicking his pants aside, he lowered himself to one knee and ran both hands up her thighs. She trembled as a current radiated from his hands through her body.

She dropped her head back on the sofa forcing herself to breathe. Darius had found her ticklish spot. She tensed up and almost sprang from the sofa as his mouth came down on the silky fabric between her legs.

His head came up. "Are you okay?" he asked in a thick, hoarse voice.

She giggled. "Yeah, you just found my ticklish spot," she said, up on her toes squeezing her thighs.

"Where? Right here?" he asked, kissing the inside of her thigh.

Alicia closed her eyes and bit her lip in sheer agony, not wanting him to stop, but unable to stand it another moment. "Uh-huh," she responded, pushing her hands down on the sofa and pulling herself away from him.

He kissed her other thigh, and Alicia reached out for a nearby pillow to squeeze. Then in one quick movement he wrapped his arms around her knees and yanked her farther down the sofa. She looked up in time to see her red silk panties being worked down her legs.

Heart pounding, her fingers dug deeper into the pillow as her butt almost hung off the sofa. As she realized where he was headed, her legs began to quiver. But, to her surprise Darius reached down and lifted her leg onto his shoulder. She trembled as he planted scorching hot kisses from her knee to her ankle, stopping to unfasten her sandal and slip it off.

"You look hot in high heels you know that?" he said, in a voice so sexy all she could do was nod her head. He reached down for the other leg and repeated the same action, before lowering her feet to the floor.

Unable to speak a single word, she nodded.

Now completely naked and totally uninhibited she sat back while he shed his boxers. An overwhelming desire to reach out and stroke his manhood would have to wait.

"Relax," he murmured, while rubbing his scalding hot hands up and down her thighs. "This won't tickle," he said, winking at her.

"Sometimes a girl likes to be tickled, if you know what I mean." The sight of him kneeling between her legs aroused her to the point of drunkenness, and she hadn't had a drop of liquor all night. She licked her lips.

When he planted his lips at the epicenter of her existence,

she melted into the sofa like hot butter. She closed her eyes and clutched the pillow tighter as he tongued her ever so exquisitely.

She squirmed and wiggled as her needy body teetered on the edge of an orgasm. His arms clamped down tighter holding her to his mouth. Gasping for air, her head thrashed from side to side as she dug her nails into the pillow.

Then, Darius pulled away. Alicia took a deep breath and relaxed her muscles. He loosened her grip on the pillow and threw it on the floor. She looked up into his smoldering hungry eyes as he lowered her to the floor, and placed her head on the pillow.

"Where's your purse?" he asked, in a deep voice looking around the room.

She pointed behind him.

He grabbed it from the sofa and handed it to her. She opened it and pulled out a condom.

For the next hour, the only sounds in the apartment were their combined moans and cries of pleasure. Exhausted, she fell asleep in his arms, as they lay naked on the bed.

The next morning Darius woke to find Alicia sitting in his shirt, across the room looking out the window. Her hair was tousled all over the same way it was the first time he met her. With one leg tucked underneath her, she looked erotic as hell. He'd give anything to know what was on her mind at that very moment.

"Good morning," he said, sitting up against the headboard.

She turned to him and smiled. He felt his heart explode when he glimpsed his future in her eyes.

"Good morning sleepy head," she replied.

"How long have you been up?" he asked, wiping the sleep from his eyes.

She shrugged. "Not long. It's time for breakfast. Are you hungry?" she asked, getting up and coming over to the bed.

He threw the covers back inviting her back to bed. "I'm starving, and I'm looking at my breakfast."

She smiled and unbuttoned his shirt.

Sterling turned down the narrow road that once led to an active beach entrance used exclusively by blacks. He stopped and got out when the thick, overgrown vegetation wouldn't let him drive any farther. He leaned against his car drinking a beer when the black Infiniti pulled in behind him.

Mike Denton stepped out of the car. Carefully watching where he walked, he approached Sterling. "Drinking on the job?" he commented, pointing to the bottle in Sterling's hand.

"I'm on my lunch break," Sterling replied.

Mike snorted and shook his head. "What's so important you had to drag me down here?" he asked, frowning. He looked down at his shoes and wiped them on the back of his pants. Sterling hurled the bottle as far as he could into the woods. "I need a job," he said.

"You have a job," Mike retorted.

"Not for long."

"What happened?"

Sterling gave him a nonchalant shrug and stopped pacing. "The younger brother, Luke, he wants my job."

Mike lowered his arms and wiped a spot off to lean against Sterling's car. "He owns the hotel, and you expect me to believe he wants your job?"

"He's digging through old files and trying to come up with some way to fire me, I know he is."

"What's there for him to find?"

Sterling glanced at Mike a second before looking off into the woods and shaking his head. "Nothing, but I wouldn't be surprised if he didn't try to trump up something. I'm afraid he'll find the papers we tried to get old man Monroe to sign."

Mike pulled away from the car. "I thought you destroyed all those papers?"

"I did. Or, at least, I hope I did. You never know; there might be one floating around somewhere."

"Okay, you've got my attention. What do you really want? More money?"

Sterling laughed. "No, sir. What I want and need is a way to feed my family. I want a job in one of RCE's hotels, as general manager."

Mike sniffed and wiped his nose as he walked up to Sterling. "You listen to me," he said between clinched teeth. "I've given you over ten thousand dollars, and in twelve months you haven't gotten me one step closer to owning that property."

"The old man was about to sell wasn't he?" Sterling shot back.

"He's dead." Mike turned and headed back to his car.

"Hey, you need to help me out here. You wouldn't want anybody to find out I've been working for you."

The stubby little man stopped and turned around. Sterling had his attention now. "Just get me something with RCE. It doesn't have to be a general manager position, I'll take some other manager position."

Mike moved his fat little legs faster than Sterling had ever seen him do before and stood waving his fat finger in Sterling's face.

"You have no way of proving that I gave you a dime for anything. And look at you." He nastily roamed his eyes up and down Sterling. "Underneath that suit is a drunk who's not fit to work in any of my hotels. You can pretend you're the man at Hotel Paradise, but I know all about everything you've done at that hotel—everything." He turned and marched back to his car. When he spun around, dust and gravel shot back at Sterling.

He harked and spit on the ground as the car drive off.

Sterling stomped through the hotel lobby. He frowned at the guests, stalked right by his front desk staff, and then hurled himself through his office door. He slammed the door behind him. Beads of perspiration formed on his forehead as everything started slipping from his fingers.

His secretary burst in right behind him.

"Mr. Simpson, I need to talk to you."

"Not right now Mary." He searched his desk looking for a file.

"But, sir."

"I said, not right now!" he shouted.

She jumped back and took a minute to get her composure, then placed a hand on her hip. "Well, your mother called—twice."

He stopped fishing around his desk and looked up at the woman.

Wide-eyed, she started backing out. "She said it was important."

"Thank you. And please close the door."

He called his mother, and tried to keep the bitterness and rage from his voice as they spoke.

"You had no business talkin' to that girl about somethin' ain't yo' business," Ode said fiercely.

Sterling could hardly keep his mind on his mother. He had to devise a way to keep his job. "She asked for my help." He drummed his fingers against the desk.

"Well I never told ya' nuttun' about Venetta bein' pregnant. So where did you hear that?"

"I don't know, I must have heard it somewhere. I don't see what's the big deal?" He ruffled through the papers on his desk again.

"I don't want nobody walkin' round here lying on my baby sister. Now because of your lies, Alicia's gonna leave on Sunday."

He stood up. "This Sunday?"

"That's what she said. Now I hope she—"

"Mama, I gotta go. I'll stop by after work, but I've got something to do right now." He hung up, without giving her a chance to respond.

Alicia was leaving. And she just might be his last chance at getting a hold of some money. He had the information she needed, now was the time to see how much it was worth to her.

After packing one of her suitcases, Alicia moped around her suite. She hadn't initially intended to leave on Sunday, but since her aunt didn't seem to care, she might as well go on home. It was going to be hard to leave Darius, but harder to stay around knowing her family was intentionally keeping secrets from her.

She opened the door to put her overflowing garbage can outside. Standing on the other side of the door was Sterling.

After a few seconds, he asked her if he could come in because he had some news for her and it would be best if she was sitting down.

Alicia thought she detected beer on his breath. Her stomach knotted as she lowered herself on the sofa next to him.

He took a deep breath. "I heard you were leaving Sunday, but you might want to give it a second thought after what I have to tell you."

Chapter 23

The hairs on the back of Alicia's neck stirred. She crossed her legs to keep her knees from quaking. The serious expression on Sterling's face scared the hell out of her.

A spastic smile framed her mouth as she tilted her head up to him.

"I talked to a woman who used to be Dr. York Bailey's nurse in St. Helena."

Alicia nodded impatiently.

"He was the only doctor on the island, and your mother went to him when she was pregnant."

A sparkle of hope shot through Alicia as she sprang from the sofa. Crossing her arms, she walked over and looked out the window. "You already told me she was pregnant when she left."

He walked over and stood next to her. "Yeah, but this woman knew who the father was," he lied.

Biting her bottom lip, Alicia stared up at him. Her world

started spinning as the bottom fell out of her stomach. He was right; she needed to sit down. She walked back over to the sofa and tucked her foot underneath her.

Sterling stood in the middle of the room. She was scared for him to keep talking and scared for him to shut up. This is what her father couldn't tell her when he was living, but wanted her to know after his death.

"You already know she was working here at the hotel at that time. And…well quite a few young men worked here too. Uh, including Willie Monroe's sons."

Her stomach tightened. "Are you saying one of Willie Monroe's sons is my father?"

He looked at her for a few minutes before turning to look out the window again. "She said they were in love and your mother couldn't tell her mother or anyone else."

"Which son?"

He didn't answer.

"Sterling," she called his name between trembling lips. He crossed his arms and turned slowly, his face pinched. A sickening wave of fear welled inside of her.

"Alicia, she's an old woman, her memory may not be what it used to be," he reasoned. He came away from the window and returned to the sofa. "I know you're fond of Darius and everything, that's why I felt I had to tell you right away. Before…well, you know."

Oh God, did she know! The desire to hurl Sterling, herself, or anything off her second-floor balcony consumed her. Flabbergasted, she didn't know how to respond. Her body went numb. He was trying to tell her that Charlie Monroe was her real father. Darius's father!

Sterling got up and paced around the room talking about something. She saw his mouth moving, but didn't hear a single word. Darius had told her about his father falling in love when he was younger and working here at the hotel, and his father would have been much older than her mother. Is that why her aunt said she never liked her mother working at the hotel?

Alicia stumbled up from the sofa. "Sterling, would you please leave?" she asked, hoping to make it to the bathroom before the bile rising in her throat escaped.

"But we need to talk," he said, following her. "I mean, before you say anything to Darius, I think we should talk."

"I can't talk to you right now." With a hand held over her mouth, she slammed the bathroom door, raised the toilet seat, and retched until her eyes crossed.

A few minutes later, a soft tap at the bathroom door startled her. She thought Sterling was gone.

"Alicia, are you all right?" he whispered.

"Thank you Sterling, but I need to be alone right now."

"I understand. I didn't mean to upset you. Maybe we can discuss it when you feel better."

"Sure," she managed to say, knowing she had no intentions of discussing this with him any further.

A couple of seconds later, she heard the door close.

Alicia spent the next hour in the shower, crying, screaming, and scrubbing everywhere Darius had touched. The love they'd made, and the things he'd done to her were so special, she couldn't conceive it had been wrong.

She climbed out of the shower and wrapped her wet body in her robe and fell across the bed. Huddled into a fetal position she lay there staring at the television and listening to the phone ring. She couldn't answer it. If Darius called she didn't know what to say to him. *Guess what? I'm your sister.* Thinking of it sickened her.

A little while later, with a clearer head, she pulled her

mother's journal from her suitcase. When she first received the journals, the pages confused and saddened her, but lately she'd found peace on the pages. She had a better understanding now of whom her mother was when she wrote the journal. After reading several pages she realized something. Her aunt may not have known her mother had such strong feelings for her lover. If she had, maybe she would have told Alicia anything she knew. Ode needed to read the journal to understand the depth of their love.

Exhausted, Alicia buried herself under the covers, and made up her mind to show her aunt the journal tomorrow. She needed concrete proof that Charlie Monroe was her father.

Unable to face what she'd possibly done, Alicia packed up her other bag and called a bellhop. She informed the front desk that she was checking out.

Right now, she wasn't able to face Darius, but she didn't want to go back to Atlanta without explaining her actions to him. So, she called a hotel in Brunswick and made reservations there.

She could hear the commotion from the front porch. Alicia stood there clutching her journal as Juanita opened the front door. The look on her face was a mix of surprise and happiness.

"Hey girl, come on in." She stepped back and opened the door. "Mama said you were leaving Sunday?"

Alicia's nerves were shattered, but she tried to smile. "I may stay an additional day, but after that it's time for me to go home."

"I hope it wasn't anything I said?" Juanita asked with a hand over her chest.

"No, it's just about that time. I hadn't intended to stay any longer than a month." The usual cast of little people ran from room to room. They giggled, screamed, and cried at the top of their lungs.

"Well come on in. I'm gonna hate to see you go. We were just getting to know one another. Mama's back in the kitchen as usual."

Alicia followed Juanita into the kitchen, rehearsing over and over again how she wanted to present the journal to her aunt.

In the kitchen, the sisters helped their mother prepare what looked like a feast. One pie was already on the table. Next to it was a large bowl of fried chicken, and Ruth Ann was putting the lid on a container of potato salad. They stood around the kitchen and chitchatted for several minutes.

Ode wouldn't look at Alicia for more than a few seconds. She had a feeling her aunt knew what Sterling had told her. A few minutes later, the sisters left them alone. Alicia knew this was the do-or-die moment for her.

"Aunt Ode, I came by to show you something." She picked up the journal she'd placed out of the way when she entered the kitchen.

Ode looked at Alicia with such intensity, she knew the old woman knew something was up.

"Sure honey," she murmured, without stepping away from the stove.

Alicia gripped the edges of the journal afraid to let go. However, she was positive this was the right thing to do. "I know you never liked the fact that my mother worked at Hotel Paradise, and I think I know why."

The chill in the look Ode gave Alicia made her skin crawl. Sterling had been right.

"She was too young, that's all."

"I think she was involved with a young man over there that maybe people didn't approve of, and I think that man was Charlie Monroe."

"That boy don't know what he talkin' 'bout."

Alicia continued when she didn't get the emotional response from her aunt she wanted. "My father gave me a set of journals a few weeks before he passed. I didn't sit down to read them until he was gone. By then it was too late to question him about anything I read. So, I came down here for clarification. This is one of my mother's journals." She held the book up and saw fear in her aunt's eyes as she looked at it. "She started it when she worked at Hotel Paradise," Alicia concluded, holding the journal out to her. "I want you to read it."

Ode's face glazed with shock, and her wide eyes moistened with tears as she reached out for the journal.

"I believe my father wanted me to know who my biological father was; that's why he passed the journals on to me. So you see, I won't be satisfied until I learn the truth."

Ode slowly opened the book. A tear slid down her cheek as she glanced at the first page.

Darius stammered with rage through his meeting with Timothy and Luke. It was only early this morning that he'd finally found time to finish the file Luke gave him about the Golden Isle Sons.

The muscles in his jaw twitched as he stared sharply across the room feeling like a fool.

Timothy shook his head. "I knew something wasn't right, that's why I brought it up. But I had no idea he had gone that far."

Luke reared back in his seat looking confident and vindicated. "I never trusted the man. I won't be surprised if you uncover more than that after the audit."

"I can't believe he smiled in my face everyday knowing he was stealing from us." Actually, Darius could believe it.

Things like that happened everyday in Chicago, but he'd come to this small island with blinders on.

The door opened and Kamora poked her head in. "Sir, Mr. Simpson isn't home, so I left a message with his wife."

"What did you tell her?"

"That you called a mandatory emergency managers' meeting and he needed to reschedule his afternoon off. Just like you told me to, sir."

"Thank you, Kamora."

The young woman smiled and closed the door. Darius noticed a flicker of apprehension on Timothy's face and had second thoughts about including him in the proceedings. After all, turning in your boss for theft wasn't an easy thing to do.

"So how are you going to handle this?" Luke asked.

Darius clasped his hands together and stretched them out on his desk. "I'm going to give the man a chance to admit it first. If he doesn't, then I'll be forced to fire him. I've got all the proof I need."

An hour later, Darius stood in the lobby with Luke and Timothy when Sterling walked in. Fear registered in his eyes the moment they made eye contact.

"Hey, where's everybody else?" he asked, his eyes eagerly studying their faces.

"Change of plans," Darius said.

He saw Sterling's jaw drop and the realization flash across his face that he'd been had.

"Let's step into my office." Darius held out a hand as all three men preceded him.

The more Darius thought about how his grandfather trusted this young man and gave him total access to everything at the hotel, only to have that generosity thrown in his face, the more infuriated Darius became.

Luke and Timothy stood back and let Sterling sit down first. In doing so, that forced him to face Darius, unable to walk or turn away. Darius came in and closed the door behind him.

"Sterling, I think you know why you're here." Darius took his seat. He placed his hands on the gold envelope containing the evidence.

Looking at the envelope, Sterling pushed his glasses up on his nose then glanced over at Timothy. "I'm afraid I don't know what you're talking about," he responded.

"I think you do. And this meeting is your chance to explain yourself." Darius opened the envelope and pulled out the contract, handing it to Sterling.

After examining the contract, Sterling looked across the room at Luke. "This isn't the copy I gave you."

"No, it isn't. That's the copy I got directly from the band. The one you lost. That's what their monthly payment is based on. I think you'll see the discrepancy."

"Sterling, I need you to tell me what happened," Darius requested.

The contract came sailing across Darius's desk as Sterling stood up. "We never enforced that contract, it's old. The contract I gave you was a good one." He turned and pointed at Luke. "You did this. You want my job? You've been after me ever since you got here."

"This isn't about Luke. It's about you and your stealing from the hotel," Darius shouted.

Sterling whirled on Timothy, and Darius thought the little guy would pee his pants.

"You started this didn't you?"

Innocent eyes and all, Timothy held his hands up in a helpless gesture.

"Could you guys leave us alone a moment?" Darius asked

Luke and Timothy. They walked out, and Sterling returned to his seat.

"Darius, your brother doesn't like me, that's no secret. But, I'd never steal from this hotel."

"We've already uncovered the split payments. How you thought you could keep this from everybody I'll never know." Darius leaned into his desk and pleaded with Sterling. "I need you to tell me what happened. Why did you do this?"

The expression on Sterling's face changed and he puffed out his chest. "You can't prove anything."

"Sterling, I have enough to press charges."

Shaking his head, Sterling leaned back in his seat staring at Darius. "I haven't done anything wrong. I'm the general manager of this hotel. For all I do, I deserve a few perks, old man Monroe would have approved."

"Consider yourself unemployed," Darius said, coming to his feet.

Sterling bolted from his seat.

"You can't fire me. Nobody knows more than I do about this place. What are you going to do—promote Timothy?" he said with a sneer. "He's afraid of his own shadow." Sterling laughed. "You see, Darius, you can't run this hotel without me. Try, and you'll find yourself so short-staffed you'll have to shut down."

"Is that a threat?"

"No, it's a promise."

"Sterling, clean out your desk. I want you off my property in fifteen minutes. You're fired."

Chapter 24

After the security guard escorted Sterling outside, Luke walked back inside and found Darius standing at the front desk talking to Kamora. "Are you sure, suite forty-two?" Daruis asked.

"I'm positive, sir," she replied.

"Did she say where she was going?"

Kamora shook her head.

"Sterling's gone," Luke confirmed.

"So is Alicia," Darius said, turning around to face his brother.

"What do you mean? She checked out?"

"Yeah." Darius flipped open his cell phone and called hers. His frustration in all the latest developments, coupled with the fact that he couldn't reach her, caused his head to ache.

Until this morning, he hadn't spoken to Luke since he stormed out of his office the other day. He'd wanted to thank him and apologize for everything he'd said, but he hadn't figured out how to say it.

Luke kicked around a white wicker chair next to him and plopped down into it. "I tried to tell you something was up with them. I bet he had something to do with that kitchen fire. He probably had her keep you away from the hotel long enough for him to set it up."

Darius wasn't having any better luck with Alicia's cell phone. She wouldn't answer. He clipped the phone back to his belt and looked down at his brother. "You're wrong about her."

Luke stood up. "Yeah, well, we'll see won't we? I need to take a ride. Got something I need to check on." Then he turned and gave Darius a nod. "Unless you had something else around here you needed my help with?"

Darius shook his head, and then Luke walked out the front door.

The front desk was abuzz. Not with guests checking in, but with employees asking Kamora about Sterling. News traveled fast in a small hotel. Darius headed back to his office.

He dialed Alicia's cell phone once again, but still received her voice mail. He didn't believe for one minute what Luke had said about her conspiring with Sterling. But, she had spent a lot of time with Sterling's mother. He picked up the phone and called the front desk.

"Front desk," Kamora answered.

"Kamora, do we have Sterling's mother's phone number?"

"No, sir. But I have his home number. Did you need me to ring his wife again?"

"No, I need his mother's number. Can you get it for me?"

"Uh, yes, sir. His secretary's not in today, but I'm sure it's somewhere in the files. I'll look for it and bring it right in."

"Thank you." Darius hung up and made a mental note to promote her as soon as he could. She worked the front desk, played secretary, assistant, operator, or whatever else he needed her to do, and Darius appreciated it.

He pored over the employee manual working out how to handle the situation with Sterling when Kamora called back with the number.

Darius thanked her, and sat there staring at the phone wondering what to do if she wasn't there. What if she'd checked out and flown back to Atlanta?

He snatched up the phone and dialed the number. A young woman answered the phone on the third ring and he asked to speak to Mrs. Simpson.

"She isn't available at the moment, may I help you?"

"Yes, I'm looking for her niece, Alicia McKay. Have you seen her?"

"Who am I speaking with?"

"My name's Darius Monroe."

"Oh, from Hotel Paradise?"

"Yes." He hoped she wouldn't bring up Sterling's name. He didn't want to discuss him.

"This is Ruth Ann, her cousin. And no, Alicia's not here, though she was earlier. She's going back to Atlanta on Monday."

Jolted by her words, Darius asked her to repeat what she'd said, and then tried to swallow the lump in his throat.

"Where is she now, do you know?" he asked.

"If she's not there at the hotel, I don't know."

He ended the conversation in a state of utter panic. He couldn't let Alicia leave; he had to find her. What in the hell had transpired after she left him the other day other than Sterling being fired?

When the sun set, the underbelly of the city came out. Sterling climbed down from his bar stool and walked in the back to a pay phone. He'd been stopping at Our Place, a

locals' bar, every night after work for at least one drink.
Tonight he'd called Catherine and told her he'd be later than
usual since he was out with a few folks from work. He
couldn't tell her yet that he'd been fired. All hell was going
to break loose once she found out. What about his children?
How was he going to feed them and keep a roof over their
heads? Most of the hotels on the island were owned by RCE.
The ones that weren't required college degrees and had never
had an African American general manager before; and
Sterling didn't think they ever would.

He finished his beer and slapped the mug on the bar.
Without being prompted, the bartender swiftly replaced it with
a fresh beer. After glancing at his watch, it was time to move
to a table. He picked up his fresh mug and found an empty
booth. He set his beer down with a trembling hand. What he
was about to do he couldn't tell anyone. He clasped his hands
together to keep them from trembling and closed his eyes.

His eyes sprang open when the table moved. Sitting across
from him in a black T-shirt, a baseball cap turned backwards,
with a thick silver chain around his neck, was Coco. This
reformed criminal was now in the make-a-wish business.

"Sup," Coco said with a quick nod.

"I hear you can help me out."

"Correct-a-mundo."

"You already know what I want?" Sterling asked, peering
around the bar to make sure no one had taken a special
interest in them.

"Yep."

Sterling had never needed Coco's services before, but he
came highly recommended by some well-respected business
owners. If you needed some money, buy a building, hire
Coco, and make a wish.

"Then I guess the only thing left is to pay you?" Sterling

reached into his pocket. "Half the money up front, and the other half when the job's done, right?"

A young waitress approached and set a tray on the table. "I'll take that, sir," she said.

Sterling looked up at the blonde he'd never seen in the bar before, and then over at Coco. He nodded his head toward the tray, where Sterling placed a white envelope. The waitress strutted away and Coco stood up.

"How will I know when the job's done?" Sterling asked.

"When I send for the second half," Coco replied and walked away.

If the Monroe brothers thought they could steal that hotel away from him, they had better think again.

Tracy heard the front door slam and knew to make herself invisible. She hated when she stayed at her uncle Sterling's house and he came home drunk. Her aunt Catherine always argued with him, and she could hear everything.

Her cousins Sandra and Donna jumped up. "Come on, let's go to our room," Sandra said. Everyone knew what was coming.

Once inside the bedroom with the door closed Tracy heard her aunt Catherine shout, "You're drunk." It had begun. She tried not to listen to the fight, but there was no television or radio in the bedroom. All they could do was sit and listen. Before long, her uncle Sterling would come in and check on them, like he always did.

Tonight, when the shouting ended no one came into the room. The girls fell asleep, but Tracy had to use the bathroom. She was scared because she had to pass her aunt and uncle's bedroom, and she didn't want to hear them fighting again. But, she didn't want to wet herself either.

She crept down the hall to the bathroom. The house was quiet. After using the bathroom, instead of going to bed, she wanted a glass of water. She tiptoed down the steps, but heard her uncle's voice before she reached the bottom. She stopped. Her heart beat faster as she turned around and tried to tiptoe back upstairs.

"I'll burn that piece of crap down. They don't know who they're messing with. I'm the one who's kept that hotel open for the last five years."

She froze as she heard him yell into the phone. She sat down and listened to everything he said before she ran back upstairs and climbed into bed. He was going to set Hotel Paradise on fire.

A few minutes later the bedroom door opened. Tracy held her breath praying her uncle didn't know she was downstairs listening. He tucked the girls in and kissed them on the forehead. When the door closed, she sprang up in bed. What was she going to do? She had to tell somebody; her cousin Alicia was at the hotel.

"How did you know I was here?" Alicia asked, surprised that Sterling had found her. She hadn't told anyone where she was staying.

"May I come in?" he asked.

She stood back, letting him in.

"I heard you checked out, and I was afraid you were leaving today."

"In light of what you told me, I cancelled my flight. But, how did you know I was in this hotel?" she insisted.

He forced a stiff smile. "I've got friends in almost every hotel around here."

"Oh," she uttered. She should have figured that out. She closed the door and walked over to sit on the edge of the bed.

Sterling walked over and looked out the window. "Nice view."

Downtown Brunswick didn't compare to an ocean view, and she knew he was fully aware of that. "Sterling, I'm not going back to Hotel Paradise if that's why you're here," she stated.

He shook his head and turned around. "That's not why I'm here." He walked over to the desk and pulled out the chair to sit down. Slowly, he lowered his glasses and wiped the lenses with the edge of his T-shirt. "Darius fired me yesterday."

"What!"

"Yep. He called me in for a phony meeting and fired me. He's one heartless, cold, son-of-a—"

"Did he say why?" she cut him off. She didn't want to hear him bash Darius, no matter what had transpired between them.

"Luke pulled out some old contract and tried to say I'd been stealing from the hotel. But, it's all a lie. I'll get me a lawyer and fight it. When I finish with them, I'll own that hotel."

"Well, you told him it wasn't true didn't you?"

"Of course, but who do you think he listened to, me or his brother? Luke's had it out for me ever since he arrived, I told you that."

"I can't believe it. You've been working there for so long."

He stood up and returned to the window. "Neither can I. I'm still in shock. But I need to find the money for a lawyer. I can fight this, I know I can."

Alicia felt her heart sink. He was going to ask her for the money to fight Darius.

Sterling turned from the window to face her. "I know an excellent lawyer, but he's not cheap."

After swallowing the large lump in her throat, she shook her head. "Sterling, I don't know," she began.

"Alicia, you're the only one I know with the money to help

me. I wouldn't ask if I wasn't certain I could win. I just want to clear my name so I can get a job at another hotel. Without that, I can't feed my family."

She closed her eyes to his pleading look. Money wasn't the issue. She couldn't believe Darius would fire him without concrete proof he'd done something wrong. But then again, she couldn't believe Sterling would steal from the hotel either.

"How much do you think you'll need?" she asked, to see what he'd say.

"Ten thousand."

She blinked in surprise repeating the amount. "Why so much?"

"Lawyers aren't cheap, and I'm sure Darius will fight me. If you're worried about him finding out, don't be. I won't mention to anyone where I got the money. Nobody has to know. Not even the family."

Alicia had trouble believing all of this was happening. She climbed off the bed and grabbed a cup from the desk. She walked into the bathroom and filled it with water. "Sterling, you're going to have to let me think about this." She walked out and found him sitting down wringing his hands. "I mean in the last two days you've given me a hell of a lot to think about." Too much, she thought, for somebody who had such a hard time making decisions.

He let out a nervous laugh. "I know, I'm sorry. You're my cousin, and I was just trying to protect you. I'd hate to see you get hurt." Then he cleared his throat. "How fast can you get me the money?"

She looked into his peering bloodshot eyes and wondered if he wasn't on something other than alcohol.

Chapter 25

In the twenty-four hours since Darius fired Sterling, Luke had taken over the refurbishing efforts and discovered critical supplies hadn't been ordered. Darius made two bill adjustments because guests were dissatisfied when their room complaints weren't answered promptly. And to top things off, one of the two front desk computers had crashed.

The young man who worked the front desk on Saturdays was so slow, Darius would have fired him on the spot if he hadn't already been short-handed.

Then, like a ray of light, Timothy came waltzing through the lobby.

Darius couldn't contain the smile on his face. Saturday was Timothy's day off and Darius couldn't bring himself to call him in since Timothy had been working so hard.

"I figured you could use some help," Timothy said as he approached the front desk.

"If I were a woman, I'd kiss you," Darius said coming from behind the counter.

"I'll settle for a thank you. Heard anything from Sterling?"

"No, should I expect to?"

"I don't see him taking this lying down."

They stood alongside the front desk discussing Sterling, as Luke walked up.

"Last night I talked to some people over at Our Place, a local bar in Brunswick, and found out Sterling's been hanging around drinking pretty heavily. I suggest we put some extra security around the place for a couple of days," Luke suggested.

"Maybe call the police," Timothy said.

Darius shook his head. "The police aren't going to come out if he hasn't done anything. Let's give it a day or two and see if anybody sees him lurking around. Timothy, can you notify the staff to let a manager know the minute anybody sees him?"

"Yeah, I'll run do that right now as a matter-of-fact." Timothy hurried off.

Darius was standing out front with a silver tray full of chilled mimosas as a large group checked in when Rodell pulled up in the hotel van with two more guests inside. After he helped them inside, he walked over to join Darius and Luke.

"Darius, can I speak to you a minute?" He jingled the keys in his pocket.

Darius handed his tray to Luke. "Sure Rodell, how's everything going?"

"Fine, sir." He nodded at Luke who picked up a conversation with another bellhop.

"Uh, remember you asked me to keep an eye on Ms. McKay for you?"

Darius nodded with interest. "Yeah."

"Well, yesterday afternoon I had to go down by the dock

for a pickup when I passed The Clarion and noticed her getting out of the car and taking her luggage in."

A sudden spurt of adrenaline coursed through Darius as he reached out and grasped Rodell's shoulder. "Are you sure it was her?"

Rodell smiled. "I'm positive, sir."

Luke stepped back over. "I can handle things around here. I'm sure you want to go talk to her," he said.

Darius turned around half expecting a cocky grin from his brother, but Luke fooled him.

He tilted his head. "Get on out of here. I'll call you if I need you."

"I thought you didn't trust her?" Darius asked.

"I didn't trust her cousin. I told you he was a thief."

"Sterling?" Rodell questioned.

Luke put his arm around the young man's shoulder. "Rodell, let me fill you in on what's been going on around here."

They walked off and Darius went back to his office for his car keys.

The persistent knocking at Alicia's door was nerve-wracking. She rolled over on her other side and held the pillow to her head. It had to be Sterling coming back; no one else knew where she was. She figured if she didn't say anything he would just go away. But, he didn't.

Finally, unable to stand it a minute longer, she sprang from the bed and walked over to peek out the peephole. It was Darius. How in the world had he found her? Obviously, he wasn't going away so she opened the door.

"Hello, I was in the neighborhood so I thought I'd stop by and find out why you deserted me."

She lowered her head, holding on to the doorknob. God, how could she tell him until she was positive?

"Mind if I come in?" he asked.

"How did you find me?"

"I've got eyes all over this town. Now the front desk clerk thinks you're my wife."

"Darius, I can't talk to you right now." She tried to close the door, but he stuck his foot in.

"Alicia." He reached out to touch her face, but she pulled back.

"I'm not leaving, so you might as well let me in. I don't think you really want to close my foot in this door."

She sighed and stepped back. He walked in and closed the door behind him. He was upset. She could see the tension in his stiff body as he entered the room.

"So, what's up? Why did you check out and come over here? I've been looking all over the place for you. Is your aunt okay?"

"She's fine. I just needed some time to think. Things were moving way too fast. I needed some space." She felt horrible for the things she had to say, but she had to find a way to get rid of him. She pulled her hair up off her neck and walked around him.

"That's why you left the hotel? Come on, I'm not buying that. If that's how you felt, you could have just told me."

"Darius, we kind of fell into each other, but we never should have."

He stepped back. "Bull! Don't give me that. So what's with this fuck-him-for-a-few-days-until-I-feel-all-better-and-then-disappear attitude?" He turned around and walked over to her open suitcase.

"Where is it?" he asked, pulling clothes out and tossing them on the bed.

"What are you doing?" she ran over to the bed grabbing her things. He was throwing her clothes around like a madman.

"Where's your journal?" he asked, with his nostrils flaring.

"My journal?" She stopped catching clothes.

"Yeah." He slowed down. "The red journal I saw in your bathroom the night you threw up on me. I read where you wanted to kill yourself at Hotel Paradise. Don't you know every time I called your cell phone and you didn't answer I freaked?"

She eased down on the bed and stared up at him. "You read my journal?"

He made half an effort to look under one more stack of clothes, before stopping. He sighed. "I didn't mean to, it was sitting open in the bathroom. I sort of read one page, that's all."

"And after reading one page you thought *I* wanted to kill myself?"

His shoulders relaxed along with the lines in his forehead. "What else was I supposed to think?"

She threw her clothes back in the suitcase. "For starters, you could have asked if the journal was mine. Is that why you asked me out, you thought I was going to commit suicide?"

He shifted his weight from one leg to the other and scratched his nose with his thumb. "If it's not your journal, then whose is it?"

"It belonged to my mother. It's the reason I came down here."

He pushed her suitcase aside and sat on the edge of the bed. "I thought you came to meet your family?"

"I did and to find my real father."

Darius's brows shot up.

Alicia spent the next half hour explaining the purpose of her trip and what she'd found out so far. Everything except what Sterling had told her. She wasn't ready to mention that just yet.

"Why didn't you tell me any of this before?" he asked.

She shrugged. "I don't know, it just didn't seem important where we were concerned."

He looked at her sharply. "And why is that?" When she

didn't respond, he answered for her. "Because *we* aren't important? To you, I'm just an extended one-night stand?"

"That's not true." She shook her head, but somewhere in the back of her mind she knew he was right. All she'd wanted was a summer fling. She had seduced him just like Rorie had suggested, but she hadn't been prepared to fall in love with him.

He stood up. "I called your aunt and your cousin told me you're leaving Monday. I can't believe how you came stumbling into my life, but now you want to sneak out like we never met. Were you even going to say good-bye, or were you just going to leave and hope to never run into me again?"

Afraid of what irrevocable damage she'd done to them both, she averted her eyes, not wanting to give away how bad she felt. How should you tell the man you've had the best sex of your life with that he is your brother? The thought of it made her sick. Her insides were churning she was so heartbroken.

He walked around to her side of the bed and reached out for her.

"I know who my father is," she announced before he could touch her.

He stopped within inches of her face. "Who?"

"Charlie Monroe," she revealed, paralyzed with fear.

He let out a resounding, "What!" before pulling his hand back. "Is that supposed to be some type of a joke?"

She bent over as her eyes filled with tears. He stood in the middle of the room with his hands braced against his hips. Then he came over and consoled her as she sobbed openly.

"Come on now, you don't believe that do you?" He rubbed his hand over her back. "Alicia, believe me, we don't have the same father. Who told you that anyway?"

Her sobbing dissolved into sniffles as she found her voice. "Sterling. He found a nurse who worked in the doctor's office when my mother was pregnant. She told him."

"Alicia, Sterling is a liar and a thief."

She jumped up and went into the bathroom for a tissue. "I expected you to say that. He told me you fired him."

"I had to. He gave me no choice."

She blew her nose and poked her head out of the bathroom. "Because your brother said he stole something? Come on Darius, Sterling isn't a thief."

"I have the proof. He's stolen over fourteen thousand dollars. We're running an audit now to see what else we find. So if he's stealing from me, what makes you think he's telling you the truth?"

"He's my cousin. He wouldn't lie to me about something like that."

"Alicia, how can I prove it? Can't we go take a DNA test or something?"

"I don't know. I gave the journal to my aunt. I'm positive she knows who my real father is, but for some reason she won't tell me. I'm hoping after she reads the journal, she'll change her mind."

She stood in the bathroom doorway while Darius sat on the bed. The room was dead silent. All she could think about were the things they'd done to one another in the heat of passion. She didn't know why she hadn't considered it before, but on an island so small the chances of their parents hooking up were pretty good.

"And what if your aunt really doesn't know?" Darius asked, finally breaking the silence.

"Then I'll find somebody else who does."

Alicia followed the directions given to her at the hotel and found Shiloh Baptist Church. She sat in the car gripping the steering wheel as all the Sunday afternoon revival-goers crossed the parking lot.

She had butterflies in her stomach. Maybe she should wait back at the house for her aunt. All she wanted was the journal back.

Who was she kidding? She wanted more than her journal back. She needed confirmation from her aunt's lips that Charlie Monroe was her father. She let go of the steering wheel and pulled down the sun visor to check her makeup in the mirror. She was going into that church, and she was going to look her aunt square in the eyes. If Ode was truly a Christian, she wouldn't lie in church.

By the time Alicia talked herself out of the car and into church, it was crowded. The usher tried to sit her in the back, but she shook her head and pointed toward the front. The usher obliged and found her a seat in the second row, directly across from the pulpit.

When the young-adult choir came out, Tracy stood in the front row. They exchanged a wave and a smile. Alicia had missed her new buddy.

Throughout the service Alicia glimpsed several other family members, but not her aunt. Finally, the preacher asked Sister Ode Simpson to come share a word with the church.

Suddenly, their eyes met and Alicia detected a hint of sadness from her aunt. As Ode addressed the congregation, Alicia realized she'd read the journal. She wiped at eyes moist with tears, and then left the pulpit.

After the service Tracy ran up the aisle toward Alicia.

"Hey girl, I didn't know you could sing like that," Alicia teased her.

Tracy blushed and shrugged. "Cousin Alicia, I need to tell you something, but I don't want nobody to hear me."

Alicia looked around. "Okay, let's go outside. I've got some chewing gum in my car."

They walked outside. "When I stayed with Aunt Catherine last night, I heard Uncle Sterling talking on the phone to somebody about the hotel where you stayin'."

Alicia smiled. Tracy probably heard him telling someone he was fired. "Yeah, he likes that hotel doesn't he?" She started feeling sorry for the guy.

Tracy shrugged. "He said he was gonna make a wish that the hotel burned down," Tracy added.

Alicia's eyed widened. "Do you know who he was talking to?"

She shook her head. "He was in the kitchen on the phone when everybody else was upstairs asleep. I was gonna get some water, but he was in the kitchen drunk, so I went back upstairs."

"Smart girl. Well, thanks for telling me. I'll make sure he doesn't do anything like that," she assured her, as they returned inside. Tracy ran off to eat with some of her friends, while Alicia fixed herself a plate and joined her cousins. The sight and smells of the food made her forget all about Sterling for a few minutes.

After a feast in the basement of the church, Ode came over and sat next to Alicia.

"Did ya' enjoy the revival?" she asked.

"I did," Alicia said warmly.

"So did I." Ode looked up reflectively. She reached a wrinkled, arthritic hand over and held it against Alicia's back. "When ya' finish ya' ice cream we need to talk."

Alicia looked into her aunt's elderly face with its sagging jowls, but flawless, creamy coco complexion and knew she was about to tell her everything. She set her bowl down. "I'm finished."

Chapter 26

Ode pulled the journal from a large bag she'd used to bring food into the church. Alicia joined her on the back pew of the sanctuary.

"My mother read the Bible every morning when she woke up," Ode began. "Even before we went to school we had to read the Bible. Lemme tell ya', wasn't nuttun' gonna keep Nancy Simpson from raising her girls to be Bible-fearing good mothers and wives." Ode dabbed at her eyes with a tissue.

Alicia squeezed her hand and pleaded into Ode's bleak eyes, encouraging her to continue. Her own eyes were moist with tears from this breakthrough.

"Back in those days girls and boys didn't date like they do now," she laughed. "My grandsons come around with a different girlfriend every week, I don't see how they keep up." She paused and ran her open hand across the journal.

"Once I graduated from high school, I married Fred and

moved to Bluffton. Two years later, Venetta graduated and started workin' at Hotel Paradise with some friends. Mama and Papa didn't want her to move, but they couldn't stop her.

"She wrote me almost every week though. She'd met a man and fallen in love. For a long time she wouldn't tell me his name. All I knew was that he worked in the hotel with her and she wanted to marry him."

Ode wiped her eyes again and looked up at Alicia as if she were begging to be forgiven. "But she couldn't, because he was already married with his own family. Venetta kept their love affair a secret. I suppose that's why his name ain't in this book. If somebody had found it and said somethin', they could have lost their jobs."

"So, she wasn't in love with Charlie Monroe?" Alicia clarified, squeezing her aunt's hand a little harder now.

"Oh, I imagine every girl from up home that worked there was in love with him. Willie Monroe had two handsome sons. Charlie was the best lookin' and flirted with all the girls. But, yo' mother said her man was as black as the night. His nickname was Coffee, and he had curly black hair, and a quiet way about himself. She said he was a real gentleman, not no boy."

More tears welled in Alicia's eyes when she remembered that Mr. Billy in St. Helena called her father Coffee.

"They carried on for over a year," Ode continued. "I told her to be careful, but she came up pregnant. After a couple of months, she had no choice but to come home. She couldn't let old man Monroe see she was pregnant, he'd fire her for sure."

"What did her parents say?"

"You see, Mama was on the board at church and Papa was a dike. That's what we called a deacon back home. Well, they couldn't let their unwed, pregnant daughter come to church with them every Sunday, so they sent her to New York to live."

"With whom?"

"I don't remember. Papa knew a lot of people in the community, and around that time folks was leavin' the island in droves. Lots of them became Yankees and moved up north."

"Did she ever see my father again?"

"Before she left, he came up to St. Helena to visit once or twice. He'd go by to see her, but Papa would run him off. He must ah' been ten years older than ya' mama. I don't know if she ever told him about you. But, I can't imagine he didn't have an idea. She left for New York and I missed her so much. By then, I had two babies of my own and a husband to take care of."

"Ya' mama was introduced to Steven McKay right after she arrived in New York. She said he fell in love with her pregnant and all. That's why, when you came along, he put his name on the birth certificate. He wanted to be ya' daddy."

"Wow, now I know why his family was so distant toward me. After my mother died, we went to live with my aunt Vivian in California for about a year. I don't talk about that experience because everyone was cold and distant toward me, even my grandmother. Then we moved to Atlanta and things were better. My father and I bonded I guess."

"And you say he gave you this journal?"

"Yes, ma'am. There's two of them, but that one—" she pointed to the journal in her aunt's lap "—she started when she worked at Hotel Paradise. I wanted you to read it so you'd understand why it's important for me to find out what my father wanted me to know."

"He loved ya' so much he couldn't tell ya' he wasn't yo' real father. Not after what he'd done. He probably figured it would be too shockin' for ya'."

Alicia laughed. "There were times I wondered. He practically left me on my own to grow up, and at times I thought maybe he didn't want me. But, I guess being a single father and building a business at the same time wasn't easy. I know he loved me."

Ode reached over and stroked her hair. "Ya' father was a good man."

Alicia lowered her head and the floodgates opened. She cried because the man she'd called Daddy all her life wasn't her biological father. And, she cried because he'd raised her as if she carried his genes, even after her mother died at such a young age. He could have sent her to St. Helena to her grandmother, but he didn't. Until now, she hadn't realized how truly blessed she'd been.

Ode held Alicia until she stopped crying. "Thank you. I know it wasn't easy for you to tell me all this, but I truly appreciate it."

Through sniffles her aunt said, "My mother was a very proud woman. She never told anyone at the church or anywhere else that Venetta left because she was pregnant, and she swore me to the same vow of secrecy. I'm so sorry."

Ode hugged Alicia again and shed a few of her own tears. After a few minutes, she pulled back and held Alicia's head up.

"Do ya' want to meet yo' daddy?" she asked Alicia.

Alicia squeezed Tracy's hand as they stood on the porch of Alicia's father's house. *Her father's house.* Those familiar words took on a new meaning for her today. She was scared out of her mind. Would she look like him? Would he welcome her? Or, would he deny he ever knew her mother?

Juanita had parked her car in front of an old white house with a beautifully landscaped yard. The house looked recently painted. From the outside, it looked like whoever lived inside was a friendly person.

Alicia and Ode stood side-by-side as Ode rang the doorbell.

The front door opened and Alicia's knees almost gave out.

They'd turned to blubbering balls of Jell-O. When a teenager stepped into view, she breathed a sigh of relief.

"Where's yo' granddaddy, baby?" Ode asked, reaching for the screen door.

The young man gave them a quick once-over before turning around. "Granddad, there's some folks here to see you," he yelled as he opened the door.

Ode hobbled through the entryway first and into the formal living room ahead of the others. The sparse accessories and big, comfortable cushions spelled bachelor to Alicia. They were all seated on the sofa when a tall, dark-skinned man with salt-and-pepper curly hair walked in.

Alicia's jaw dropped.

He glanced down the sofa before he reached out to take Ode's hand. "Ode, how you doin'?" he asked, looking a bit confused.

"Fine Nate." She shook his hand, unable to get up from the deep cushions of the sofa. She instead pointed to Alicia. "I want to introduce ya' to somebody. Do ya' know this young lady?"

He looked over at Alicia squinting his eyes, then smiled. He stepped over and reached out for Alicia's hand as she stood up. "Hey there, you're a guest at Hotel Paradise, Ms. Alicia, right?"

She nodded, unable to speak. Nate was Nathan, the driver for Hotel Paradise.

"Nate." Ode shifted in her seat, struggling to get up. Then, she gave up and settled for leaning on the arm. "Nate, Alicia is Venetta's baby girl. Her only child."

Alicia's knees trembled as she stood by the mere grace of God. If Nathan let go of her hand right now, she would collapse.

He remained speechless.

"Nate, ya' knew Venetta was pregnant when she left here didn't ya'?" Ode asked, as if they'd always been aware of it, but hadn't mentioned it.

He let go of Alicia's hand and backed into the chair next to the sofa. "I always had a feeling," he murmured, not taking his eyes from her.

And she couldn't take her eyes off him either. She lowered herself back onto the sofa. She licked her lips, now aware of where she'd inherited their fullness. Nathan was her father!

He looked a little apprehensive, but managed to smile and nod. "I see ya' mother in yo' eyes. She had beautiful big brown eyes too."

"Nathan, Alicia was born six months after Venetta got to New York."

He lowered his head for a moment, and when he looked up, tears stained his cheeks. "Why didn't she tell me?" he posed the question to Alicia.

She shrugged helplessly.

"If I'd a known…" he trailed off.

"I didn't know myself," Alicia volunteered, before he started to apologize. "Until my…father passed away a year ago."

Nathan stood up again and pulled Alicia to her feet, and into his arms. She'd found her biological father.

Juanita took Tracy and Ode home, giving Alicia and Nathan time to talk. By the time she returned, Alicia had met her nephew and discovered she had two stepsisters, and a stepbrother. Only one sister lived in the area, and she hoped to meet her soon. Nathan's wife had passed away over ten years ago.

"Before ya' go, I've got somethin' for ya'," he said before disappearing down the hall.

Alicia gave Juanita a skeptical look. What could he have for her when he hadn't known she existed until a few hours ago?

He returned with a picture in his hand and gave it to Alicia. "I found that about a month ago when I was looking through some important papers."

It was a picture of Nathan and her mother posing by the pool. Hotel Paradise was in the background. Her mother had a big smile on her face and looked happier than she'd ever seen her.

"We used to have what was called 'employee appreciation day,' where old man Monroe would let the employees take over the hotel and have one big party. I want ya' to have that."

She held the picture as if it were the most precious jewel in the world. "Thank you," she whispered through fresh tears.

Chapter 27

Alicia pulled into the Clarion and looked over to see Sterling sitting in the car next to hers.

All she could think of was how he'd lied to her, and she wanted to know why. They exited cars at the same time. Something Darius's brother Luke said came to mind. He'd asked her how well she knew Sterling. She'd assumed that by spending more time with him than anyone else in the family they would have bonded and he'd have no reason to lie to her, but she guessed she didn't know him at all.

"Hey Alicia," he said, jumping down from the hood. "I was wondering if you've had any time to think about what I asked you?" he inquired with a smile on his face.

His suit was wrinkled as if he'd slept in it all night. She guessed he'd given up on shaving; he'd started growing a beard.

"Sterling why did you lie to me?"

He flinched and looked at her with furrowed brows. "What are you talking about?"

"Charlie Monroe is not my father." She pulled out the picture Nathan had given her and shoved it at him.

He eased back onto the hood of his car as he took the picture. Not recognizing Nathan right away, he stared at the photograph shaking his head.

"That's my mother and father. My real father. His name is Nathan Morris."

Sterling's head snapped up at the mention of Nathan's name. "Our Nathan?" he asked.

"The hotel driver, yes."

"Are you sure?"

"He gave me that picture," she said as clarification.

Sterling cocked the right side of his mouth into a nasty grin. "I guess that means you weren't doin' your brother then."

Alicia snatched the picture back and shoved it into her purse. "Why did you lie to me?" Her tone was hard and forceful.

He shook his head. "I didn't say he was your father, you did. I said the guy worked at the hotel."

She jabbed her finger into his chest. "You said it was one of the Monroe boys. And you let me believe it was Charlie Monroe."

He stood up pushing her hand away. "I tried to tell you that old lady might have been wrong. Nobody told you to jump to the conclusion you did."

The strong stench of beer and liquor was heavy on his breath. He probably hadn't been sober since he lost his job, Alicia thought.

"You wanted me to think he was my father didn't you?"

He turned around and walked back over to his car door and

reached inside pulling out a pack of cigarettes. She'd never seen him smoke before.

"What are you talking about?" he asked, as he lit a cigarette and blew the smoke into the air.

"Sterling, I know how you feel about the Monroes. You'd do anything to hurt them wouldn't you? Is that why you told me Charlie Monroe was my father? You wanted to hurt Darius?"

"You don't know what you're talking about. Besides, I didn't come here to talk about them. Are you going to give me the money or not?" he asked, squinting his eyes from the cigarette smoke.

She crossed her arms and stared at him with complete disgust. "How dare you ask me for money after you lied to hurt me?"

He was oblivious of her stare as he sighed and flicked the lit cigarette across the parking lot.

"Why did you steal from the hotel?" she asked. "Sterling, your whole family is proud of you and your success. Why are you throwing it all away?"

"I didn't take anything." He pointed his finger in her face. "And you don't know nothing about me or my family." He jerked open his car door.

"I know how much you love them, so why did you do it?" she pleaded.

"I could have gotten into a hotel management program years ago, that would have given me the education to be general manager for any hotel on this island. But, I didn't. I stayed at Hotel Paradise because Willie Monroe told me he had nobody to leave the hotel to. His boys didn't want it, so one day it would be mine." He climbed back into his car and slammed the door.

Alicia stepped closer to the car. "He promised you the hotel?"

"Yeah, he just forgot to put it in his will. Then Darius showed up." He started his car.

"Sterling—" she reached out and put her hand on the car door "—come inside, we need to talk."

He shook his head. "Keep your damn money. I don't need a lawyer after all."

He threw the car in reverse and sped back out of the parking space and then out of the lot.

"What about the fire?" Alicia screamed to herself as he drove away.

She now believed what Tracy heard wasn't Sterling merely wishing the hotel would catch on fire. He'd planned to set the hotel on fire. She ran inside her hotel room.

Alicia paced around her room wondering whom to call first. She could call her aunt first, but if there weren't anything to the story she would upset her for no reason. But then again, would the family believe her? After a month, she'd finally broken through to her aunt and now felt like a member of the family. Would they shut her out again and say she was trying to cause trouble for Sterling?

Or, she could call Darius first. But, he would probably tell her it was another one of Sterling's lies.

If there was something to it, Alicia didn't have time to ponder this decision. She had to do something. Sterling looked out of control and was mad as hell at Darius. She had to stop him before he did something he'd regret.

She walked over and picked up the phone. Staring at the numbers for only a few seconds, she made up her mind faster than she ever had before. She dialed the hotel.

"Hotel Paradise, how may I help you?"

"May I speak to Mr. Monroe?"

The woman on the other end hesitated a moment before responding. "One moment please."

Alicia thought she heard the woman put her hand over the receiver. Seconds later a man's voice came on the line.

"Hello, this is Mr. Monroe."

"Darius?" She didn't recognize the voice.

"No, this is Luke. Who's this?"

"It's Alicia."

"Hey, hold on a moment. I need to talk to you."

The hair on her arms stood up. What did he want? She'd gotten the impression that Luke didn't like her.

She could hear him asking to have the call transferred to Darius's office. A few seconds later, he picked up.

"Alicia, Darius isn't on the property right now, but I wanted to apologize for the way I talked to you a couple nights ago. A little case of displaced anger. My beef was with your cousin, not you. I hope you'll forgive me?"

She was stunned, but happy. "You're forgiven," she said with a smile. She liked Luke. He seemed like a fun guy.

"I guess you've heard Darius fired him?"

"Sterling told me. Luke, I'm not sure how true this is, but a family member heard Sterling talking on the phone to somebody about making a wish that the hotel would burn down. I didn't give it much thought at first, but Sterling was just here and I believe he's mad and drunk enough to make that wish come true."

"Thanks for the heads up, I'll be sure to let Darius know."

"Okay. He told me something else I think you should know." She repeated everything Sterling told her about being promised the hotel.

"I find that hard to believe," he said. "I've been hanging out in Brunswick looking for some local musicians, and in doing so, I heard that Sterling was working with RCE to get the hotel from my grandfather. I haven't found any proof of that yet, but I'm looking for it."

Alicia sighed. "I hope that's not true."

"I'm pretty sure it is. I haven't told Darius yet, but I think he'll listen to me about Sterling now."

"If you don't mind me asking, you two don't get along too well do you?" The strain between them bothered Darius so much she could see it in his eyes when he talked about Luke. And she didn't like to see him hurting.

"He's the businessman, I'm the screw up."

"That's not true is it?"

"No, it's not. But, that's what he thinks."

"Why do you let him think that? Aren't you proud of your musical accomplishments?"

"I used to play them down because I thought he regretted not having a musical career." Luke chuckled. "Then last week he admitted he never really wanted it. His beef isn't really with me, I'm just the closest he can get to it."

"Your father, right? He told me a little about his childhood and the riff between you two."

"I should have known. Yeah, our father. He's gone, so Darius takes his resentment out on me. Nobody held him back though. Look at all he's attained in his life. Then look at what I've got. A guitar collection and a few bucks. But, you don't see me sulking."

"I don't think he cares about the stuff. He can't get over the relationship he missed."

"Yeah, he told me. But he did have a relationship with him. It was just different than the one I had. He doesn't know this, but I'm here because my father asked me to come. Before he passed, he asked me to help Darius run the hotel. But I had to think about it. He wanted me to give up my music career to live on an island with a guy who'd always treated me like a second-class citizen." He let out a nervous little laugh. "I needed to think about it, so I toured Europe before I ultimately decided it was the right thing to do. So, here I am doing what's right by my family. Just like Darius."

Alicia was almost brought to tears. "Have you told him any of that?"

"No."

"I think you should."

"Yeah, maybe."

Later that night, the blaring siren of the fire truck drowned out the radio in the hotel's van. Luke's ears perked up and he snapped his head around. Behind them, the headlights of a fire truck shined through the back window.

"Oh crap, I messed up," he yelled as Rodell pulled over out of the way.

Luke snatched his cell phone from his belt and dialed the hotel's front desk. No answer.

"What's wrong?" Rodell asked, pulling back into the road.

"Speed up, I think that truck's headed for the hotel."

Rodell picked up speed. Luke dialed Darius as the van turned the corner and he could see the fire truck pull into Hotel Paradise.

"Yeah, what's up?" Darius answered.

"I think we've got trouble."

The van pulled in behind the fire truck and Luke saw the smoke.

"Where are you?" Darius asked.

"Get back over here quick. The hotel's on fire." Luke snapped the phone closed and opened the van door as Rodell slowed to a stop. They jumped out and ran around the fire truck to see flames shooting through the roof, and employees running everywhere. Guests crowded away from the building at the far end of the lawn watching the firemen work.

* * *

Darius excused himself from the Chamber of Commerce reception and shot out to his car. The hotel was only a few miles down the road. He sped down Beachview Drive looking up to see if he saw flames. He didn't, so he prayed to God his father and grandfather's legacy wasn't destroyed.

Minutes later, he pulled in behind two fire trucks and a couple of police cars. Billows of smoke came from the building, but the hotel looked intact. He jumped out of the car and ran over to Luke, who was talking to a fireman.

"It's out now," Luke assured Darius.

"What happened?" Darius asked.

Fire Chief Mills introduced himself before explaining what he'd detected so far. "Well, it looks like it started in one of your guest rooms on the ocean side. Damaged four units, but the fire walls kept it from spreading too fast. You were lucky."

"Did everybody get out okay?" Darius asked.

"Yeah, the smoke alarms went off and the staff evacuated everybody. No casualties. The burned units were vacant," Luke informed him.

"Do you know how it started?" Darius questioned the fire chief.

He shook his head and removed his hat. "Not yet, but we'll conduct an investigation. As soon as we have something I'll let you know."

"Thank you," Darius said.

The burned units were several yards away from Darius's apartment, which luckily hadn't been damaged. As night fell he and Luke stood on the beach watching the four ocean-side units smolder.

"Man I should have been here to prevent this. We'd been

warned Sterling would try this. I should have kept my butt here," Luke chastised himself.

"It's not your fault," Darius assured him. "So don't sweat it."

"What about the renovation plans?" Luke asked.

Darius shrugged. "Nothing's changed. We'll work around these units. When we get the investment money, the whole building's coming down anyway."

Luke nodded and stared at the remaining puffs of smoke slowly escaping the building.

"You know, I didn't get a chance to thank you for solving that contract discrepancy and working things out with the band," Darius remarked.

Luke slowly turned to him and chuckled. "That's the first time you've ever thanked me for anything."

Darius shook his head. "That's not true."

"Okay, you thanked me for letting you ride my bike when you were twelve, but that was the last time."

"It was my bike and you whined until I let you ride." Darius shot Luke a big smile.

"Whatever." Luke held out his hand grinning. "We cool?"

Darius released all his inner resentment and jealousy toward his little brother and grabbed his hand, pulling him into a bear hug. "I'm sorry man," he whispered in Luke's ear.

"It's okay. Let's just make the old man proud. He wanted us working together. So let's whip this place into shape."

When Darius turned around to head back to the lobby a silhouette of blue headed their way. It was Alicia.

Chapter 28

Alicia found Darius walking along the beach with Luke. They met in the sand. "I heard about the fire. Is everybody okay?" she asked.

"Yeah, thanks for coming by," Darius said, standing close enough to touch her, but not doing so.

Alicia turned to Luke. "Did you give him my message?"

"Yep, we were just talking about Sterling."

"Darius, I'm so sorry. I didn't think he'd be crazy enough to do something like this. If he did do this."

"We'll know what started the fire pretty soon." He reached out and stroked Alicia's arm. "But, I need you to tell the police everything you told Luke."

She nodded. "Sure, when?"

"Now."

The police took statements from all the employees, and then Alicia had her turn. She told the officer everything she knew. Darius sat in the office for all the interviews. Afterwards, he brought Alicia into his office and closed the door.

"Alicia, thank you." He walked back over to his desk and flopped down in the chair.

His face, haggard with worry and marred with stress lines across the forehead, tugged at Alicia's heart. She'd do whatever she could to help him. "I'm just sorry I didn't go to the police the minute Tracy told me what she heard. But I thought he was just blowing off steam."

"Luke and Timothy suggested I hire extra security, but I thought the same thing. Then again, we won't know for sure if he set the fire or not until the fire chief finishes the investigation."

Alicia wanted to go to him and comfort him.

"How are you doing?" he asked.

She laughed. "Your hotel almost burns down and you ask how I'm doing. I'm fine. How are you?"

"I won't be any good until you tell me you've talked to your aunt."

In reality, Alicia was bursting with excitement, but she'd held it in not wanting to say anything until they finished discussing the fire.

"I did, and my father is Nathan Morris."

Darius blinked. "Our Nathan Morris?" he asked.

She smiled and nodded. "Yes, your driver."

Darius fell back in his seat, mouth open, smiling. "You're kidding?"

She laughed and shook her head. "Nope. My aunt took me by there earlier this evening, and we talked." She pulled the picture from her purse. "He even gave me this." She walked around the desk and handed Darius the picture.

He pulled her closer to stand between his legs as he examined the picture. "This is Nathan and your mother?"

"Yeah."

"This was taken here at the hotel," he pointed out.

"He said it was on employee appreciation day. He was married, so they kept their relationship on the down low. He didn't even know she was pregnant."

Darius handed the picture back and pulled her closer to him. "I'm happy for you."

She shrugged. "I am too. I was a little sad, but when I think about what my dad did for me and for my mother, I wish I could tell him all over again how much I love him."

"You know what this means don't you?" he asked. He turned her backside against his desk, trapping her between his legs.

"Yeah," she laughed. "I wasn't doin' my brother, as Sterling so eloquently put it."

Darius cringed and shook his head. "I can't believe he started all that mess. And I thought he was my right-hand man."

"No, he wanted to be *the* man. He didn't want to sit on anybody's right or left side."

Darius pulled Alicia down onto his lap. "How would you like to be *the* woman in my life?

She blushed. "Mr. Monroe, are you trying to seduce me?"

"Baby, I already did that. I'm trying to make you my woman, and keep you in my bed."

She met his mouth to taste what she'd been missing so desperately the last couple of days. His lips were soft and the kiss sweet, leaving the promise of much more.

He took a breath and looked around his office. "I've gotta get a sofa in here."

"What for?" she asked, smiling wickedly.

"Because I like taking chances, don't you?" He buried his face between her breasts, kissing her hot flesh.

She laughed.

"I'm so in love with you it's crazy." Alicia threw her head back enjoying his warm, soft lips, until he abruptly stopped.

"So you gonna be the woman in my life and stop disappearing on me?"

She took a deep breath. She wanted more than anything to be Darius's woman. "But, I live in Atlanta, and you live... I don't know, will you live here or Chicago?"

He planted a soft kiss on her cheek. "How does Chicago in the summer and Jeykll Island in the winter sound?"

"What happened to Atlanta?"

"Oh yeah, I guess after you open your spa in my new hotel, you'll want to visit Atlanta every now and then."

"You're crazy," she said with a big smile.

He smiled down at her. "I'm crazy in love."

The next morning, Alicia and Darius rushed to the police station where Luke was being questioned for suspicion of arson.

They walked into the station surprised to see Ode, Catherine, and Juanita. While Darius talked with the arresting officer about Luke, Alicia ran over to see why her family was here.

"Aunt Ode, what happened?" Alicia asked, as she approached them.

Catherine sat in a chair with her face in her hands crying, while Ode rubbed her back. "It's Sterling. He was in an accident and arrested for drunk drivin'."

"He's in big trouble," Juanita added.

Alicia took the seat on the other side of Catherine. "Catherine, I'm so sorry. He came to see me yesterday and he'd been drinking heavily then. I should have called somebody."

Catherine looked up at Alicia and reached out for her hand. "It's not your fault. He's been drinking pretty heavily for a long time now. I don't know what happened to him." Then she started bawling.

Darius joined them and Alicia stood and introduced him to everyone. Knowing that Darius had fired Sterling made Alicia feel a little awkward.

Ode stood up and Alicia feared she might say something horrible to Darius.

"Mr. Monroe, I'm sorry for anythin' that boy done did to ya' hotel or to you." Tears rolled down her cheeks.

"Thank you, but that's not necessary. I'm just sorry things turned out this way. Sterling was—"

"Excuse me folks." A detective walked up to them.

Everyone turned to him, eager for some news.

"Mr. Monroe, we'll be letting your brother go." Then he turned to Catherine. "But, Sterling Simpson is being charged with driving while under the influence. We also found some towels and an empty kerosene container in the trunk. So, I'm afraid Gibb Underwood along with Mr. Simpson will be charged with arson in connection with the fire at Hotel Paradise."

"Gibb?" Darius asked in surprise.

"Yes, sir. He confessed to helping Mr. Simpson set the fire and leaving items taken from Mr. Monroe's room to make it look as if he set the fire. The only problem was Luke Monroe has witnesses to say where he was at the time the fire started." He turned to Darius. "Mr. Monroe, may I speak to you a moment."

"Sure." Darius excused himself and followed the officer into another room.

Catherine continued sobbing as Juanita helped her up. "Come on Catherine, let me get you home."

Alicia reached over and helped Aunt Ode up.

"Oh, that knee's really actin' up today. It must be fixin' to storm this evenin'." She struggled to her feet with the help of Alicia.

"Let me help you out to the car," Alicia said, as she

wrapped her arm around her aunt and followed Juanita and Catherine out.

Once they reached the car, Ode turned to Alicia and gave her a big hug.

"Want me to ride back with you?" Alicia asked, not quite sure what she could do to help.

Ode shook her head. "Ya' take care of your young man right now and don't worry 'bout us. We'll get Catherine home and see to the kids. Everythin's goin' to be okay."

Teary-eyed, she climbed into the car and closed the door.

An hour later, Darius, Alicia, and Luke emerged from the police station and drove back to the hotel. Alicia had checked out of The Clarion and moved back into Hotel Paradise early that morning.

"Can you believe they tried to pin that on me?" Luke reeled in astonishment.

"You were never really a suspect," Darius said. "I talked to the detective, and he told me they locked up a guy a couple days ago whose business consisted of taking contracts to burn down buildings. He called it his 'make-a-wish foundation.' You gave him an agreed-to amount of money, and let him know what you wished would burn down. A couple of days later, poof, it was gone."

"That's what Tracy heard," Alicia said.

"Yep, but he didn't get to do Sterling's job. He was in jail. So, Sterling did it himself."

"And Gibb was working with him?" Luke asked. "I never suspected him."

"Neither did I. According to the detective, Gibb goes by the nickname of Trouble. Which is what he's been causing the hotel for months. He doesn't have a record but the police have had more than one run-in with him. They've just never been able to arrest him for anything, until now," Darius explained.

"I bet they were working with RCE to get Poppy to sell the hotel," Luke suggested. "Then we came along and messed up their plans. If it's the last thing I do, I'm going to find that connection and expose RCE somehow."

Darius sighed. "I don't know if we'll ever be able to prove that, but they didn't get the hotel, and they never will."

They stopped at a red light and Darius reached over for Alicia's hand. He squeezed it until she turned to him. Then he mouthed, "I love you."

Epilogue

One Year Later…

"Hurry up, you're going to be late for your own wedding," Rorie scolded Alicia.

"I'm moving as fast as I can. Who's down there?" Alicia asked, slipping on her shoes.

"Your whole family. Now come on." He grabbed her veil and stuck the comb into the top of her hair as they opened the door and hurried out of the room and down to the beach.

Alicia beamed at the site of her family sitting in the new gazebo built especially for weddings at the newly renovated Monroe Bay.

Ahead of her, the flower girl, Tracy, had already started down the path tossing rose pedals. Rorie, making last-minute adjustments, tugged on Alicia's dress.

Alicia swatted his hand. "Rorie, stop it. I'm fine."

"I'm sorry. I just can't help myself. You look so beautiful."

"She sure does," Nathan agreed as he joined them.

Standing at the east wing of the hotel, Alicia smiled at Nathan, as he waited to escort her down the aisle. Her father was going to give her away. He held out his arm. Beaming up into his face, she wrapped her arm around his and proceeded down the path adorned with her family and friends.

Darius looked up at his beautiful bride coming down the path and felt his heart explode. She was the most beautiful woman in the world, and she completed his life like no other woman could.

He felt a hand on his shoulder and turned his head. His best man, Luke, smiled at him and whispered, "She's beautiful man."

Darius nodded and smiled at his mother sitting in the front row. She dabbed at her eyes with a tissue and smiled at him.

"I wish Dad were here," Luke whispered.

Darius had a feeling he was there. Sitting right beside their mother, witnessing his boys working together, and getting along better than they had in the last twenty years. This is what his father wanted. Darius knew that now. This is what would have made Charlie Monroe proud. He wanted to bring his boys back together. He didn't want them fighting and distant like he'd been with his brother and father.

Nathan stepped aside and handed Alicia over to Darius, who took her hand and looked down into her face. This time he saw a house full of beautiful children. All heirs of Monroe Bay.